BAD Bl

CASTLE

An Alison Cameron Mystery

Myra Duffy

www.myraduffywriter.com

cover design by Mandy Sinclair
www.mandysinclair.com

Also by Myra Duffy

THE ISLE OF BUTE MYSTERY SERIES

The House at Ettrick Bay
An unexpected discovery at an archaeological site leads
to murder

Last Ferry to Bute
Mysterious deaths at a nursing home and a shady
antiques dealer.

Last Dance at the Rothesay Pavilion
Past events cast a long shadow over the present as the
Pavilion is renovated

Endgame at Port Bannatyne
The world of film-making hides a deadly secret

Grave Matters at St Blane's
A proposal to build a theme park is the catalyst for
violent events

Death at the Kyles of Bute
The Kyles of Bute Hydro Hotel is again open for
business, but someone has murder in mind.

The prequel to the Isle of Bute Mystery series

When Old Ghosts Meet
Dangerous events are sparked off by a chance sighting
on the Edinburgh to Glasgow train.

For Rosie, who gave me the idea and for Nuala whose favourite building is Rothesay Castle.

PROLOGUE

Helena stopped at the entrance to the Gatehouse of
Rothesay Castle and watched as the Heritage
Adventurers clustered around her.

Two weeks of employment as a guide for this party
of American tourists was a godsend after the terrible
experience of her divorce. And once the settlement was
confirmed, there'd be no need to work, thank goodness.
In the meantime, this money was useful, though
sometimes she felt like a Primary School teacher,
constantly having to gather up any strays who'd
rambled off to explore during one of the many activities
on their schedule. Only a moment before she'd had to
warn them to be careful crossing the water-filled moat
as they leant far over the side of the timber bridge to
watch a pair of swans elegantly swimming past.

'If you come over this way. That's right. Can
everyone see?' She marshalled them one by one to a
space over by the wall. The wind funnelled through the
Gatehouse, in spite of the warmth of the day, and she
pushed her long blonde hair off her face.

'If you come in closer, you'll have a better view.'
The members of the group obediently inched nearer.
'These iron steps lead down to the old dungeon,' she

said, indicating the set of narrow stairs. 'High status prisoners were lodged in the castle, but others weren't so fortunate and were kept here in what was called The Pit. Pretty unpleasant.'

'Gee, Mrs Gibson, were people actually imprisoned here? In this awful place?'

Helena nodded, 'Yes, Jerome, this was the main dungeon for Rothesay Castle. If these stones could speak, they'd tell many a gruesome tale. And do call me Helena.' The fewer reminders of her ex-husband the better, she thought grimly. Only a few more weeks now. Everything would work out fine.

She could sense the excitement: that was the great thing about Americans, they loved these tales of horror, the grislier the better. And they were all from the United States, except for one dark-haired, bubbly woman at the back, her badge identifying her as Susie, eagerly telling anyone who would listen, 'My husband and I were married here a few years ago.'

A stocky teenage boy, noisily chewing gum, detached himself from the others and sidled up to her. He peered over into the dimly-lit depths. 'Guess we can't go down there? Suppose it ain't allowed?'

Helena forced a smile. She'd expected this, anticipated someone would be sufficiently intrigued by the stories about the castle to want to explore the dungeon. 'Of course you can. It's perfectly safe, Ricky.'

She nodded encouragingly. 'Anyone else?' The silence was answer enough.

'Oh, be careful, honey.' Ricky's mother rushed forward, but he shrugged her off and she moved back, biting her lip.

'Stop fussing, Mom.' The boy hitched up his baggy jeans, turned his baseball cap back to front, opened the little gate and, grabbing the guide rail firmly, began climbing down, pausing mid-way to gaze up at the crowd, as though regretting his decision. But spurred on by calls of, 'You can do it, Ricky,' he resumed his descent.

Helena didn't take her eyes off him as he began to move down slowly, one careful step at a time.

'Are you sure he'll be okay?' Ricky's mother tapped Helena on the shoulder.

Helena spun around, unwilling to look away from the boy as he negotiated the remainder of the steps to disappear from sight. Her heart was beating fast. 'Don't worry, Kimberley. It's perfectly safe. There's no way anyone would be allowed down there if it wasn't.' Even so, she'd feel happier when he was safely back with the rest of the group.

The crowd bunched together near the top of the stairway, a few holding on tightly to the iron railings as they peered over into the depths to watch for Ricky's reappearance, the stillness occasionally punctuated by a nervous cough from Kimberley.

'He won't come to any harm,' Helena said, but as the seconds dragged out into minutes, she felt a pang of doubt. He seemed to have been in the dungeon an awfully long time. What was he doing?

'I'll go down and check,' she said brightly, trying to hide her fear. The last thing she wanted to do was follow him. 'I won't be…'

Her final words were drowned out by an ear-splitting scream and Ricky came clattering up the steps a good deal faster than he'd gone down. He stumbled

3

on to the little platform at the top, then stood up and charged through the gate, bending over to catch his breath.

His mother grabbed him, hugging him tightly. 'Oh, honey, I knew you shouldn't have gone there, down into that awful place. It's far too scary. Are you okay?'

Ricky struggled to extricate himself from his mother's ample bosom and Helena cursed herself for letting the youngster take up the offer to explore the dungeon. If she'd waited a few moments surely one of the others would have volunteered.

Shakily, the boy pointed an accusing finger at Helena. 'You told us the dungeon wasn't in use.'

'Of course it isn't.'

'Was it a ghost?' An elderly woman, Connie according to her badge, moved forward, her brown eyes magnified by her gold-rimmed spectacles. 'I've heard these places often have ghosts and you can feel the presence of those who once lived here, if you are in tune with the spirit world. I read somewhere a princess had an accident here, haunts the castle…'

Ricky had recovered his self-confidence and cut in. 'It weren't no spook,' he said, adjusting his cap, which had fallen over his eyes. He paused and looked from one to another. 'It weren't no spook,' he repeated with growing boldness, 'it was a real person, and he wasn't moving, just lay there.'

'Did you speak to him, honey? Try to help him?' His mother's eyes were wide with fright. 'If he's hurt we should call an ambulance.'

'How could I talk to him, Mom? He's dead.'

His mother let out a shriek. 'Dead? Are you sure?'

4

Ricky was scornful. 'Course I'm sure – we did that First Aid course at last year's summer camp.'

'So what happened to him?'

Ricky shrugged, clearly relishing being in command of an audience. 'Guess he might have fallen down those slippery steps.' He nodded towards Helena, 'They ain't as safe as she makes out.'

'That's nonsense,' she said in a steady voice. 'The castle is well looked after and if there was the slightest chance of danger, the dungeon would be closed to the public.'

Susie came forward and whispered, 'Where's Max? He should be here with us.'

Ignoring her, Helena said, 'If you would all remain where you are for a moment,' and began to count aloud the number in the group, aware Susie was standing behind her, counting with her.

Susie muttered, 'There should be eleven of us in the group, but I make it ten.'

'I'll phone for help,' said Helena briskly. As she pulled her phone from her jacket she saw Susie was standing quite still, staring at Ricky. Helena followed her gaze. The boy had turned away, but not before she noticed the smirk on his face as he hastily pushed something into his pocket. What had he been up to?

CHAPTER ONE

Susie was standing at the far end of the pier, waving her arms in some strange kind of semaphore, trying to attract my attention.

There was no need. From my vantage point on the upper deck of the MV Bute as it slid gracefully into Rothesay harbour, she was easily identifiable from afar by her brightly patterned yellow top and matching trousers.

She was calling out to me, but her words were carried away on the breeze that frothed the tops of the waves lapping on the beach known as Children's Corner: a popular spot in the days when Bute was a holiday destination for workers escaping the grime of the nearby city of Glasgow.

I hurried back to the Passenger Lounge to join the queue waiting patiently to disembark. I always experience a surge of excitement on the short crossing from Wemyss Bay to the island and this time the lone seagull who appeared to be keeping guard on the top deck was surely a good omen.

No sooner was I on dry land than Susie came rushing towards me to catch me in a hug. 'It's great to see you again, Alison.'

I stood back to look at her. She hadn't changed much in the couple of years since our last meeting, though she'd grown her hair and it was a mass of tumbling dark curls, almost obscuring the dangling silver earrings she favoured. 'You've lost weight,' I said. 'You're looking well.'

She grinned. 'It's a bit easier to resist comfort food when you live in a sunny climate like California.' She did a twirl, then stopped, frowning. 'Though I have to say being back on this tour has presented a lot of temptation. Especially the cream doughnuts from the Electric Bakery. Luckily Dwayne's also finding them irresistible.'

We linked arms as we left the Ferry Terminal and crossed the road to Guildford Square. 'Married life seems to suit you, then.' It was still hard to believe Susie and Dwayne were so compatible. Susie is vivacious, never still, while Dwayne is the type of person who copes with any problems with an unfailing calmness.

'So how did Simon react when you said you were coming back to Bute?'

Her question reminded me of the conversation my husband and I had had one evening a few weeks earlier, after Susie's phone call.

'I thought you'd decided you weren't going back to Bute, at least not any time soon?' he'd said in astonishment when I told him of my plans. 'Anyway, isn't it all very short notice?'

'Yes, but this is something special. Susie is in the U.K. with a group of Americans – the Heritage Adventurers, they're called. They'll be on Bute for over two weeks, the final leg of the tour. Although it's a long trip, I gather it's such a tight schedule there's no time for her to come south to meet up here in London.'

'Well, it's important to keep in touch with old friends,' he said. 'How long will you be away? A couple of days?'

'Nooo… a bit longer than that. Susie's asked me to take on a small project.'

He frowned. 'Alison, you're not going to get involved in any trouble on the island, are you? I would have thought you'd had enough of that…' He began to run his fingers through his hair, his way of signalling frustration and I suddenly noticed how much greyer he'd become.

'No, no,' I interrupted, anticipating a reminder about the incidents I'd been involved in on previous visits to Bute. 'This group are all Stuarts, except Susie and Dwayne of course, and they're visiting sites of interest around the country. Having learned about the history of the early Stuarts on the island, they've decided some ancestry research would be interesting. Nothing too complicated.'

Simon threw back his head and roared with laughter. 'That's some task you've set yourself. They'll be expecting links with Bonnie Prince Charlie or Mary, Queen of Scots. Good luck with that one, Alison. Sounds like one of Susie's hare-brained schemes to me.' He hesitated. 'You're not a genealogist. Why choose you?'

8

'From what Susie told me, they do want a bit of investigation into the Stuarts, into their own families and any island connections, but it's more about having a memento of their holiday. Besides,' playing my trump card, 'you'll be at a conference in Brighton while I'm away. It will give me something to do.'

'You seem busy enough to me. You're never at home. You've only recently finished that project on Learning Design materials and you spend a lot of time with Maura and Connor.'

'Well, Maura's our daughter and Connor is our only grandchild,' I retorted and as a loud, 'Hmm' was the only response, I knew he was reconciled to my decision.

'So what did Simon say?'

I pulled myself back to the present and to Susie's question.

'He asked why the people in your tour group couldn't borrow a book about the Stuarts from the library or order something from the Print Point bookshop on the island.'

'That's so like Simon. And your reply?'

'I explained as best I could that the aim was to find some personal information about each person's ancestry and weave it in with more general information about the Stuarts.' I didn't repeat what he'd said about Bonnie Prince Charlie. 'What persuaded him was being told the payment could go towards another trip to Canada to see Alastair. Our son's not good at keeping in touch and our last trip was such a success.'

'That's because he's an academic, taken up with his research,' grinned Susie.

'I suppose so.' Certainly since moving to the University of Maple Ridge Alastair's career has prospered.

'You'll have to tell me more about this project,' I said.

'When we're back at the hotel. We're so pleased you agreed to do this. No one else could have taken it on at such short notice.'

'It sounds interesting. I'm looking forward to it.' Then, 'Is Dwayne not with you?'

Susie shook her head, setting her long earrings dangling.

'Uh, uh. He decided to wait at the hotel. Give us a chance to meet up first.'

As we linked arms and left Guildford Square to head for the Stuart Hotel on the High Street, she stopped suddenly.

Over by the Post Office a young man was walking aimlessly up and down. He spied us and waved.

'Who's that? He obviously recognises you.'

Susie hesitated before acknowledging the greeting. 'That's Ricky. He's one of the group.'

I raised my eyebrows. 'Seems a bit young to be travelling with the Heritage Adventurers?'

Susie shrugged. 'He's with his mother. I'll tell you the story another time.' She gnawed at her lip. 'And there's something else I should say to you before we join the others.'

All my light-heartedness, my pleasure at being back on the island vanished in a sense of foreboding.

'What is it, Susie?' I said in a quiet voice as she stood scuffing her feet on the pavement, fiddling with one of her earrings.

'One of our party had an accident a few days ago when we were on a tour of the castle. I didn't want to tell you. I thought it might put you off, that you might change your mind about coming over.' Her words came out in a rush and she hurried on without pausing for breath, 'But it's nothing to do with you or any of us. It was an accident and it appears it was entirely his own fault. From what we know he decided to go off alone to explore and slipped on the steps leading down into the old dungeon in the Gatehouse at Rothesay Castle.'

I heaved a sigh of relief. 'So, it was an accident?'

'Our tour guide, Helena, says it couldn't have been anything else. Max was given to wandering away from the rest of the party. Of course,' she said, hurriedly, 'as it was a sudden death there's to be a post mortem, but everyone knows he was always disappearing like that. We almost lost him on the trip to Carlisle Castle. It took ages to find him. He was a historian and much more intrigued by the details of the places we visited than the rest of us. Even in the short time we'd been on the island I'd the impression Helena was pretty fed up with him, to be honest.'

'So how is everyone? About his death, I mean?' Thank goodness it had happened before my arrival.

Susie raised her eyebrows. 'It was Ricky who found him. He volunteered to go down into the dungeon when we were on a visit to the castle. I think he's pretty upset. At least he's been very quiet since. The tour will continue, that much has been agreed. Max wasn't the most popular person, always going on about how he was about to realise a great inheritance.'

'What did he mean by that?' In spite of my doubts, perhaps this was someone with a famous Stuart connection after all.

Susie shrugged. 'To be honest, no one paid much attention to him. I suspect it was just talk, a lot of boastful nonsense – that's the kind of person he was.'

Now I was confused. 'I thought I was investigating possible ancestral links Heritage Adventurers might have on the island?'

'Yes, yes,' said Susie. 'But he was the one who really set everyone else off, with his stories and his bragging…'She frowned.

Hurrying to reassure her, I said, 'Don't worry. It'll be fine. I'm sure I'll be able to produce an interesting booklet for them to take home as a souvenir.'

'That's why I thought of you, Alison. You've so much experience in this kind of thing.'

'And it's an opportunity for us to catch up.'

In spite of my hope that all would be well, I'd no intention of mentioning the accident in the castle to Simon. Not yet at any rate. Time enough when I was safely back home.

CHAPTER TWO

As Ricky disappeared towards Albert Place, Susie put
up her hands, as though suddenly noticing my luggage.
'Sorry, Alison, are you okay with that? I should have
asked someone to come with me to meet you.'

'It's only a light suitcase and a holdall,' I said. 'If
we're staying in the Stuart Hotel, it's no distance.'

Susie moved off towards the High Street. 'Fine,
then, let's go.'

Rothesay was busy, busier than I'd seen it on any of
my previous visits: a sign that all the efforts of the
various community groups were paying off in attracting
visitors to the island. The old gap site in Guildford
Square now boasted a newly built retail unit with flats
above and a retro Diner, all red and cream leather and
shiny chrome, occupied one of the old shop units. In
front of the castle, in Montague Street, a circular paved
area with a series of plaques on the low stone walls
traced the history of Bute, with the old Rothesay town
bell a prominent attraction.

'It's great to see the town looking so good,' I said.

'Yes, there have been a lot of changes, but much has
stayed the same.' She grinned. 'And the tearoom at

Ettrick Bay is still there, you'll be glad to hear, though there's now a smart new entrance. A must for a chance to gossip away from the rest of the tour group.'

As we continued up the High Street the vast circle of the ruined grey stone castle, dominated by the remains of the square towers, loomed large on our right. Several visitors were waiting patiently at the entrance to the wooden cabin that served as a ticket office and gift shop. I shivered a little as we passed it. Did any of those so eager to explore know what had happened there recently?

In the moat, a family of swans gracefully ignored this interruption to their territory. One of the adults waddled out of the water to spread itself out on the grassy bank, ruffling and preening its feathers, much to the delight of a couple of children peering through the iron railings surrounding the castle grounds.

I was tempted to ask Susie for more information about the death of Max, what exactly had happened, but I didn't. She'd tell me in her own good time and besides, it was nothing to do with me, though I had to admit to a certain curiosity. Ancient buildings were carefully managed these days so surely the steps down into the dungeon weren't dangerous?

Almost as quickly as I considered this question, Simon's admonition as I left for Bute, 'Don't get involved in anything that doesn't concern you,' echoed in my head. So instead of giving in to my natural inquisitiveness, I said, 'Have the members of your group considered what they want from this project?'

'Mmm.' Susie sounded dubious.

I stopped and put down my suitcase. 'What does that mean? Don't tell me there's another reason for persuading me to come back to Bute.'

She laughed. 'Don't look so alarmed, Alison. It's all above board. I'm not a Stuart so it'll be better if you discuss the details with Lloyd - he's the group leader and the one who was most interested in the project. The one who first suggested it in fact, though I think a bit of that was to do with being fed up with Max and his stories. Max was always trying to tell him about that so-called "inheritance" of his.'

We started walking again, a thousand questions jumbling in my brain. 'As long as he understands there is a limit to the amount of detail I'll be able to manage in the short time available. You'd need a properly qualified genealogist for more.'

'Of course, of course,' she said eagerly. 'But if you come across anything that's of PERSONAL interest, that's what we want.'

'How come you and Dwayne are involved if this is a group of Stuarts?'

'One of the leaders had to drop out because of illness and as Dwayne knew Lloyd it seemed a good opportunity to make a trip back to celebrate our anniversary.' She grinned. 'We got the tickets at a very good price and as I'd been to Bute many times, I was given the job of assistant leader. It suited us fine.'

As we reached the hotel I gazed in surprise at the building rising before me. Last time I'd been on Bute this had been very shabby, run down, a bit of an eyesore if I was being honest, having gone through several incarnations since closing in the early nineties. Now, the cleaned stone, the new bay windows each with a small wrought iron balcony, the sparkling paintwork, the building topped by crow stepped gables, all spoke of a confident future.

A little further along the street the Mansion House had also been restored and the beauty of this building, newly painted, was properly visible for the first time in many years.

'I must say I'd doubts when you first told me where you'd booked. I remembered it as it was, very run down.'

Susie grinned. 'Me too. When Lloyd told me where we'd be staying, I couldn't think what to say, but he was adamant, insisting what a great deal we were getting, I decided to keep quiet and suffer what I expected to be a very uncomfortable couple of weeks on the island.' She gestured towards the canopied entrance, a portico of fretwork metal, gleaming black in the late afternoon sunshine. 'Wait till you see the rest of it – I had to pinch myself when we arrived. They've done a great job of modernising it while keeping all the original features.'

I turned my back on the castle and together we pushed our way in through the large wooden doors.

Susie hadn't been exaggerating: immediately we were in a spacious hallway with a chequered marble floor leading to a grand foyer, the original Victorian features and dark wood panelling lovingly reinstated. An imposing marble fireplace boasted a warming fire. It might be Spring, but evenings, and even days, could still be chilly in this part of the world.

On the opposite wall, behind a semi-circular reception desk of polished oak, a smart young woman, neatly attired in a dark blue uniform, looked up and smiled at Susie as we approached. 'Good evening. Is this your guest?'

As she tapped my details into the computer in front of her, I gazed around. Through the archway opposite there was a lounge and a small bar and the double oak doors beside Reception led to the dining room.

A few minutes later, formalities completed, I was on my way up in the silent lift to the bedroom I'd been allocated on the top floor, but not before catching a glimpse of the ornamental garden at the back of the hotel, set out with wrought iron tables and chairs in expectation of good weather.

'I'll see you later. I'll be in the bar with the others, so come and join us when you're ready. I've still to tell you about something else that will interest you: the last day of our trip there's to be a medieval fair in the castle followed by a pageant of a Viking raid on the castle and a firework display. Everyone is excited about it.'

'You didn't mention this.' I could hardly contain my astonishment.

Susie winked. 'Yes, I wanted it to be a surprise for you. I'll fill you in when you come down.'

It was clear she was hugely enthusiastic about this way of ending the tour and I could scarcely wait to hear more, but she repeated, 'You'll hear the details later,' as the lift doors closed. This was so like Susie. What other surprises was she going to spring on me? I'd only been on the island less than an hour and already there were two unexpected events to deal with: the death of one of the tour group and some plan or other for a pageant. I wondered what she might come up with next, but in the meantime I had to check my room.

The bay-windowed bedroom facing on to the castle was every bit as luxurious as the rest of the hotel, with a large ensuite shower room, a separate area with a squashy sofa, a coffee table and a little writing desk. The bed looked so comfortable it was all I could do not to kick off my shoes and flop down on it, suddenly overwhelmed by a feeling of tiredness. It seemed like years since I'd left London, though it had only been early that morning Simon had taken me to the airport. Then I reminded myself I'd agreed to meet Susie and the rest of the group downstairs in the bar. There was no time to unpack my few belongings.

With a sigh I made do with splashing my face with cold water and reapplying my make-up. Now that I was back, my life in London seemed a million miles away. Bute was beginning to work its magic and I was looking forward to my time on the island.

CHAPTER THREE

It was a few moments before I spied Susie in the far corner of the Stuart Hotel bar. Or rather, heard the noise before spotting her sitting with Dwayne and a group I assumed to be the Heritage Adventurers.

Dwayne saw me first and rose to his feet to saunter over, a grin splitting his amiable features. He bent down to greet me with a kiss on the cheek and a, 'Gee, Alison, how good is it to see you again,' reminding me why I'd been delighted when Susie had married him. He was so laid back, so easy-going, exactly the right balance for my friend's highly excitable nature. It looked as if marriage also agreed with him, for he too had lost weight, though he still reminded me of a large bear.

He steered me by the elbow. 'Come and say hello to some of the tour group. They've been so looking forward to your arrival, but you can meet the rest of them later.' He grinned. 'I'm sure there'll be plenty of opportunities.'

My first impression as I approached the group was of a riot of colour. There were several people settled in the easy chairs around a large, low table on which a variety of drinks, equally colourful, sat.

The man seated furthest away stood up and came over to stand beside me. 'Gee, you must be Alison,' he said. He grasped my hand in a powerful grip. 'I'm Jerome Stuart. I used to be in the movies.'

'Pleased to meet you, 'I replied, taking in his strange attire of knee length red shorts and brightly coloured shirt patterned with what appeared to be parrots, wondering if this was his standard attire.

'Perhaps I should introduce myself to Lloyd?'

'Lloyd should be here, but guess he's gone into town.' He winked. 'Lots of good places to have a drink in Rothesay. We're looking forward to Alison helping us find out about our links to the Stuarts, aren't we folks?' He waved his hand and the others in the group nodded in unison, murmuring in assent. There was an eager, expectant silence as they gazed at me.

A man at the table nearest the window stood up, grabbing at the bundle of papers in front of him as they began to slide to the floor. He bent down to retrieve them, then straightened up saying, 'I'm Oscar. Yes, Ma'am, we're so eager to hear what you can tell us about our Stuart heritage.' He put the papers on the table and fidgeted with his small moustache. 'Connie and I are very interested in our connections, aren't we?'His large doleful eyes reminded me of a spaniel we'd had at home when I was a child.

Connie, a neat grey-haired lady sitting beside him, adjusted her gold-rimmed spectacles and leaned forward. 'What are we doing about connecting?'

'Connections, connections.' Oscar shook his head. 'My wife is a little deaf, I'm afraid, Ma'am. We're so looking forward to having our ideas confirmed.' He indicated the pile of papers now securely moved to the middle of the table. 'Some of my most recent research,' he said proudly. 'I'm sure it'll be of interest to you.'

I jumped in before Oscar could get the wrong idea about tracing their ancestry, to make it clear there was only so much I'd be able to do. Best to quash any false expectations.

'Please remember there are lots of people related to the many branches of the Stuarts and to be honest, it's very unlikely any of you will have royal blood in your veins.' I said this in a joking manner, but no one laughed. Instead one or two faces registered disappointment, especially Oscar's. For a moment I felt out of my depth, but surely with all my recent experience of this kind of research I'd be able to find some tasty morsels in the history of the Stuarts to satisfy them?

I nodded as Jerome said, smiling encouragingly, 'Oh, I'm sure you'll do just fine.' Now was not the time to let my imagination run riot, to remember my previous intrigues on the island.

'Have this chair, Alison,' said Dwayne, leaning over to drag one across from the nearest table as

Susie brought a glass of wine from the bar and set it in front of me.

'Thanks.' We've known each other since our days at college and there are some things there's no need to ask.

I sipped my drink, aware of the silence as everyone gazed at me. Attempting to change the topic of conversation I said, 'Tell me more about the Pageant, about this re-enactment.'

21

'Ah, knew you'd be interested. There's to be a medieval fair in the Castle during the day – coracle building, basket weaving, wool spinning, that kind of thing. And there will be stalls selling Medieval food and drink.' Jerome looked animated at the prospect. 'It reminds me of the time I had a part in Knights of the Silver Sword. What a movie that was…' His eyes grew misty.

'Sounds very exciting. And the Pageant?'

'That's being arranged by a lecturer in the college up at the Rothesay Joint Campus, Zachary Benford. He teaches drama and he's had this great idea of staging some of the episodes from the early history of the castle. It'll all take place on the final day of the tour and the re-enactment will end with a mighty battle where William the First defeats the Vikings and takes control of the castle. Lots of the children from the primary school are also involved – it should be quite a spectacle, ending with a firework display,' Susie's voice was squeaky with excitement.

'So this was set up especially for your group?'

Connie, who'd been sitting quietly, piped up, 'No, it was lucky we happened to be on the island when it was taking place.'

'And Zachary has said we can go up to the college and watch one of the rehearsals,' added Jerome. He sighed. 'It'll remind me of the ole days.'

'You can see how enthusiastic everyone is.' Susie's face was flushed. In spite of earlier attempts to appear unimpressed, I could tell she was thrilled.

A woman on the far side of the table said, 'And of course we're eager to see what you'll find out about our connections to the Stuarts.' I squinted to see her name badge. Though not young, Margie was attractive-looking, immaculately dressed and conveyed a kind of resolute fierceness. 'You will be able to find out about our ancestors, Alison?'

Fortunately, before anyone else chimed in, the main door to the lounge swung open and a skeletal figure wearing black jeans and a black t-shirt strode over to join us. All the time I was with the group I didn't see him in any other outfit: he wore it as a kind of uniform, doubtless (or hopefully) having several changes of identical clothes.

'I'm Lloyd,' he said leaning forward to shake my hand. He grinned at me, but the smile didn't reach his dark, unfathomable eyes.

'Has Jerome been filling you in? Telling you a bit about us?' He leaned further in and I recoiled a little from the whisky fumes.

'Yes, though I believe one or two of your group are out in town at the moment.'

As though he guessed my thoughts, Lloyd said, 'We like to keep these tours to a limited number of guests. We think they get more out of it that way.'

'And that's it, a couple of weeks on Bute?'

He threw his head back and laughed, revealing a set of highly veneered teeth. 'We're having just over two weeks here: it's our 'chill out' time, if you like. But we've also taken in Glasgow, Edinburgh and we've been to Stirling and to Carlisle. Many of us are particularly interested in the history of Bonnie Prince Charlie.' It was almost a question, an assumption that there would be some connections and there was a gleam in his eye as he spoke.

23

No point in starting with a complaint, but if anyone thought I might be able to dig up a link between anyone in the group and that particular Stuart they were very much mistaken. However, I did laugh to soften my response, 'Ah, the Young Pretender. That's a branch of the Stuart family none of you is likely to be related to, I'm sorry to say. Died out long ago.' Best not to get their hopes up, make the scope of the exercise clear at the beginning, though I made a mental note to check out the history in greater detail.

Oscar shifted his chair. 'But it's not impossible, is it, Alison? Some of us may have a link?' He sighed. 'We were so intrigued by the display about the story of the taking of Carlisle Castle during the '45 Jacobite Rising.'

'It's not entirely impossible,' I said, injecting a note of caution into my voice, 'but it's VERY unlikely.'

Good heavens, what had Susie got me involved in? There was a look of expectation in the group, in spite of my attempt to play down the possibility of such an illustrious ancestor. As a way of cutting short this discussion I said'And you're in the U.K. for how long in total?'

'A whole four weeks, Alison,' said Margie. I crossed my fingers that they would all continue to sport the large name badges they wore on a chain around their necks. It would make that part of my task so much easier.

Ah, so the tour was longer than I'd realised. Even so, I didn't say that if they were spending a lot of time on Bute, it must be a pretty tight schedule for the rest of the trip. But then, perhaps being American, they were used to that. Coming from such a vast country, distances weren't quite what they were to us in Britain.

Before we could continue, there was a commotion at the far end of the room. A large, very large, middle-aged woman with clearly dyed blonde hair and a heavily patterned dress that did nothing to disguise her size came towards us, grasping an equally large teenage boy by the arm.

This could only be Ricky and his mother, Kimberley. 'What I say goes,' she was repeating in a loud voice. 'I'm your mom and you'll enjoy the rest of the holiday, for sure.'

The sulky teenager wrested himself free. 'I didn't ask to come on this boring 'holiday' to be dragged around all these ancient ruins. I wanted to go to New York to see dad. You knew that.'

'You see plenty of your dad, Ricky,' his mother replied. 'I'm due some of your time too. Besides, surely you want to find out about your roots and how we might have famous ancestors?'

'That's as may be, but you weren't the one who found the body,' he replied.

'Sure, honey, I know that was a shock, but Max shouldn't have climbed down there, not with his heart problems and not without telling anyone what he was doing.' She wagged her finger at him. 'Be warned, Ricky. That's what happens when you go wandering off.'

In spite of his air of bravado, discovering Max's body in the dungeon must have given him quite a jolt. His mother didn't appear to be sympathetic, but perhaps she was also hiding her feelings well.

'Yes, we're all sorry about what happened to you,' said Dwayne, laying a hand on his shoulder. 'It's nothing to do with you – none of us can guess why Max wanted to go down into the dungeon on his own like that.'

Ricky sniffed and turned away, but not before I caught the sly look on his face.

Suddenly my confidence in my ability to carry out this project plummeted, but as quickly as this thought entered my head, I dismissed it as cowardly.

I sighed and turned my attention back to the group. I'd have to make the best of it, think of it as an opportunity to see Susie and Dwayne. It might be a long time before we met up again.

Decision made, I tuned in to the conversation, in time to hear Susie say, 'Are you absolutely certain?' and realised she was addressing a tall well-built man, younger than most of the group, who had joined us.

'Yep. Sorry to say there ain't no doubt about it.' There was a sheen of sweat on his dark skin and he ran his hand through his close cropped curly black hair.

A silence, a complete stillness had fallen over the group, then there was a sudden explosion of noise. Damn! I should have been paying more attention. I tugged on Susie's arm. 'What did I miss? I'm sorry, I was miles away.'

When she turned to look at me, her eyes were as wide as saucers. 'Didn't you hear?'

'Sorry, no.' I shook my head.

'It's Max. Wesley has been in touch with the police to find out about the arrangements for getting the body back home to the States and apparently there's a problem.' She hesitated and looked at me with some concern, probably realising this was the last thing I wanted to hear.

'What is it? What's the difficulty?' I asked, though with a sinking heart I'd a strong suspicion about what she was going to say next.

Susie spoke slowly. 'They're going to do further tests on Max's body. They have some questions about the cause of his accident and we'll all have to be interviewed again.'

My first inclination was to laugh, but that would have been wholly inappropriate in the circumstances. It was true I hadn't been in the castle when the death in the dungeon happened, but now, merely by being here, I'd some involvement.

Untangling the family history of these members of the Stuart clan was my sole purpose. Whatever the reason for Max's death, I had to keep my distance. Then I thought, a chill seizing my heart, was it possible she too had concerns about the circumstances of Max's death? Surely not. She'd arranged my visit before Max died. But then she might have had some worries about the group before the accident? I was beginning to see conspiracy everywhere.

I tried to catch her eye, but she was deep in conversation with Oscar and Connie, shaking her head from time to time. Then, as though Wesley hadn't spoken, the chatter in the room began again, discussing arrangements for attending the rehearsal for the Viking re-enactment at the school the following afternoon and the problem of Max seemed to have been quickly forgotten.

Susie turned back to me.

'I can't believe everyone is so unconcerned about Max?' I muttered. 'What's going on?'

She shrugged. 'As far as we know all the police want to do is conduct more tests. It'll probably be no more than routine. You heard what was said. He had a dicky heart and he shouldn't have been down in that dungeon without letting someone know where he was going. He thought he was a cut above the rest of us, always going on about some idea he had that would make him famous, how he'd get the benefit from his inheritance. Of course when you asked him for details, he clammed up. A lot of nonsense.'

'Hmm,' I said. I knew nothing about Max and very little about the others in the group, but there must surely have been a good reason for Max behaving as he did, going down into the dungeon. Then I said to myself, Stop this, Alison, it's no business of yours. It's no more than an unfortunate coincidence that this man died just before you arrived.

Susie grasped my arm, interrupting my thoughts. She smiled. 'Even if there is a problem, Alison, it's nothing to do with me, or indeed with you. There's plenty else going on with helping us explore any possible Stuart ancestry. Now dinner calls. I expect you'll want to have an early night after all your travelling?'

'Sounds an excellent idea.' And putting all my fears to the back of my mind, I followed her through to the dining room.

CHAPTER FOUR

There was an air of expectancy as I entered the lounge area of the Stuart Hotel late the next morning. After a restless night, I'd decided to skip breakfast, making do with coffee and the packet of biscuits on the hospitality tray in my room while I tried to come up with a strategy for conducting interviews with the Heritage Adventurers. Several attempts later I'd decided to keep everything simple, do a general chart of the Stuart line, then do a little summary about each of their families. Provided they had enough information. Having met them, I suspected only a few were really keen to do the work required to uncover their origins and the others would be happy with something that was a pleasant reminder of their links to the Stuart name.

I picked up the latest edition of The Buteman lying on the table in the foyer. The headline 'Mystery Death at Rothesay Castle,' jumped out at me. I scanned the article and the large photo of Max Stuart accompanying it. He had a pleasant face, his high domed forehead exaggerated by his receding hairline and the accompanying story gave details of his post as a History Professor at the University of California. I put the paper down with a sigh. The Heritage Adventurers must be hoping the Police would be able to close the case quickly.

The Americans were sitting together in a tightknit group near the large window at the far side and Wesley and Jerome stood up as I approached. Wesley saluted with a, 'Morning, Ma'am,' which threw me for a moment. Unused to being treated as if I were royalty, I indicated that they should sit, then covered my confusion by smiling.

By way of conversation I said, 'So you're also a Stuart?' then realised how critical that might sound. He didn't appear to be in the least offended as he replied with a grin, 'Well, I guess one of those darn Stuarts might have strayed a little far. Get my meaning?' He winked and I only just stopped myself winking back.

Lloyd was standing at the bar and now came towards me, clutching a glass. By the looks of him, this wasn't his first drink. 'Hi, Alison,' he said. 'Ready to roll?'

'Almost,' I smiled and was about to turn to speak to Susie when he said, 'I don't know if I said how great it is that you could make it. We were a bit worried for a while.'

Seeing the puzzled look on my face, he laughed. 'As I'm kinda heading up this little expedition to the homeland I'm responsible for all the arrangements. Susie was a bit concerned you'd decide at the last minute that this wasn't your kinda thing, this ancestor searching.'

Susie stepped forward. 'Yes, Alison is very experienced and will do all she can to help us, but let's not expect miracles, Lloyd.'

30

That should settle it, but Lloyd ignored her comment, taking a long swig of his drink and narrowing his eyes. 'Now that Max isn't here, annoying us all with his claims about his inheritance, I'm sure we'll get on fine.'

No one commented on his thoughtless description of the dead man, but a little murmur went from one to another in the group and I hurried to lighten the atmosphere with, 'At least we'll have fun looking into the possibilities,' before adding in a firm voice, 'but, as I said, anything I can come up with in the limited time is likely to be an overview.'

'Yes, sounds good,' said Oscar, fidgeting in his chair. 'I could show you what I've found out about my family. Some of it you'll think pretty good.' He began scrabbling through the pile of papers and I raised my hand to stop him.

'Perhaps later?'

'I don't think she's being rude,' said Connie, frowning.

Oscar shrugged and raised his eyes heavenwards. 'Let's have a walk along the seafront,' he said and together they walked slowly towards the door, Oscar all the while clutching his papers, by now secure in a cardboard folder.

It would take me a little time to get to know them, but fortunately they seemed to be taking seriously the requirement to wear their name badges.

The only person who appeared little interested in what was going on was Ricky, lurking in the shadows in the corner. Perhaps he was more upset about finding Max's body than any of the others realised. No one was giving him special attention, helping him come to terms

31

with what had happened. It wasn't that I was unsympathetic, but I'd had enough of sulky teenagers in my previous career as a teacher at Strathelder High School.

Lloyd moved to the front and climbed on to a chair to bring the group to order. This didn't seem to me to be a good idea as he stumbled and almost fell. But somehow he managed to regain his balance and said in a loud voice, 'You've already met Alison Cameron, but I wanted to say a few words about what she plans to do. She's been good enough to come over to join us at short notice and I guess we owe her a debt of gratitude for all her work.'

Bit of an exaggeration, I thought, as I hadn't actually done anything yet, so I smiled weakly, trying to look confident.

There was a little cheer as he concluded, 'So let's welcome her and give her all the cooperation she needs. She's going to start the interviews now, so if you have any special information about your ancestors, now's the time to tell.'

He came down from the chair without incident, much to my relief. One accident on this trip was more than enough.

There was no time to lose and I began to move among the group, taking some basic notes. There was no problem about their surnames, but in some ways that made it all even more confusing.

From these first brief meetings, it was clear it would be better to record the interviews: they all spoke quickly and tended to wander off into long irrelevant anecdotes about relatives not connected to their direct line. One thing was certain: from these initial discussions I was sure there were no illustrious ancestors lurking in the background, waiting to be discovered.

I was in the middle of a conversation with Margie Stuart, once again impressed by her elegant appearance and full make-up so early in the morning in contrast to my own hasty attempts to look presentable, when Connie and Oscar reappeared.

'Thanks, Margie,' I said, 'I'll get back to you later.'

'I'm so pleased I managed to get a place on this tour. It was full, but then someone dropped out….'

I smiled as I left her. It was important to have a preliminary word with every member of the group.

'Perhaps I can have a quick word with you, Connie,' I said as they sat down. Remembering what Oscar had said about Connie being slightly deaf, 'So you and Oscar have a connection with Bute,' I said, leaning forward.

'Yep, my grandfather. And Oscar's mother was from Scotland.'

'Ah, your grandfather came from Bute?'

'He certainly was a beaut of a man,' she replied proudly. 'That's what my ole Grandma used to say.'

'So,' I said leaning even closer so that my face was only a couple of inches from hers. She recoiled and I tried again, speaking as slowly and distinctively as I could. 'And that's why you're interested in this trip?'

'Yes,' she replied, a puzzled look on her face. 'Why are you speaking so slowly? I'm not deaf.'

I stood up. 'I'll be recording interviews later. I'll catch the details then.' I smiled encouragingly.

She had clearly misinterpreted this statement also, but before she had the opportunity to ask me to repeat what I'd said, there was a hubbub at the other end of the room and I looked over in time to see Lloyd rushing out, swaying a little as he did so, closely following the receptionist.

'What's going on?' I asked, sidling over to Dwayne.

He shrugged. 'Seems that the police have arrived to speak to Lloyd.' He looked upset. 'No idea what that's about.'

Wesley leaned over. 'I wouldn't worry, bro. It's probably nothing. They'll have a few questions for him as leader of the group. Probably want to confirm Max died accidentally and the funeral can be arranged. They have to check all possibilities before the body is released.'

'Suppose so.' He frowned. 'But I thought we'd cleared all that up when we were questioned by them earlier.'

'Yes, but Lloyd is the leader. That's all. Wait till he comes back. He'll tell us then and you'll see there's nothing to worry about.' With that Wesley slouched over to sit beside Jerome, leaning back in the chair and stretching out his long legs.

Susie joined us. 'Dwayne has some concerns about the police visit, 'I said, 'though Wesley is convinced there's nothing to worry about.'

Susie grabbed his arm and hugged him. 'Oh, I know this isn't the trip we planned for our anniversary, but I'm sure Alison's right and there's nothing to be anxious about. We only met Max on this trip so we know almost nothing about him. Don't worry.'

'I don't want your holiday to be spoiled, honey. That's all.'

'I think I've done enough for today. I'll organise recording the interviews. There's a lot more to consider than I thought.' I was beginning to feel a headache coming on and a breath of fresh air, a walk along the prom at the seafront was beckoning. An escape from the febrile atmosphere of the hotel, to stand in the warmth and watch the yachts coming in and going out of Rothesay harbour would be exactly what I needed.

'I could come with you?' Susie frowned. Perhaps she thought that I intended to escape on the next ferry to Wemyss Bay.

'No need. I won't be long. I'm probably a bit out of the way of doing interviews. I'll be fine now I've made a start.' I smiled to reassure her.

But I didn't make it as far as the front lobby as Lloyd reappeared, walking slowly this time, his face deathly pale.

'What's wrong, Lloyd? You okay?' Dwayne moved forward to catch his elbow as he looked as if he might fall. 'Come and sit down over here. What's happened?'

Lloyd made no protest, allowing himself to be led over to a comfortable seat in the lounge.

For a moment he sat there with his head in his hands, breathing deeply while we stood around in silence, waiting for him to recover.

Finally, curiosity got the better of Susie and she said, 'What's going on? What did the police say?'

Lloyd looked up, almost as if he'd only just realised she was there, then bowed his head again and started to talk without looking at her, gazing fixedly at his feet.

'It's Max,' he whispered. 'The police are treating it as a suspicious death. There has to be a full investigation. What am I going to tell the others, eh?'

35

This piece of news had certainly sobered him up and an idea flitted through my head. Was this drunken behaviour of Lloyd an act? I quickly dismissed this thought. I had to focus on the task I'd been recruited for. Nothing else concerned me and certainly not the death of a complete stranger.

No one replied to Lloyd's question. Susie turned to look at me, raising her eyebrows as though encouraging me to speak, but I'd no intention of being drawn into this against my better judgement and I went to stand by the door, ready to make my escape as soon as seemed proper. My hands felt sticky with sweat and I wiped them on my trousers. This is not your concern, this is not your concern, I repeated to myself.

There was a slight scuffling noise behind us. No one else seemed to notice, intent as they were on what Lloyd had said, waiting for him to speak again. I glanced around in time to see Ricky disappearing towards the lift, but not before I noticed the guilty look on his face. Had he been listening in?

CHAPTER FIVE

This news, the discovery that Max hadn't died as the result of an accident, caused great distress among the remaining Heritage Adventurers.

'It must be a mistake. This was the first time Max had been on the island,' said Connie in a shrill voice. 'Who could possibly want to kill him? What reason could there be…'

'Of course it's a mistake.' Jerome added. 'Nonsense. The police have got it wrong. It's exactly like the plot of a movie I was in some years ago when…'

Wesley narrowed his eyes, interrupting his tale. 'What makes you think he was killed by a stranger?'

This sudden intervention provoked an initial silence, then a flurry of responses.

'No way,' and 'How could you say that?' 'It must have been some madman.'

'You're not meaning it was one of us?' Lloyd's question was asked in honeyed tones, but the effect was immediate. The room fell silent and Wesley glanced over at him thoughtfully.

I took a deep breath, feeling as though there was a tight band across my chest.

Wesley gave a sad smile. 'Well, there ain't no other explanation, is there?' He stood still, looking from one member of the group to another, but everyone avoided his gaze until Margie said shakily, 'Does that mean the rest of the tour is cancelled?'

Lloyd shook his head. 'We'll have to be here yet awhile, so no sense in not going on with our plans.' Then, as though aware how callous that sounded he added hastily, 'We're all really sorry about Max, but…'.

No one replied. It was clear Max hadn't been the most popular person in the Heritage Adventurers and the group appeared to be more concerned about continuing with the tour than worrying about what had happened to him.

'The police will sort it out,' said Connie, peering over her spectacles. 'Anyway, I'm sure they got it wrong. Who would want to kill Max? He wasn't best liked, but even so…' Her voice trailed away to vigorous nods from several of the group, seemingly pleased someone had articulated what they were thinking.

'Let's get out of here,' croaked Susie and, grabbing Dwayne's arm, she ushered both of us out of the hotel to stop a little way down the High Street.

'Sorry – I couldn't stand being there a minute longer,' she said, toying with one of her earrings. She ran her fingers though her dark curly hair, destroying any attempt at a smart hairdo she might have made.

'We can't up and leave,' protested Dwayne, in a not unreasonable tone of voice. 'We're part of the group too. We have to support one another, Susie.'

'Yes, yes,' she sighed, 'but I wanted a couple of minutes away from it all.'

'How well did you know him?'

Susie looked over at Dwayne and indicated he should reply, though surely as one of the group leaders she'd have known the dead man better than the others?

Dwayne said roughly, 'None of us were that well acquainted with him, not really, so we didn't notice he was missing from the group. He was a bit of a loner. I tried to be friendly for sure, but he ignored me. Heck, why would he want to go down into that awful dungeon? Ricky was only up for it because he's a youngster, a bit of a daredevil. And there were plenty of people on hand if he got into trouble. It must have been an accident. Ain't possible one of our group was involved.'

'Max was a bit strange, you have to admit,' Susie mused, adding, 'Damn,' as her earring finally gave up the unequal struggle and fell to the ground.

I bent to pick it up as Dwayne muttered, 'Wasn't he a professor of something?' He frowned. 'I only spoke to him once or twice, but I kinda remember he said he was here because of some inheritance he was chasing down.'

'Everyone has a connection to the Stuarts, that's why they're here on Bute,' said Susie much more sharply than was usual for her. 'Max would be no different from anyone else.'

'Yes, but even so,' I waded in to what threatened to become an argument, 'surely there's no one in the party who would have wanted to kill Max?' This was no concern of mine. I hadn't even met the man. Here you go again, I rebuked myself, getting involved where you shouldn't.

Susie shrugged. 'Someone with your experience should realise the strangest things can happen, that there can be the most bizarre motive for killing someone.'

That logic I couldn't refute. On my various times on Bute, I'd been involved in many exploits that had defied explanation, so I kept quiet. I was determined to have nothing to do with this mysterious death, though in spite of all my good resolutions I had to admit to a certain sneaking interest.

'Let's get back inside,' said Dwayne as a couple of locals passed us, eyeing us strangely. On this small island news travels fast and it was likely they'd heard about the death. If they were curious, they were too polite to say anything and contented themselves with nodding, 'Good Afternoon.'

Inside the hotel all was quiet, as if the members of the group had, for the time being at least, exhausted all possibilities and explanations regarding the death of their fellow traveller.

'What's happening now?' I whispered.

'We're supposed to be going on a trip this afternoon to the Rothesay Joint Campus. It's all arranged and Zachary is expecting us. It's too late to change arrangements, I guess, and no one wants to sit around in the hotel thinking about Max.' She sounded not the least bit enthusiastic about the outing.

'There's no point,' I replied. 'Far better that people have something to occupy them, take their minds off what's happened.'

'She's right, Susie,' said Dwayne. 'We have to go on with the rest of the events planned for the tour.'

Lloyd was one step ahead, had clearly thought through all the options. He moved to the middle of the group, clapping his hands. 'Listen up everyone, I know it's really difficult for y'all, but Max would have wanted us to go on with the rest of our tour.'

'So you've had word from beyond the grave, bro,' muttered Wesley from the back of the room, but if Lloyd heard he ignored this remark.

He was right, of course. No purpose would be served by curtailing the trip at this stage. Rearranging their schedule would only cause more problems, leaving everyone at a loose end. Besides, no one seemed to be clear about what the police would want us to do. If Max had indeed been murdered, the leaders of the party might have to remain on Bute while investigations continued.

Lloyd's words seemed to hearten the rest of the group and there was a low murmur of approval. Picking up on this he added, 'So let's meet back here in half an hour in good time for the bus out to the Rothesay Joint Campus.'

In ones and twos, the company began to drift off.

'Guess we'd better get organised,' said Dwayne and he and Susie headed for the lift. 'What are you going to do, Alison?'

'I'll go up to my room in a minute,' I said. As Susie looked puzzled, I racked my brains to come up with an excuse for remaining behind. 'I'm really in need of a cup of tea,' was the best I could manage, but this left Susie more baffled than ever. I'm sure she was about to say, 'But there are tea making facilities in the room,' but instead she said, 'Fine, we'll see you here later.'

I waited patiently, watching to make sure Susie and Dwayne were on their way upstairs in the lift.

The last thing I needed was a cup of tea, but I'd spotted Ricky skulking in the far corner of the lounge, almost hidden behind a large potted palm tree. It was nothing to do with me, not really, but I was curious as to what information he had about the body in the dungeon at Rothesay Castle. I'd this strange feeling he knew more than he was telling us.

I tiptoed over, concerned he'd spy me and take off, but he was too engrossed in some game or other he was playing on his Tablet and as I said, 'Well, hello, Ricky. Aren't you getting ready for the trip to see the rehearsal for the Pageant,' he looked up, startled, only just catching his Tablet as it slipped from his grasp.

He tried to switch it off quickly, but not before I'd glimpsed what he'd been looking at. I had to focus because my first thought was he was playing one of those games teenagers seem to be addicted to. But the more I thought about it, the more certain I became that Ricky had been looking at a webpage concerned with Stuart family inscriptions. Given his apparent lack of interest in his family links to the Stuarts, why ever would he be interested in that, I asked myself?

CHAPTER SIX

There's something about Spring on Bute. How suddenly the air becomes softer, smelling of brine and the southerly winds that caused disruption to the ferries in the winter now have a gentler feel. Swathes of daffodils grace every verge and the burgeoning greenery tumbles over ancient stone walls, giving promise of fine days to come.

Outside the Stuart Hotel, I stood enjoying the feeling of the sun on my face, relishing the moment as I waited for the others to appear.

There was a sense of suppressed excitement as we boarded the coach for the short journey to the college. I'd have been happy to walk up the High Street, given that I'd had few opportunities to enjoy the bracing air of the seaside since arriving and the college wasn't far from the hotel. But with the short timescale of this project, I had to remain with the members of the group. Hoping that informal opportunities to ask questions might prove useful, I selected a seat in front of Margie and Wesley. While both were inclined to be chatty, their expectations of any direct connection with famous Stuarts were tempered by common sense.

Helena was accompanying us and as the driver started up the engine with a cheery, 'Everyone sitting comfortably?' she slid into the seat beside me.

'Have you been a tour guide for long?' I asked, trying to find a way to engage her in conversation as she appeared to be content to sit in silence, something that doesn't suit me one little bit.

She shook her head and pushed her long fringe out of her eyes. 'Only this year, but I'm lucky to have this job.' She made a face. 'I had to come back to sort out my mother's effects. She died a few months ago.'

'Oh, I'm sorry to hear that,' I said quickly.

She acknowledged this with a nod of her head. 'She'd been ill for some time. But you know how it is. I haven't lived here for many years. I left to go to art college, but there were no jobs in that field on the island.'

'Or in many places,' I muttered. 'My daughter, Deborah, found that out. She's had a whole variety of jobs since leaving art college. So what made you come back to Bute?'

Helena shot me a sidelong glance. 'I was divorced recently and left penniless. One of the reasons I returned to the island. This kind of work suits me fine, but it will only be temporary.'

'A pamphlet about those Stuarts will be a great souvenir of our time on Bute,' said Margie, leaning forward from the seat behind, putting an end to our discussion.

Margie and I continued to chat about the Stuarts until we turned into the entrance to the Rothesay Joint Campus. The car park was busy and the bus drove around twice before finding a bay close to the college on the far right hand side. A long building, with the appearance of being low in spite of having three stories, sat square in front of us: to the left was the primary school, to the right was the college and the academy sat in the middle.

As we came off the bus a tall, skinny, frenetic man came out of the main entrance to the college and hurried towards us. As he came closer, we could see clearly his cropped hair, a shade of red which surely wasn't natural, the colour much at odds with his dark straggly beard.

'Is he wearing eyeliner?' I whispered to Susie.

She giggled, 'Looks like it. Perhaps he's in stage make-up.'

'But he's the director, not one of the actors.'

'Oh, don't be so stuffy, Alison. If you lived where I do, you'd be used to the strange ways of these artistic types.'

Zachary grinned and stretched out his hand to Lloyd, who'd strode forward to the front of the group.

'Delighted to meet you. I'm Zachary Benford.'

Suddenly he registered the silence as we stared at him and his attire of tight jeans and an equally body-hugging t-shirt embellished with the slogan Fair Play for Actors. He broke out into a peal of laughter, clearly amused by the reaction he'd caused. 'Oh, sorry, I should have said at once. We're all ready for you.' He winked. 'Even me. I thought you'd like to see things as close to the final version as possible.'

Lloyd blustered, 'We weren't quite sure what to expect,' but it was hard to tell if he was talking about the rehearsal or Zachary's strange appearance.

Still chuckling, Zachary said, 'If you'd like to come with me, we'll go straight to the college theatre and I'll talk you through what's happening. I'm sure you'll find it exciting.'

Now, as though to make up for the earlier silence, the members of the group chattered noisily as we followed him through the double doors and into the main entrance hall.

'The theatre is right at the back,' he said, waving to the woman on the reception desk and indicating the way along the corridor leading from the foyer. He picked up speed and began to race ahead, shadowed by Jerome who was attempting to establish his credentials as a fellow actor.

As the rest of us trooped obediently behind him, some keeping up with difficulty, I noticed the walls were adorned with old theatre posters, many of famous people, but several with Zachary in the cast. I stood for a moment looking at one of him in the role of Eric Birling in An Inspector Calls, clearly a part from his younger days, then pushed through to the front to catch up with him. He was biting his nails, but stopped as I came up alongside him, turning to give me the benefit of a dazzling smile.

'So you've spent some time in the theatre? Or so I see from the posters.' Close up, I realised he wasn't as young as I'd first thought.

'Yes, indeed.' He made a mocking little bow. 'Had to give up when the parts dried up. It's a great game when you're young, not so good as you get older. I was lucky enough to go back as a mature student and get a teaching qualification.' In spite of his assertions that

46

he'd been 'lucky' I detected an underlying note of bitterness in his reply.

As we reached the theatre Zachary fetched a key from his pocket to open up.

I don't know what I'd anticipated. Something like a school hall with a slightly more upmarket set of chairs perhaps, but this was a proper theatre, modern in design and, even to my inexperienced eye, the polished wood of the beamed ceiling, the impressive stage and the gleaming floor appeared to be best quality.

Judging by the murmurs of astonishment, I wasn't the only one so surprised and Zachary grinned, pleased by the impression the room had made.

'Yes, it's quite something, isn't it?'

'How on earth was the college able to afford this?' The words were out before I'd time to think.

Zachary pointed to a large plaque in the far corner of the room, near the stage. 'That tells the story.'

Now intrigued, I wandered over to inspect it as the others settled themselves in the plush red velvet seats, Zachary calling out, 'Come right down to the front. You'll get a better view here.'

The plaque was made of highly polished brass and the message on it was short.

Funded by subscriptions from members of the Stuart Clan worldwide.

I turned to say to the group, 'Have you seen this?' But it was too late. Zachary had bounded on to the stage, his face alight with excitement. Once an actor, always an actor: he was clearly delighted to be in front of an audience again.

He raised his voice and the last of the chatter died away. 'Could give me your attention for a minute? I'm delighted to welcome you all to our theatre. During this rehearsal you'll see several extracts from the show we're planning to put on at the castle on the last night of your tour. Sit back and enjoy it.'

He loped to the front of the stage and swung down into the orchestra pit to fiddle with a series of buttons on the large console there. There was a clicking sound, setting in motion an array of lights, and then the music started.

From the wings a group of children, dressed in full costume as Vikings, suddenly appeared and began a mock fight as the music grew louder and louder. As though on a word of command they stopped and stood stock-still and a young man, clearly one of Zachary's drama class, came striding on, dressed as King William the First, followed closely by another actor wearing a more sombre outfit of a brown jerkin and leggings. This was Walter, the High Steward, or Stuart, I assumed.

'I seize Bute for my people,' intoned the King, waving his sword about and narrowly missing one of the children now surrounding him. A boy in the far corner nudged his companion and they began to giggle, making mock of the actor portraying the king as he continued to declaim about 'a great victory' and 'freedom for Bute'.

There was a scuffle at the back and one of the Vikings lurched forward.

'Careful, Frida,' called Zachary from the orchestra pit. 'We don't want any accidents.'

Frida giggled and resumed her place in the group of Vikings, whispering to the girl beside her.

48

This tableau was swiftly cut short, to be followed by a succession of similar scenes: women wailing over their dead Viking King Magnus, peasants rejoicing as King William walked among them, shadowed by Walter.

Zachary was clearly in his element and the rest of the rehearsal was a lively affair as he went bounding up on to the stage to give directions, then back down into the orchestra pit to alter the lights or the music, all the while pointing and pulling faces to show his displeasure or pleasure. It might have been only a rehearsal, but the whole event had a curiously disjointed air thanks to Zachary's inability to stay in one place for long.

If someone fluffed a line or missed a cue, he would make a great fuss and call out in his high-pitched voice, 'No, no, no. What's your problem?' as he made a play of rubbing his brow as though in anguish. It was evident the cast were well-used to this kind of behaviour because they ignored him.

'Is it time to go yet?' a little voice piped up and one of the children was pushed to the front of the stage.

'Not yet, Bronwyn. Just one or two little tweaks and that will be all for today.' He rushed back down to the console, then back on to the stage, moving people this way and that until he was satisfied.

Bronwyn retreated behind the other Vikings to a great deal of giggling and nudging. I heard her whisper, 'He promised there'd be cake for our break, but I can't see any.'

Zachary pretended not to notice, saying as he turned to us, 'The finale is being kept as a surprise. I'm sure you'll be impressed by it. Everyone in the cast has been sworn to secrecy.'

49

Then, as suddenly as it had begun the rehearsal was over and Zachary leapt down to shut off the console before running back onto the stage.

'That's only to give you a flavour,' he said. 'The finished production will be much more polished and we'll have the whole castle to work with.' He waved his hands wildly to give us a feeling of the scope of the final performance. 'We won't be constrained as we are here.'

No one could fault his enthusiasm, but it all seemed rather ramshackle and I wondered how he'd manage to turn in a professional performance in the time left.

Zachary gazed out at the members of the Heritage Adventurers. 'Any questions?'

There was a shuffling of feet and just as it appeared he'd get off lightly, saying, 'Good. Well, then…' Ricky stood up. 'I gotta question. How come the Vikings are half the size of the Scotch fighters? Don't seem fair to me.'

He gazed around, a look of triumph on his face, expecting approval, but there was silence, though one or two muttered at his audacity and I was tempted to correct his use of the word 'Scotch'.

'It's meant to be symbolical,' replied Zachary, an icy edge to his voice.

'Symbolical?' Ricky sneered, making it perfectly plain he'd no idea what Zachary was talking about.

'Yes,' said Zachary patiently, standing still for a moment. 'The Vikings aren't as good as the Brandanes and that's shown by the difference in size.'

Ricky's mother tugged at his sleeve. 'Sit down. You're making a spectacle of yourself.'

'Seems crazy.' Ricky wasn't going to be deterred. Now that he had the attention of the room, he was determined to continue.

Frida came up beside me and hissed in my ear. 'And he was told if he didn't involve the Primary School he wouldn't get the funding for the Pageant. There will be a lot more going on at the castle than this play. It's only one of a number of events on the day, but Zachary wants to make out this is the most important.'

Ah, that made more sense. If it was to be a community venture, there would have to be as many of the locals involved as possible.

'Besides,' said the King, 'this is only part of the performance. Zachary's keeping the best bits for the night. Wants to surprise everyone.'

Inspired by Ricky, there were a few further questions, but none was difficult and Zachary looked well pleased as he ended the session. 'Thanks for coming along. I look forward to seeing you all at the performance on Saturday night at the castle.'

We trooped back to the bus, as I again pondered why Zachary had to be in make-up to press a few buttons and jump about telling everyone else what to do.

'It looks as if it'll be a great evening,' said Connie, coming up beside me. 'How exciting to see this in the castle.'

'Yes, it should be quite a spectacle,' I agreed, not mentioning my concerns about the one thing that might cause a problem – the unpredictable Scottish weather. I hoped Zachary had a contingency plan. Most likely it would be staged in the Great Hall if the weather was wet.

The mood on the bus as we returned to the hotel was merry, the problem of Max forgotten or at least ignored for a while. This little peek at the rehearsal was a bonus they hadn't expected and if the performance went well the tour would end on a high note.

Susie came up and sat in the empty seat behind me: as Connie had latched on to me and was talking nineteen to the dozen about anything and everything, I was pleased at this interruption.

She leaned over, talking quietly. 'What did you think of Zachary?' as Connie turned to chat to Oscar.

'He seemed very enthusiastic and everyone is looking forward to the performance.' Best to be non-committal until I'd a better idea of her reason for asking the question.

'Mmm. Don't you think it odd that he should want us all up there for the rehearsal? The surprise element of the actual performance might be lost.'

'Oh, Susie,' I said. 'Please don't go making difficulties. Did you notice that plaque near the stage?'

'What plaque?' She frowned as though trying to recall.

'The inscription said the theatre had been funded by subscriptions from members of the Stuart clan. It's clear he's very proud of it. And if we hadn't gone to the campus for the rehearsal we might not have seen it. Don't you think that perhaps that was his reason for bringing us up there? A party of possibly rich Americans might be exactly what he needs to get more funds for his performances. It can't be cheap running something like that and from what I know of Simon's time as a head of department in a further education college, their budget wouldn't be able to support such a venture on a long term basis.'

'Possibly.' She didn't sound convinced. 'I thought there was something decidedly shifty about him.'

I laughed. 'It was difficult to tell under that make-up and his frantic way of working.'

Whatever was worrying Susie about Zachary, I'd no intention of playing to her concerns. The Heritage Adventurers would only be here for a short time longer. I wouldn't be drawn into events that had nothing to do with my assignment, no matter how intriguing Susie thought they might be. Nor how much she thought I might be able to help solve any mystery. I'd had quite enough of that in the past.

CHAPTER SEVEN

Susie and I have been friends for years, have supported each other through difficult times, but even so I was less than happy at her suggestion we go over to Rothesay Castle and, 'Have a look around, in case there's anything the police might have missed.'

'That's most unlikely,' I pointed out. 'From what I gather they've been over the place with a fine toothcomb. How on earth do you think we might spot something they've missed? Anyway, it's not a job for an amateur. Leave it be, Susie.'

She shrugged. 'I know it seems unlikely, but the thing is, we know the people in the group, have a better idea of what they might do.'

'Uh, uh.' This wasn't going to persuade me. 'You might know them, but I've only met them, so I've no idea what you think I might contribute. And I didn't know Max at all. Besides,' playing what I thought might be my trump card, 'Simon would be furious if he thought I was involved in another mysterious death. He's always worried about my safety.'

Most people, faced with my steely resolve, would quietly back down, but then Susie isn't most people.

She caught me by the arm. 'Simon doesn't have to know anything about it. I'm not proposing you become involved, only that we have a quick look at the Castle. I feel some responsibility to the group, given that I volunteered to be one of the leaders. Surely you're willing to help me, Alison.' She didn't actually say, 'After the many times I've helped you.' She didn't have to.

This conversation was taking place outside the hotel, across from the Castle and well away from anyone who might overhear. I glanced over at its vast grey bulk, topped by the ruined tower, the water of the moat glittering in the afternoon sunshine. Perhaps if I did as she suggested, we could put this mad idea of solving the mystery of the death of one of her fellow travellers to rest and leave it to the police. Then I could focus my full attention on the task I'd been recruited for.

Dinner the previous night had been a subdued affair, with few opportunities to elaborate on the information gleaned so far from the Heritage Adventurers. The good spirits engendered by the visit to the Rothesay Joint Campus had been short-lived. After several half-hearted attempts to engage the more promising of the group I decided to wait another day before resuming the interviews, allow them time to remember any information that might be helpful.

'Okay,' I said, adding in an effort to assert my authority, 'but it will have to be later this afternoon. I have to go to the bank.' Perhaps by the time I returned she'd have thought better of her idea.

'Fine, fine,' she agreed eagerly. 'That suits. We've a free afternoon and Dwayne and some of the others want to have a walk out to Craigmore. I've already said I wouldn't join them, so there's no problem about getting away without being noticed.'

'About two thirty then,' I agreed and began to walk down the High Street towards town. Rothesay has a good variety of shops, with the added advantage of being free of the jostling crowds you find on the mainland. It was true I had to go to the bank: in my haste to leave I'd not had time before boarding the train from Glasgow Central. But I also wanted to have a wander along the main street to see what changes had taken place since my last visit to the island.

To my delight little had altered in this part of the town. Yes, one or two of the shops had relocated, but only further along Montague Street. The Electric Bakery still dispensed its selection of savouries and pastries to an eager clientele, the Bute Tool company catered across a wide range from DIY to the latest toys, all set out in imaginative window displays and the merchandise in the clothes shop of Fraser Gillies continued to offer a selection for the more traditionally-minded visitor and local alike.

One or two passers-by nodded to me, probably curiously aware that my face was familiar, but not sure why. I smiled and waved – it was good to be back in this island community after the anonymity of a large place like London and my spirits lifted. Could I persuade Simon to join me for a holiday here at the end of my contract? By then the Americans would have left the island and we'd still have time to visit Deborah in Glasgow before returning to the bustle of London. He'd been working long hours of late, was due some leave, and a couple of days to unwind in the peace and tranquillity of Bute was exactly what he needed.

The visit to the bank took longer than I'd bargained for, partly because I needed a mini statement and the ATM printer appeared to have run out of ink. Inside the bank I joined the queue, but those in front of me were clearly in the mood for gossip as much as for business. On Bute, life proceeds at a comfortably slow pace.

I was standing behind a young woman with shoulder length brown hair, pondering what I'd learned to date about connections of the Americans to the island, when suddenly I was startled out of my daydream by her words. Without thinking, I leaned forward and tried to catch what she was saying, conscious I might have misheard.

'That Max, the one found dead in the dungeon at Rothesay Castle? He wasn't born in America, though he claimed to have been.'

I couldn't hear the reply from the teller behind the glass partition, but it was clear from the expression on her face and the way she was nodding that either this piece of information wasn't news to her or else she was being polite.

This was an intriguing scrap of information, encouraging me to shuffle closer to find out what the young woman would say next, almost bumping into her as I did so. She swung around and looked at me in surprise and I said, 'Sorry,' before swiftly moving back and making as though I was engrossed in the contents of my handbag.

Whatever her intention, this action of mine put an end to her conversation with the teller and she quickly concluded her business and left, giving me a wary look as she passed.

I moved to the counter and explained my request for a mini statement.

'Not a problem,' she said with a smile as I gave her my bank card. I stood waiting, speculating if I dare quiz her about the conversation I'd heard a few moments before. How best to introduce the subject? As she handed over my money with the statement, I said in a matter-of-fact way, trying hard to sound as though I was merely passing the time, 'I'm with that group of Americans at the Stuart Hotel. It's been a rather dreadful experience for them, the way one of the party died so unexpectedly.'

There was a moment's hesitation, enough to make me realise she was weighing up how she should reply and I reproached myself for being so blunt.

She seemed to consider for a few moments before saying, 'Yes, it's terrible about the death of one of them.' She looked over my shoulder to the person behind me in the queue to indicate the conversation was at an end.

I nodded, choosing my next words carefully, hoping she wouldn't suspect I'd overheard the discussion with the previous customer. Now I'd started, I had to go on. 'Yes, to come all the way from America and die so tragically here.'

She stared at her computer screen, carefully avoiding making eye contact, so that I had to lean forward to catch what she was saying. 'Mmm. There's a rumour that he wasn't American at all. That he'd some connection to the island.'

She looked up suddenly, a worried expression on her face, as though she'd said more than she should, but I'd no intention of stopping now. 'Oh, indeed, why would that be?' I wanted to encourage her to continue, but she pursed her lips. 'No idea,' she said, once again staring past me to indicate I should make way for the next customer. 'Is that all I can help you with today?'

As I hurried outside, the young woman with brown hair was standing at the Bute Tool Company, gazing in at the window and as I passed she turned towards me.

What made me speak to her? I've no idea and if she hadn't turned around, I suspect I wouldn't have stopped. But she did, so I said, 'Hello, don't I know you from somewhere?' It wasn't exactly a lie as I did recognise her from the queue in the bank and it was the best I could come up with on the spur of the moment.

She regarded me with a puzzled look, as though trying to recall where we might have met, but then good manners got the better of her and she said, smiling broadly, 'I'm sorry, your face is familiar, but I can't place you.'

'Oh, probably at some event on the island,' I replied, introducing myself but not wanting to be too specific. Best if she didn't remember me from previous trips. There was no point in being hesitant. 'I couldn't but help but overhear what you were saying to the teller in the bank…about Max Stuart? He wasn't an American?'

She looked alarmed. 'It's only gossip,' she said quickly. 'I didn't know him or anything.'

'But gossip says he was well acquainted with the island?'

She frowned. 'It was old Mrs Halson who lives out at Ardbeg. I work with Social Services and she was one of my clients before she went into a nursing home. I still visit her from time to time. She saw the photo of Max Stuart in The Buteman after they found his body in the dungeon at the castle.'

'And…' I prompted.

The young woman shrugged. 'As soon as she saw it Mrs Halson said, 'That looks very like young Max Colpin. I haven't seen him for a good number of years of course, but it's impossible to mistake that long nose. Runs in the family.'

'Perhaps being elderly she was wrong?' This seemed a very strange story indeed.

'No. I did say to her, ask her how she was so certain. Working with old people as I do, I know eyesight can fade or they can forget. But there's nothing wrong with Mrs Halson except old age and a touch of arthritis.'

'So did you know about him?'

She shook her head, sending her mass of brown hair swinging. 'I was born on the island, but the family moved away when I was a teenager. I only came back to take up the job in Social Services because my husband has a building job on the island.' She hesitated. 'But people here have long memories, that's for sure.'

She didn't seem to have any other information, or else decided she'd already said too much. 'I have to go or I'll be running late for my next client.'

I stood aside to let her pass, bidding her goodbye. Could her story be correct? It didn't seem likely. More like old Mrs Halson had made an error, confused him with someone else who looked similar.

And yet, and yet. The girl was right – people here had good memories. In a community like this, family recollections lingered.

But Max Colpin? As far as I knew everyone in the party, except for Susie and Dwayne, was a Stuart. That was the purpose of the trip. And why pretend to be a Stuart? I couldn't imagine what use that would serve. And yet, there was a strong suspicion his death had been no accident. If so, someone must have had a motive. What had I got myself into?

CHAPTER EIGHT

Now I was faced with a dilemma. I could either forget what I'd heard at the bank and the conversation about Mrs Halson or I could tell Susie. The last thing I wanted to do was become enmeshed yet again in events that didn't concern me, but on the other hand if Max's death was suspicious surely I should let someone know what Mrs Halson had said? Then I thought about what would happen, about the consequences of my discovery. Susie would rush off as usual without considering all the possibilities and I'd be in trouble if it turned out to be a blunder, no more than island gossip or most likely, a case of mistaken identity.

There was also my growing concern that this was supposed to be an anniversary trip for Susie and Dwayne. And so far, they'd had precious few opportunities to celebrate. No, best not to confuse matters.

Perhaps it would be an idea to go directly to the police and tell them what I'd learned, but would they believe me without any evidence? Besides it wasn't a crime to change your name, was it? Max may well have had a good reason for doing so.

Why not be honest about it? And why pretend you'd lived all your life in America when you'd been born on Bute, were a real Brandane, especially on a trip like this?

There seemed to be no easy answer and I weighed up the pros and cons of the various options as I walked slowly back towards the hotel, arriving at the entrance without coming to any firm decision.

One thing struck me forcibly – there was little grief being exhibited by other members of the party about Max's death. No one had said much, as though having handed it over to the police, the feeling was that they could forget all about it, get on with the remainder of the holiday.

Then I rebuked myself for these unkind opinions. How did I know what was happening behind the scenes? Lloyd was in charge and no doubt he was liaising with the police, dealing with any family Max might have. Once again I reminded myself it was no concern of mine.

As I came into the hotel I could hear sounds of laughter from several of the group seated in the far corner of the bar. My views about the reactions of the group to Max's death were quickly confirmed as Lloyd came sauntering over as if he hadn't a care in the world, though there were dark circles under his eyes.

'Hi, Alison, we were looking for you.'

'I had to go to the bank. Did Susie not tell you?'

He grinned, but again I noticed how that grin didn't reach his eyes. 'Guess she did, now, but there's been a development and I have to speak to you.'

A feeling of panic seized me. What on earth was he going to say?

As though able to read my thoughts, he said, patting me on the arm, 'Don't look so worried. We've been offered another tour of the castle, since we had to cut the last one short. Pretty decent of them, ain't it? And I guessed you'd want to come along with us. Pretty convenient too, as this was supposed to be a free afternoon.' He leaned over to whisper in my ear. 'Got to be better than last time.'

So I'd guessed correctly. There'd been little love lost between Max and Lloyd, or any of the group it would appear. Even so, how did the other members of the group feel about going back to the place where the death had taken place so soon after the event?

I tried to catch Susie's eye, but she was busily chatting to Dwayne and to Oscar.

Better to agree. I shrugged. 'Yes, I'll come along with you,' though I'd no intention of going anywhere near the dungeon. In a way it was a piece of good luck as it would allow Susie and me to carry out the search she'd suggested, without raising suspicions or having to make a separate visit to the castle.

Susie came over and I said, 'I thought Dwayne and some of the others wanted to spend the afternoon having a walk out to Craigmore?'

Susie shrugged. 'They're happy with the change of plan, the opportunity to have a tour of the castle.'

After checking no one could overhear, I leaned over to say in a quiet voice, 'It will let you have a proper look.'

She stared at me as though I'd said something odd. 'No, no. I've realised we won't have access to the dungeon and that's the important place to search.' She shook her head. 'There's no option: we'll have to make an arrangement to visit some other time.'

'But surely you're mistaken, should…' Before I could finish, there was a noise at the other end of the room and, 'Lunchtime, folks,' Lloyd boomed, interrupting the little groups clustered around the bar. If nothing else the bar was doing a roaring trade. Every time the manager appeared he had a huge grin on his face.

We dutifully trooped behind Lloyd into the dining room. I'd have to try to catch Susie on her own, persuade her to give up this mad idea. I'd noticed that, with the exception of Susie, everyone in the party kept together as though, mindful of what had happened to Max, they were afraid some misadventure might befall them if they strayed too far.

I sidled up to her. 'Who's leading the tour this afternoon? Is it the same person as before?'

'Uh, uh. Not sure. Probably Helena. I think Lloyd booked her to be our guide for the whole trip to Bute.' She wrinkled her nose.

I tried one more time to persuade her. 'We'll see what kind of opportunity we have to search the place. Remember the dungeon will still be out of bounds.' This seemed to me to be a positive advantage, but there was no time for further speculation as we made our way to our table.

Make the best of it I told myself, you're only here for a very short time. And the death of Max Stuart or Max Colpin, if that indeed was his name, is no concern of yours.

Determined to be positive, I made a start on my soup, but I'd tasted no more than a mouthful when

65

Connie, who was sitting beside me, put down her spoon and whispered in my ear with relish rather than anxiety, 'Any more word about what happened to Max? Was he really murdered?'

Unwilling to indulge in gossip, I replied, more sharply than intended, 'I know nothing about it,' and resumed eating.

She wasn't to be so easily put off. She patted me on the arm. 'I can tell you something. There have been several rumours about him, y'know. The word is his signing up for this tour was a bit of a mystery. Understand?' She winked at me as though we were both privy to some secret about Max. 'He was a history professor; so why would he want to come on a tour like this?'

Best to make it clear I wasn't going to start speculating about Max with someone like Connie whose refusal to admit she'd problems with her hearing could lead to misunderstandings.

'I'm sure it's best left to the police. They are very capable, you know.'

She wasn't so easy to dissuade. 'Indeed. But I've heard he wasn't quite what he seemed. For one thing, there's a rumour that he wasn't a Stuart, not a real Stuart any road. Now ain't that suspicious. It explains a lot.' She stopped. 'You should have a word with Margie.She'll be able to tell you a thing or two about Max.'

But surely not why he was murdered, I thought, as I applied myself to finishing my soup. How come Connie also had this idea that Max wasn't a Stuart, unless he'd told her. Perhaps I was making a great fuss about nothing. Determined as I was to stick to my brief, I was being slowly sucked in to this mystery. And I'd yet to make a decision about whether to add to Susie's worries by telling her about Mrs Halson.

CHAPTER NINE

Rothesay Castle was directly opposite the hotel and within a few minutes we'd reached the front of the Gatehouse by walking across the bridge spanning the moat. As we passed the ticket office, I spied Lloyd standing on tiptoe, counting us. I couldn't blame him for fretting. The last thing he'd want was for someone else to go missing.

'Now, make sure you keep together. Is that clear? We'll go with the guide and I'll be keeping a close eye on y'all.'

Susie raised her eyebrows as she looked at me. 'He's being ultra-careful,' she whispered, 'as though any one would consider wandering off after what's happened.' Although at first seemingly disappointed that we wouldn't have the chance to reconnoitre the castle on our own, she'd recovered her good humour. 'We can have a proper exploration later,' she said as soon as we had a moment alone, out of earshot of the others. 'Probably best if we do it on our own, rather than starting now. We don't want to alert anyone.'

I nodded, but it wasn't a sign of agreement. With a bit of luck, there would be so many group activities lined up for the remaining days I could plead the need to maximise the time to finish my commission and duck out of this investigation she seemed so keen on.

As we grouped together in the shelter of the Gatehouse, Helena was standing waiting for us, clutching a large folder to her chest.

'I thought she might give up, leave after Max's body was found like that,' whispered Margie, coming up beside me. 'But I guess, like everyone else, she has to make a dollar.' She made a face. 'He wasn't worth worrying about.'

She moved away, nudging her way through to where Jerome was standing. I smiled as I saw the look on his face and he moved to talk animatedly to Dwayne, leaving Margie frowning.

Suddenly aware of the importance of this visit, there was a hush in the group, and a shiver went through them as they huddled closer together, as though seeking comfort.

Helena began in a brisk and efficient manner. If she was worried, she didn't show it. 'Hello, everyone, over this way please,' but her voice was low and it was left to Lloyd to shepherd us through the Gatehouse.

Susie went forward and caught her arm. 'You'll have heard the news?'

Helena looked startled. 'What news?'

'There's some problem about Max's death. It may not have been an accident.'

Helena frowned. 'Nonsense. What else could it have been? You remember how he kept going on about some inheritance, how he'd have to check it all out…'

'Yes, but in the dungeon?'

69

Helena shook her head. 'No matter. This way, everyone. Please keep together.'

We walked in under the stone arch of the Gatehouse, moving quickly towards the open area, our footsteps echoing on the flagstones. Although the roof now boasted a series of lights and the side passages where archers had once defended the castle through the tiny slits in the stone were well illuminated, it was still gloomy. One by one we quickened our pace as we passed the dungeon, still cordoned off by blue and white tape, and although some gave it a sidelong glance, most averted their eyes as though glad to be heading for the green sward in the centre of the castle.

As we emerged into the sunlight, blinking in the sudden brightness, to stand on the open space in the centre, our guide started her talk with an abruptness that showed she was well aware of how people might feel about their previous visit. Helena was evidently anxious to divert attention from what had happened. 'In Scottish terms this is a very unusual castle as it's circular rather than square.' She waved her arms around, 'Much of what you see around you goes back to the 1200s. There's an excellent model of the castle in the Great Hall in the Gatehouse, which you can view later. That will give you a better idea. This area wouldn't have been empty as it is now, of course. This was where the dwellings for the inhabitants of the castle were situated and the stabling for the horses. Remember this was like a little town in itself, designed to be easily protected from invaders.'

'Well, guess it didn't work, did it?' said Jerome. 'According to the play Zachary's putting on for us, there were plenty of successful invaders. I remember once when I was playing the part of a medieval knight in The Story of Camelot, there were…'

We didn't hear the end of his story as, 'Yes, yes,' interrupted Helena. 'You can read all about it in the various publications about the castle. I'm giving you no more than basic information. Anyway,' she concluded, 'as I said, you'll have a very good idea of what the castle originally looked like from the model in the Great Hall.'

'That's where we had our wedding,' Susie whispered to Margie who was standing beside her, grasping Dwayne's hand as she spoke.

Margie looked surprised. 'So is this a kind of nostalgia trip? I was lucky to get a place at short notice.'

Susie smiled. 'Not really. Perhaps only a few years married is a bit early for reminiscing. Truth is, we didn't investigate the castle's history at the time. We were too taken with the romance of getting married somewhere like this.'

I could see Margie mentally calculating how old Susie was and if she found it odd that she'd married so recently, she gave no sign. Margie had lost no time in telling us she was a widow and given the way I'd noticed her deliberately seeking out Jerome, possibly she'd hopes in that direction.

There was no time for further questions, however, as Helena ushered us across the grass, talking all the while, pointing out the well in the centre. 'The original castle was wooden, but by 1230 there was a stone castle on this site, built by Alan, High Steward of Scotland, or his son…'

Oh dear, I hoped she wasn't going to continue like this, with what promised to be a dry as dust history lesson. Already I detected a restlessness in several of the group, but the well, now covered by a metal grill, seemed to have caught their attention.

'Is it a wishing well?' asked Connie, pulling Helena's attention back to the mesh covered circle.

Helena frowned. 'I don't think so,' she began, but at last Ricky had found something to take his attention and with a speed that took us by surprise he pulled a coin from his pocket and knelt down to poke it through the mesh. 'Let's see how far it goes down,' he said. 'You have to count. Every number means ten feet.'

Several others from the group had come over to join him, scrabbling for change to follow his lead in throwing a coin into the well.

'One, two, three, four…' he began to count, then pulled back as there was a loud clink.

'It ain't very deep,' he said in a disappointed tone as he stood up. He turned to the others. 'Save your dough.'

His words failed to deter some of the group and there was a ripple of excitement as one after the other they tried to outdo Ricky.

'Well, of course, it isn't deep now,' snapped Helena, unable to disguise her annoyance at having her discourse on the castle interrupted. 'At one time it would have been the main source of water for the castle, but in later years it was partly filled in. Now, if we could resume the tour.'

Reluctantly the party regrouped, reconciled to moving on.

Helena was in full flow again and with some effort I forced myself to concentrate on what she was saying

'…attacked and taken by the Norsemen soon after, an occurrence which happened regularly from then on…'

I switched off again. I'd have to come up with something more exciting than Helena had if I was to grab the attention of this group with stories of their possible ancestors.

Out of the corner of my eye I spotted Ricky. Now he'd discovered the potential of the castle for making mischief, he wasn't about to stop. He'd moved to the back of the group and, with a glance around to make sure no one had spotted him, he began to sneak towards the set of stairs leading up to the rampart beside one of the ruined towers.

With a speed that belied his bulk, he sprinted up the last few stairs to lean over the railing at the top.

'Yoo-hoo,' he called, waving his arms to attract attention. 'Look where I am.'

Several members of the party turned to look in her direction as Ricky's mother screamed out, 'Come down from there, you stupid boy. It's dangerous up on that ledge.' She began to move towards the stairs, but Helena laid a restraining hand on her arm. 'Don't worry,' she said. 'It's perfectly safe, else it would be cordoned off. There's a door up there that leads to the Great Hall. We'll be going there next so you can catch up with him.'

Ricky's mother shook herself free. 'You've no idea,' she said, 'my poor baby's afraid of heights.'

He didn't seem the least bit concerned about the height to me, but she rushed to the bottom of the stairs. 'Ricky, Ricky, wait there, momma's coming.'

Who could blame her for her concern, when we remembered Ricky's experience of finding Max's dead body in the dungeon. If it hadn't been for the element of danger in the situation I'd have found it remarkably funny as the members of the group turned as one, first to watch Ricky, then back to his mother, then back to Ricky again.

Margie grabbed Jerome's arm. 'Perhaps you can help,' but Jerome gently disengaged himself and moved away to stand beside Wesley.

Ricky leaned over the railings, swayed back and forth. 'I'm king of the castle,' he sang, dancing up and down, loosening a few pebbles on the top step.

'Come down, Ricky, it's dangerous up there.' Kimberley started to follow him up, then clearly thought the better of it, pausing halfway.

Ricky ignored his mother's plea and as though to infuriate her further, continued to dance about, jumping higher and higher as he did so. More loose stones clattered down from where he was standing, gaining momentum as they banged and rattled down the stone steps.

This was too much for Kimberley and her tone changed. 'Come down out of there you little varmint before someone gets hurt. I mean it, Ricky. I'll be calling your dad to tell him.'

Finally, Ricky decided either the threat of his father or the fact he'd got enough out of the situation was sufficient and he began to climb down the steps, a sulky expression on his face, as all the while his mother, restored to her role of solicitous parent, cupped her hands around her mouth and called, 'Be careful,' and 'Mind your step as you come down. Hold on to the handrail.'

As he reached the bottom, she shuffled forward and clasped him to her. 'What were you thinking of, Ricky? You know you don't like heights.'

At least this interruption had sparked life once more into the group who had been flagging under the weight of a litany of dates and names of Stuarts and of Norse invaders which seemed to be Helena's idea of an interesting guided tour.

Ricky shrugged and wriggled his way out of Kimberley's arms saying, 'Don't fuss so much, Mom. I only wanted to see what the place looked like from up there, get a better view.'

'A lot more fascinating than it does from down here,' muttered Lloyd beside me, then coughed in an attempt to disguise what he'd said.

'I'd have thought this was of interest to anyone with the name of Stuart,' I said, but he merely shrugged.

'It would be better if we all stayed together,' Helena was saying, frowning as she counted the numbers in the group yet again. 'If you would all follow me; we'll head next to the Great Hall by going back through the Gatehouse.'

Susie squeezed Dwayne's hand. 'We're looking forward to seeing this again,' she said. 'There was so much going on at the wedding, I've only the vaguest memory of the place.'

Helena walked briskly ahead, glancing back every few paces to make sure no one else strayed as Ricky had done.

She gathered us together at the bottom of a steep spiral staircase. 'You'll have to mind your step here,' she said in a loud voice. 'If anyone is concerned about climbing, there is disabled access and even if you're fit

I advise you to hold on tightly to the handrail. As you can see it's made of rope and the stairs twist and turn, though there is a little landing halfway up.'

Margie peeped out from the back of the queue. 'What about that other stairway? Where does that lead?' She pointed to a stairway on the left.

'That one is out of bounds,' said Helena, 'and I mean NO ONE can go up it.' She looked directly at Ricky as she spoke but whether he wasn't interested or considered he'd created enough excitement for one day, he stood gazing into the distance.

'So why is it out of bounds, Helena? 'Margie persisted. 'Is it dangerous?'

'Yes, very,' was the reply in no uncertain tones.

'Wait a minute, wait a minute. Ain't there some story about a princess here? Is that why it's dangerous?' She turned to Connie. 'Didn't you say something about that… last time we were here?'

Helena sighed, probably seeing her well-rehearsed schedule disappearing fast. 'Yes, the story was that there was a princess who didn't want to marry the man her father the King had chosen. Instead she planned to run away with her lover, but as she came down these steps in the dead of night, she missed her footing and fell to the bottom, breaking her neck.'

As she saw how well this story was received, Helena added, 'They say her ghost haunts the castle to this day.'

This tale had reduced even the garrulous Margie to silence, and as we carefully made our way up the steep spiral stairway leading to the Great Hall, there were murmurs and discussions about the fate of the princess.

We mounted the stairs slowly, one at a time, to step out into the vastness of the Great Hall, its timbered roof and enormous arched fireplace made all the more impressive by the sparseness of furniture and the huge iron circular 'chandeliers' which would once have contained candles but were now lit by electric bulbs, shining and winking even on a sunny day such as this where the tiny windows allowed in only a little light.

'When it was first built,' Helena was saying, 'this would have been a very comfortable space. Look at the huge fireplace and the window seats.'

Some of the party had already discovered the window seats and were taking advantage of a place to rest after the steep climb. 'My feet hurt,' Connie complained.

Fortunately, there had been a decided change in atmosphere when we reached the Great Hall and a ripple of delight went through the crowd as they peered this way and that, examining the replica Cloth of Estate hanging above the fireplace and the latrine tower which Ricky seemed to find particularly interesting.

Oscar stood in front of the painting beside the fireplace. 'Look here. This shows how the Great Hall might have looked in the 13th Century – the King seated among his courtiers enjoying a great feast, the favourite dogs looking for titbits, the musician at the harp. This picture sure brings the place to life.'

As we wandered about, examining the details, the door to the outside parapet slowly opened a fraction and Lloyd came sidling in through the narrow gap.

No one else seemed to notice, but as I was right behind the door, he almost knocked me over as he came in. He glanced at me, but offered no apology, striding across to join the others.

'Don't miss this,' he said, as though deliberately trying to draw attention to himself. To the left of the room a scale model of the castle stood in a full height glass case, precise down to the last stone, the intricacy of the details generating enthusiastic chatter among several of the members of the group.

There was something strange about Lloyd: where had he been? I tried to remember when I'd last seen him. Was he still there when we were in the courtyard. I closed my eyes the better to focus, running through the members of the group standing at the well. No, Lloyd wasn't there.

Aware Susie was speaking, I turned my attention back to her. 'Someone is very interested in this replica. Wesley makes models for film sets. Quite a job, I'd think.'

'I thought he was a basketball player?' My mind was still on Lloyd's disappearance.

'That was some time ago. He has a new career now.'

'Gosh.' Susie's statement intrigued me. 'I'd have thought it was all CGI nowadays.'

'No, not always – there are some times when a model works better.'

Wesley was eagerly interrogating Helena and she too had become animated, no doubt glad someone was at last paying attention to her talk about the castle. Or possibly the fact that Wesley was tall and good-looking was the reason her eyes were sparkling as she spoke.

'Look, there's another one over here.' Margie had spotted a smaller version of the model in a glass case in the middle of the room.

'What's up there?' Ricky pointed to a set of stairs in the corner and went over to take down the cord roping the area off from the rest of the room.

Helena rushed over and grabbed the cord from his hand. 'Visitors aren't allowed up there. It's not safe.' She was breathing heavily, perhaps fearing another accident. Her face was glistening with sweat, though you couldn't say it was a particularly warm day. Keeping this group in order was no easy task.

'Yeah? What's up there?' Lloyd wandered over to stand beside her.

'There would at once time have been rooms for the King and on the top level there's a walkway along the parapet.'

'Sounds good,' said Lloyd.

'Yes, that well might be,' replied Helena, 'but it's unsafe. NO ONE is allowed up there.'

At these firm words, Lloyd took a step back and lifted his hand. 'Gee. Okay, okay, I get the message. Listen up everyone. Keep to the places Helena advises.' He pointed at Ricky. 'That means you.'

But Ricky turned away, making a face as he did so and realising there was no way he'd be able to slip away to the upper rooms, he lost interest in the proceedings. 'Ain't it time to go? I'm starving.' He tugged at his mother's sleeve.

Whatever else you could say about Ricky, he showed no signs of needing food any time soon. Indeed a few days without much to eat would probably have done him a lot of good.

Helena overheard and glanced at her watch. 'Good gracious – is that the time? Sorry folks, we have to go. The castle will be closing in half an hour and I guess you'll all want to spend some time in the Gift Shop. There's an excellent selection of gifts connected with Rothesay Castle and with the Stuarts. There are mugs, scarves, ties and lots of other garments, all in the Stuart tartan. I'm sure you'll find something there to suit all tastes.'

This offer to head for the shop was greeted with a murmur of approval and in little groups the party straggled off down the stairs behind her with warnings of 'Take care,' and 'Don't go too quickly,' ringing in their ears as they headed off to make their purchases. I peeped in, because the shop was small and there seemed no room for any more people, so crowded was it. The Heritage Adventurers seemed to be buying up the shop as, laden with goods, they queued at the till.

Well, that tour of the castle hadn't been a great success, though it was difficult to tell. I wondered if Helena was part of the problem. Apart from anything else, her bland delivery of facts and figures in a very flat voice wasn't likely to engage a group such as this. She showed so little animation, made no effort to involve them in the history of the castle, though I knew from my own research how interesting a history it had. I wondered why she'd taken the job, if she had so little enthusiasm. The answer must be that she needed the money, something I could well relate to.

I left the others in the shop and wandered on my own through to the Gatehouse, in time to see Helena standing inside the cordon above the steps to the dungeon.

80

About to say, 'I thought that was out of bounds,' instead I slunk back into the shadows, waiting to see what she would do next. But she simply stood there for a moment, before ducking under the tape and heading to join the others.

My curiosity about her behaviour was forgotten as Susie came towards me, clutching a bag of souvenirs. 'I said I'd only have a look,' she grinned, 'but it was too tempting.'

The upside of this contract for me was that they would have taken in so little of what had been said about the castle and its story, my task of writing up their individual history would be all the easier.

I did wonder why some of these people had come all the way from America – it appeared they had little passion for the history of the Stuarts. Perhaps it was a way of being able to say they'd been to Scotland, had been back to trace their roots. No doubt, once safely back home in America they would have a tale or two to tell, much embroidered by distance.

CHAPTER TEN

We straggled out of the castle across the road to the hotel, where most of the group headed for their rooms to relax before dinner, but a few stayed in the lounge, including Lloyd.

He headed straight for the bar, ordering up a large whisky 'soda, lots of ice,' and went to sit at a table in the far corner where there was little light. He ostentatiously lifted a newspaper lying on the seat next to his, shook it and began to read with a fierce concentration, indicating he'd no wish to be disturbed.

No one else appeared to have noticed and I supposed he was entitled to some peace and quiet away from constant questions and problems. Adrift in a foreign country, many of them for the first time, they relied on Lloyd to answer their every need.

'I'll see you at dinner,' I said to Susie.

She raised her hand in reply, deep in conversation with Helena who'd joined us for the evening.

'So, Alison,' she said, 'what have you found out about the links this group might have to the history of Bute?'

I shrugged. 'It's early days yet. I've a few more interviews to finish.'

'But there's no one with a famous connection?' There was a gleam in her eye as she spoke.

'Highly unlikely,' I replied. 'Now, if you'll excuse me.'

As I passed Lloyd, he put down his paper, looked around and beckoned. I followed his gaze, but as there was no one else in sight, I had to guess he was trying to catch my attention. I was tired, ready for a break, but it would have been unprofessional to ignore him, so I went over and sat down.

For a few moments he was silent, frowning as though deciding what to say, folding and refolding the newspaper. In an attempt to break the uncomfortable atmosphere, I said, 'How did you think the visit to the castle went? It must have been difficult for most people, given the circumstances.'

'What? Oh, that? Fine, I guess. Everyone sure came back with plenty of souvenirs. Some of them will get a big surprise at the airport when they check in their baggage.'

Silence again. I stood up. 'I'm heading upstairs to freshen up. I'll see you later.'

As I made to move he grabbed my arm. 'No, hang on a minute. There's something I have to ask you.'

My heart sank. All I wanted to do was stick closely, very closely, to my brief. I wasn't in the business of giving advice and certainly not to Lloyd, especially if it was anything to do with Max's death.

I'd guessed correctly. He ignored my uneasiness and said, after glancing around to make sure we were alone, 'What do you think happened to Max? Do you think it was an accident or was it as the police suspect, murder? As an outsider you must have some opinion?'

I shrugged. 'I know no more than I've been told. I didn't meet him, knew nothing about him.' Why should he imagine I'd a view about Max's death? Then a little niggle as I remembered the conversation in the bank, the story about Mrs Halson. A foolish thought. How would Lloyd know about that?

He caught my hand as I stood up to leave. 'Yes, but you're not part of the tour group, not connected with anyone. You must have some opinion about it, have heard others talking.' A knowing look. 'I've heard you've been involved in this kind of thing before.'

Ignoring the reference to my previous exploits on Bute or who might have told him, I replied, 'I'm not quite an outsider. Remember Susie is a long-time friend of mine. In fact, it was only because of her that I took on this job.'

'I guess you're not willing to commit to a theory, then,' he said in a flat voice and lifted his newspaper once again, effectively dismissing me.

But talking about Max had reminded me I was behind in my schedule of interviews. Out of deference to their feelings about his death, I'd tiptoed around the problem. This was over-sensitive: it appeared no one was particularly upset by what had happened, except at the level of gossip. If I didn't manage to flesh out the preliminary discussions, there'd be no time left. Sure I could write up a booklet for them, but they wanted something personal, not to have the kind of history that was available in any bookshop. This was my opportunity to involve Lloyd in the arrangements.

'Can you set up interviews for me with those members of the group with a particular interest in finding their roots? My first attempts have shown me not everyone is.' I didn't want to mention any names, but Ricky and his mother came immediately to mind.

Lloyd put down his newspaper and frowned again, as though trying to focus on my request. 'Mmm, you have a point. I'm not sure.' He downed the rest of his drink in one gulp. 'Especially as there are unlikely to be any famous connections?' The query in his voice annoyed me.

'Well, could you possibly find out? Then, aware that I was in effect the employee, I added, 'It would be important to speak to them during the next couple of days so that I can have enough details to complete the research when I'm back home.'

For a moment I thought he would tell me sorting out the interviews was part of my job, not his, but all he muttered was, 'I'll check tonight and you can do the interviews over the next couple of days,' and he went back once more to reading the paper, or making a good pretence of reading it, without making any firm commitment.

I nodded. It looked as if I'd have to be content with that, but if there was no progress the following day, I'd take matters into my own hands.

Once again I headed for my room, but this time before I reached the lift a voice said, 'I'm dying to talk to you about Oscar's mother. She was a Stuart. There's so much about her life that'll interest you.' It was Connie.

'Yes, I'm sure everyone has a fascinating story to tell. I've been talking to Lloyd about setting up more interviews.' I gestured in the direction of the far corner of the bar where he'd been sitting, but he'd disappeared, leaving the newspaper lying in a crumpled heap on the table.

This response didn't satisfy Connie. She wagged her finger. 'Ah, but we've done a lot of family research and I'm pretty sure we've got some intriguing relations in our past.'

I'd no enthusiasm for beginning an interview at that moment, but I didn't want to appear to discourage her. 'I think it would be better if we started fresh first thing tomorrow morning, don't you? And I want to record the interviews. That way I've a better chance of making sure they're accurate, that I don't miss anything.'

A look of disappointment crossed her face, but only fleetingly. 'Suppose so, Alison.' Then, eagerly, 'Maybe I could be first? With this group there's no problem about taking us in alphabetical order.' She chuckled at her own joke.

'Absolutely fine. Shall we say nine thirty tomorrow morning? There's a little side room off the breakfast room. I don't think it's ever used, so we could meet there.'

She nodded. 'That sounds just dandy. I'll be there waiting for you. I can have an early breakfast. Oscar and I will bring the documents we've managed to find so far. We can look through them together. There are a few questions you can help us with.' She added proudly, 'Oscar and I are both Stuarts.'

It wasn't worthwhile reminding her I wasn't a genealogist, but a writer. Still, I could worry about that in the morning.

I hurried off, but as I travelled up in the lift, I pondered what Lloyd had asked me about Max. I hadn't met him, had only heard snippets of conversation, so it was a pretty strange question. Then again, did Lloyd think I was somehow privy to information about Max's death? I remembered Connie urging me to have a word with Margie. What was that about?

CHAPTER ELEVEN

'So how's the project going?' Was that a note of concern I detected in my husband's voice? If it was, I chose to ignore it, answer his question as if it was a casual enquiry.

'So, so,' I replied. Hopefully he would think my lack of conversation was to do with the early hour.

'Thought I'd catch up with you before the conference day began.'

'There's so much happening. It's a busy tour,' I yawned, stretching my arms high in the air to ease the crick in my neck. I'd have to ask for an extra pillow.

'Ah, it's not turning out to be as easy as you thought?'

For a moment I considered telling him about Max, then quickly dismissed the idea. Instead I said, 'There are different levels of interest in the group. With the exception of Oscar, Connie and Margie, there's little enthusiasm for linking with their Stuart roots, no matter what Susie might say.' Why they'd signed up for this tour was a puzzle. Perhaps they'd had a different, a very romantic, idea of what it might be like to return to the land of their ancestors and the reality had so disappointed them, they'd lost all interest.

'But you'll be able to produce something useful?'

Best to put a brave face on it. No matter how anxious I might be, there was no way I was giving up. Adopting a positive tone of voice, I said, 'Oh, yes. There's still a lot to do, but I am getting to know the various members of the group. Given the short timescale it's fortunate not everyone has the same level of interest. I would say of the eight (because Susie and Dwayne aren't Stuarts, of course) there are three with a real desire to find out if they have a connection and a couple of the others have a general curiosity about the island's history.'

'And?'

'Mmm, too early to tell.' I wasn't going to admit there were difficulties. In an effort to distract him by changing the subject I said, 'And what about the conference? Going well?'

This at least had the desired effect. 'It'd be fine if it weren't that the main speaker on the first day didn't turn up and then yesterday…'

I let my mind drift as he continued with a series of grumbles about the organisation, the various factions that had developed, the stuffy meeting rooms, the poor food. 'You'd think with what the company is paying, there would at least be decent food…'

Guiltily I came back to the conversation with the realisation he was asking me a direct question.

'Sorry, I didn't catch that,' I said.

'I asked when you're planning to come back,' he repeated. 'I can't remember how long you said you'd be on the island.'

'I'm here for the remainder of this week and then I can finish the rest from home. Thank goodness for the internet.'

There was a pause, then he said, 'I've an idea. What do you say we meet up in Glasgow, and catch up with Deborah? We could revisit some of our favourite places and have a holiday.'

When we moved to London for Simon's job, our youngest daughter, Deborah had chosen to remain in Glasgow, at least temporarily. After a series of courses, including a spell at art college, an attempt at teacher training and various short-lived spells of employment, she'd at last found her niche with an advertising agency in Glasgow. Or so we hoped. The last thing we wanted to do was upset her arrangements.

'Good suggestion,' I said, 'though we'll have to book into a hotel. Her flat's far too small for her to put us up.' I laughed. 'Strange you should propose coming to Scotland, I was about to ask if you wanted to come to the island for a couple of days – after the Americans have gone,' I added.

'Mmm. That's a possibility, I suppose.' But he didn't commit himself. 'We can decide next time we speak.'

'Right. But let me know soon. It's getting to be a busy time of year on the island and I'd want to book a hotel.'

As I was about to ring off, he said suddenly, 'Oh, and Maura's planning a party for Connor's birthday. She said she'd be in touch when you get back, will come over. She didn't want to bother you while you're busy.'

'Was that all she said?' That she had contacted
Simon rather than phoning me first sounded ominous.
Although my elder daughter and her husband, Alan,
live reasonably near us as far as London distances go,
we don't see a great deal of them, busy as they are with
their careers. Last time we'd met, Maura had confessed
to feelings of guilt about the number of birthday parties
Connor had been invited to. This latest call to her dad
was a sign she was planning to return the favours and
I'd a feeling I'd be called on to help.

We said goodbye, Simon promising to phone or text
about arrangements for coming to Bute or staying over
in Glasgow.

Considerably cheered by this conversation and the
prospect of a couple of days in Glasgow catching up
with my daughter as well as squeezing in some much
needed clothes shopping, I'd a quick shower before
heading down to join the others for breakfast.

There was a buzz of conversation in the breakfast
room, more than was usual and people stood around in
groups rather than sitting at the tables, shifting uneasily
whenever someone joined them. Connie was over by
the window. She looked in my direction then as quickly
looked away again. Surely she hadn't changed her mind
about the interview?

Susie was sitting with Dwayne at a table in the far
corner of the dining room, neither of them speaking.
Dwayne was drumming his fingers on the table, a frown
on his usually placid face. This silence was so unlike
my usually chatty friend a feeling of disquiet made me
shiver in spite of the high temperature in the room.

'What's wrong? Why is everyone so nervous?' I said, drawing up a vacant chair and sitting down beside her.

She glanced around, as though reluctant to be overheard, then leaned in to whisper, 'It's Ricky.'

'Don't tell me he's in trouble again?' Really, that boy was getting to be a proper nuisance. I wasn't the only one who wished his mother hadn't insisted he come along on this trip.

'That's what we don't know,' said Susie, biting her lip. 'It would appear he's gone missing.'

'Oh, for goodness sake. How likely is that? It's probably no more than he's gone wandering off somewhere. His mother seems unable to control him. And let's face it, he's absolutely no interest in anything that's going on here.'

Susie shook her head. 'He wasn't in his room when she went to call him for breakfast this morning. She thought he'd overslept and eventually had to call the manager to open the door when there was no response to her knocking. His bed hadn't been slept in.'

Now I regretted my initial reaction: this might be more serious than I'd first thought. 'So what's happening?'

'Kimberley's very distressed, but the police reason it's too early to act. They probably believe he's done that teenage thing of wandering off because he was bored.'

'Isn't that the most likely explanation? Though where could he have gone and stayed out all night?'

'Who knows? He's been such a pest, always causing trouble.' She glanced over at Kimberley.

It was unlike Susie to be critical, but I could understand what she meant. Ricky had caused trouble several times, but in all honesty I couldn't blame him. 'He must be fed up trailing round with all these older people. I've no idea why his mother thought it was a good idea to bring him.'

Dwayne, who had been silent all this time, chimed in, 'Sure was a bad idea, but I guess his mom had no choice. She could hardly leave him behind...'

Susie interrupted. 'He's said more than once he didn't want to come – his mum and dad are divorced and he divides his time between them. It was his mum's turn to have him and as she had booked this trip...' She shrugged leaving the remainder of the sentence unsaid.

'It's of no consequence why he's here,' I said. 'The main thing is that he's found safe.'

'Don't know how we can help with that,' Dwayne muttered. I suspected he'd no inclination to get into an argument with Susie about something which didn't really concern them, especially on a trip which was supposed to be a joyous occasion, a celebration for their wedding anniversary that so far was proving anything but.

'Let's hope he's found safe and well...and soon,' I said. Whatever had happened to Ricky, I couldn't be the only one who thought immediately about Max.

The restaurant manager bustled in, smoothing her fair hair. 'If you'd like to be seated for breakfast?'

Obediently, we did as we were asked and the waitresses moved around, taking orders for cooked food.

'Best to have something to eat,' I encouraged my friends. 'This looks as if it's going to be a long day.'

93

Over in the far corner, Ricky's mother sat quietly weeping, being comforted by Margie. Occasionally she let out a loud wail, 'Oh, Ricky, where are you?'

Lloyd came over, walking slowly, unlike his usual cocky self. 'We're trying to come to an agreement about how we should spend the day. There ain't much point in all of us sitting around here waiting for news.' He stopped, scanning our faces as though willing us to agree. I didn't envy him and for once I felt sorry for him. Problem was, we weren't even sure Ricky was missing. It would have been so like him to go wandering off without telling anyone where he was going.

'Had you any special plans?' I said, to break the silence.

'Not this morning, but this afternoon we were supposed to be going back to the castle for a talk on the early Stuarts who lived there at one time. Hoped there'd be an opportunity to do some exploring of our contacts with them before then.' He gazed fixedly at me, leaving unsaid what he was surely thinking: this morning might be an ideal opportunity to complete some of the interviews.

Finally, I said, 'If Ricky doesn't appear soon, continuing with the interviews might be a good way to keep everyone busy.'

Lloyd grinned, then changed it to a grimace, aware of the solemnity of the occasion. 'Exactly what I thought, Alison. And you'll be able to learn a lot from the talk this afternoon. I'm sure it'll be of help. When we come back you might want to chat to anyone you don't manage to see this morning?'

'Sounds good.' Truth to tell, I was struggling to understand what they wanted. My suspicion was that when this commission was proposed several of these Stuarts had assumed I'd be able to discover a link to the Stuarts they knew best – Mary, Queen of Scots or Bonnie Prince Charlie.

Aware Lloyd was speaking again, I pulled myself back to the present to find I'd been complacent too soon about escaping.

'When will we see the first draft of your booklet? We thought it would be a good idea to have an event in a couple of days and you could tell us what you've discovered. Make it a fun evening. Everyone is really keen to hear your stories.'

Susie nudged me as I tried to think of a reply which wouldn't disappoint him. I mumbled something about 'needing more research,' and 'leaving it open,' hoping he wouldn't press me.

'But we can arrange a time when you'll talk to everyone together?' he persisted. 'It doesn't have to be the final version. I guess you'll want to do a bit of editing before it's ready, but we won't worry about a few missing commas.'

Ignoring Lloyd's notion of how easy it was to be a writer, I said, 'Of course.' Perhaps I could enlist Oscar's help. He'd been more than happy to talk non-stop about his ancestors. I could hand over most of the session to him, use him as a case study.

Buoyed up by this sudden brainwave, I added, 'Friday evening might be a possibility. The Medieval Fair at the castle will take up most of Saturday and then there's the Pageant in the evening.'

Lloyd gave me a thumbs up. 'Done. Great stuff, Alison.' And looking more pleased than I'd seen him for some time, he stood up and went to join another table where, from the glances in my direction, I could guess he was talking eagerly about what we'd agreed. Little did he know my plan was quietly to drop the idea.

So much for this time on Bute with the group being relaxed, finding out about them, chatting about their ancestry. It was turning out to be a lot more difficult than I could have imagined and for one moment I wondered if I could faint, fake illness and head home. But then my loyalty to Susie overcame my natural instincts, not to mention my aversion to slinking home to have Simon say, 'I told you it was a mad idea.' What I should have done was refuse when Susie first asked me. That's my problem – I'm far too optimistic for my own good and it was too late now.

Even so, I had to make sure Lloyd wasn't making promises I couldn't keep and excusing myself to Susie and to Dwayne, I headed for his table to say, 'Whatever information anyone can give me will be very helpful, but don't expect...'

But Lloyd wasn't listening and I followed the direction of his gaze as Kimberley let out a loud screech. The door to the dining room was flung open and Ricky came swaggering in.

CHAPTER TWELVE

There was an explosion of noise as Ricky's mother elbowed her way through to clutch him in a hug that threatened to strangle him. 'Oh, Ricky, honey, are you okay?' Kimberley's tears dripped on to the top of his baseball cap.

He tried to struggle free, twisting this way and that, a fruitless effort until she released him without warning and he staggered back.

'Where have you been, Ricky? We were all sooo worried about you.' Anger replaced relief at his safe return, her face red and frowning.

Ricky appeared not the least upset by the trouble he'd caused. 'Thought I'd take a bit of a stroll around the town last night and got involved with some guys. I ain't a baby, Mom. You worry too much.' He blustered on, 'Ain't nothing to do in this place in the evenings.'

'A stroll around town? You've been away all night. Rothesay ain't that big a town.' Kimberley's relief at his safe return was now overtaken by fury.

'Bunked down with some guys I met in the pub.'

Kimberley drew back. 'You did what! Going off with complete strangers?'

Ricky sniffed and rubbed his nose. 'It weren't no stranger. It was that Zachary from the college and some of his students out celebrating.' He grinned, unconcerned about being so vague. 'It was pretty late and I didn't want to cause no fuss by coming back to the hotel. The pub stayed open after it should've closed. They call it a 'lock-in' here.'

This casual approach only served to enrage his mother further. 'The pub? You ain't old enough to be going to no pubs. Wait till your dad hears about this…' A moment's hesitation. 'And where did you get the money to go to the pub? Thought you were complaining about being broke?'

Ricky interrupted this tirade, giving up his attempt to put his mother in a good mood. 'Of course I'm old enough to have a drink here in Scotland. Better than trailing from one ruin to another with a bunch of old folk, listening to boring stories about people that died long ago. Besides it wasn't as though I was with strangers.'

Connie moved forward. 'That's disgraceful. They let little children into the pubs here and let them drink alcohol?'

'What! Ain't you got no sense, Connie? It was Zachary and some of his students I met, not the fifth grade kids.'

'How can you make these remarks about the tour? I brought you all the way over here to find your heritage, Ricky. You might be related to one of those famous Stuarts. We might have what they call here 'blue blood' running through our veins. Have you no feeling for that?'

'That ain't likely, Mom. Don't kid yourself. We're not related to any Scottish nobility. If that's what you're after it's a wasted trip. Though you ain't shown much interest in finding your ancestors so far.' This barb struck home and Kimberley drew back, scowling.

A murmur ran through the crowd, comments about 'What does he know,' and 'Young whippersnapper,' being the politer of the many remarks.

'We called in the police, thought you'd met with an accident,' growled Jerome. 'You outta have more consideration for your mom, young man. Why, I remember when I had a part in Missing for a Week there was a real life incident that…'

'Not my fault if y'all made a fuss.' Ricky scowled, not allowing Jerome to finish.

I looked more closely at Ricky as he was speaking. With his chubby face and general podginess, he appeared much younger than he was. I tried to guess what age he might be. At least eighteen or surely Zachary wouldn't have included him in the celebrations, wouldn't have invited him to join them in the pub. That explained his lack of interest in the tour and I felt sorry for him. I wondered how his mother had managed to persuade him to accompany her all the way to Bute, what promises she'd made.

Ricky went red, shuffling his feet and staring at the ground. 'Ain't my fault,' he said again. Under all his bluster I detected a hint of sheepishness about the worry he'd caused. 'Any road, I'm off to have a shower and some shut eye. Didn't get much sleep last night.'

This remark made his mother even angrier, but the others in the group appeared to have lost interest in this family dispute, especially as Helena came in to join us, saying, 'Now that Ricky's returned safe and sound, I hope you're all ready for this afternoon. We've a great programme lined up.'

Perhaps inspired by Ricky's comments, someone at the back muttered, 'Yes, but will we learn any more about our connections to the Stuarts?'

'Of course. We've someone special coming along to talk to us and I'm sure you'll learn a lot.'

Helena might declare this with confidence, but I wasn't convinced. In spite of the number of interviews I'd conducted, I'd managed to find very little of excitment. I'd have to include a great deal of historical background, flesh out the meagre details with individual case studies. Ricky might well be right. In fact, if I was totally honest, he'd a proper understanding of the reality of the situation.

Convinced as I was about the disappointments awaiting the group, Helena's next words took me by surprise. She clapped her hands. 'If you could all gather round for a few minutes.' She grinned. 'I know you're all anxious to get on, but this is something I'm sure you'll be delighted to hear. A researcher from a company called Ancient Roots Discovered has been in touch. From some very preliminary research he's convinced that at least one of the group can trace their ancestry back to Walter, who was Steward to William the Lion.' She paused, waiting for the effect on her audience and it wasn't long in coming.

'Who is it?'

'Is it us? My wife and I are sure we're related to nobility.' Oscar grew visibly taller at this news.

'You gotta tell us, put us out of our misery…'

Helena held up her hand and the room went quiet. 'I'm not going to tell you right at this moment, but he'll be revealing more at the end of our talk this afternoon.'

More murmurs, a little feeling of discontent, but she was not to be swayed. 'No,' she said in response to several pleas for more information. 'It's better if we do as I suggest. I look forward to seeing you all in the Great Hall of the castle at two o'clock, immediately after lunch. Don't be late.'

'As if we would be,' said Margie, loudly enough to be heard by everyone in the room.

Helena merely smiled and swept off with the self-confidence of someone who knows she's fully captured the attention of her audience.

As one by one, or in little groups, the party drifted towards the residents' lounge or to their rooms, I remained sitting by the window, gazing out at the castle walls. Did this researcher really have something to tell, or was it no more than a ploy by Helena to make sure she'd a good attendance for the talk later in the afternoon? I'd detected a weariness in the group from all these talks and tours. And who was this researcher? As far as I was concerned, although I wasn't a qualified genealogist, that part of the tour was my remit. I'd have to catch up with Helena before the afternoon visit, find out what was really going on.

I'd grown fond of the people in this group, in spite of the eccentricity some of them displayed and I wanted to do my best for them, give them something substantial to take home. But this venture was becoming more and more muddled and I'd the uncomfortable feeling that there was more to this tour than had first appeared. Then again, there was always the chance I'd be proved wrong. I certainly hoped so. It would please the group enormously and make my task a whole lot easier if this researcher had managed to find a royal connection.

CHAPTER THIRTEEN

Surely no one would miss me for an hour, I reasoned, as I slid quietly out of the room to head upstairs. All I wanted at the moment was to close the curtains, lie down on the bed and try to ease the gremlins pounding in my skull.

Susie and Dwayne were deep in conversation with Helena and I'd no intention of alerting them to my departure. Susie would only fuss. Some of the others were still clustered round Ricky, giving him the third degree. He seemed to be bearing up pretty well, having abandoned all thoughts of making up for the sleep he'd lost. You might even say he was enjoying the attention.

Relieved to reach my bedroom without being waylaid by one of the group, I pulled over the heavy drapes and snuggled down under the duvet, telling myself I'd feel better in half an hour. There was no need to set the alarm on my mobile.

Instead, worn out by the events of the previous few days, I fell into a deep slumber. A loud banging on the door dragged me from a strange dream where I was trying unsuccessfully to climb to the top of Rothesay castle, but kept falling back to the bottom of the stairs to begin my ascent all over again, much to the mirth of the bystanders below, prominent among whom was Ricky.

I struggled into wakefulness, thankful to find it had all been no more than a dream.

'Alison, are you okay?'

I pushed back the duvet and struggled groggily to my feet, banging my shin painfully on the coffee table in my haste to open the door. 'Coming, coming.' I hopped over and tugged at the handle.

Susie stood there, frowning in concern. 'We were beginning to worry about you,' she said.

I blinked, trying to focus, still heavy with sleep. 'What time is it?'

'It's four o'clock. We missed you at the castle, but didn't want to draw attention to the fact you weren't there.'

There was a primness in her manner which was a sure sign she thought I was neglecting my duties, but I was in no mood to be contrite. And at least the headache had gone.

'I had a migraine,' I said, clutching my forehead for effect.

She watched me through narrowed eyes. 'I'd no idea you were prone to migraines,' she said, pushing past me into the room.

'I'll let Helena know why I wasn't there this afternoon, but honestly I had this most awful headache.'

Her mood softened. 'You should have said. Everyone would have understood.' She sat down on the bed and began fiddling with the edge of the duvet.

I changed tack. 'What happened at the castle? Did the researcher do the great reveal?' I was half joking. I couldn't imagine there would be anything of note, any of the Heritage Adventurers with a connection to Stuart royalty, in spite of Helena's promises.

'That's just it. There's been a development.'

'So who's supposed to be related to Walter, the High Steward?'

She frowned. 'The researcher turned up, but it wasn't what we expected. He wanted us to sign up with his company and then investigations would be undertaken' She shook her head. 'I think Helena was as surprised as anyone. If you ask me, it was a scam, a way of getting money out of gullible Americans.' She grinned. 'Or so he thought. Dwayne soon put paid to that.'

'Poor Helena. She must have felt very annoyed.'

Susie continued to sit on the edge of the bed, pulling at a thread on the top cover. 'There was something else I wanted to talk to you about. Lloyd didn't join us. The police wanted to speak to him again because he's the leader of the group. He came over to the castle later as the researcher from Ancient Roots Discovered was winding up his talk.'

'I could have guessed as much, Susie,' I said yawning. It was as I'd suspected. The story about one of the group being related to one of the early Stuarts had been a way of trying to make money, no more than that.

'So how did people react?'

Susie shrugged. 'There were a few grumbles, but to be honest I think most of the group have given up hope of being related to anyone famous. Besides, with what happened, it cancelled out any such disappointments.'

'You mean about a famous ancestor?'

'You don't understand. It was what Lloyd wanted to tell us that was important.'

I tried to shake off the rest of my drowsiness, to digest her revelation. 'I guess all is well and you'll be able to arrange for the transportation of Max's body back to the U.S?'

'If you'd listen, instead of trying to second guess everything, Alison. That wasn't what Lloyd had to say.'

'So?' Fully awake, I'd an uneasy feeling about what Susie's next words might be.

'The post mortem results are in…' she paused for dramatic effect, '...and it's been confirmed Max's death was no accident. It was murder.'

'Murder? Are they sure?'

'Of course they are and that's why everything took so long. It means we'll all have to stay here for some time yet. It's as well we've a few days in hand.'

I wasn't really surprised. It was so unlikely that someone like Max, someone with a heart condition, would go down into that dungeon on his own. Ricky had found it difficult enough. And what could he possibly have wanted down there? It was completely bare, with nothing of any interest.

'So how did he die?'

'Apparently it was a blow to the head that could only have happened before his body was found in the dungeon.'

'But that means someone else must have been there in the castle with him?'

'Well, possibly. The rumour is that he was killed and thrown down into the dungeon to make it look like an accident. We'll know more once the full report comes through.'

This was news indeed and much worse than we'd feared. 'Why would someone want to kill Max?'

'No one has any idea – there's not the least suspicion of a motive. He wasn't the most popular person in the group as you've heard, always going on about how he was about to discover something that would make his fortune, but that wasn't enough to kill him.'

'Robbery?' I hazarded.

Susie grimaced. 'No. He still had his wallet and his phone. So not robbery.'

'Well, someone must have had a reason to kill him.' I stopped. Why was I discussing this with Susie? It was none of my business.

'Perhaps you could investigate a little?' Susie said eagerly as though she'd read my mind. 'The sooner this is solved, the sooner we can all go home. I don't see how we can stay here for any length of time. Apart from the cost, some people have commitments back in the U.S.'

'Oh, no. Not me. I've had enough of dealing with mysteries on this island.' I held up my hands in protest.

'Yes, I know how you feel and I wouldn't ask you if there were any other way. The police will do their best, but as you're interviewing all the members of our group anyway...' She left the rest of the sentence hanging in the air.

She was right of course. I was the outsider and with my brief to investigate the ancestry of members of the group, I was best placed to question everyone without raising suspicions. Because if robbery hadn't been the motive for killing Max, it was likely he'd been killed by someone he knew, someone from Heritage Adventurers.

And that made things very difficult indeed. Having killed once, was the murderer likely to kill again?

CHAPTER FOURTEEN

After Susie left saying, 'Have a cup of tea and then you'll feel better,' I sat at the table beside the window, gazing out at the view of the bulk of the grey stone castle. What dramas it had seen in its long history and now there was one more in the unexplained death of Max.

How did I feel about this news? If what Susie said was correct, Max wouldn't have attempted to explore the dungeon on his own. And what purpose could his doing so have served?

What was it Susie had told me about the trip to Carlisle Castle? Max had wandered off there also. But that was different.

His death had certainly had an effect on the others. They might be called Heritage Adventurers, but after what had happened it seemed they now clung together like limpets.

I hadn't met Max, knew of him only through what others had told me, and being utterly selfish about it, my immediate concern wasn't who was responsible for his death, but what Simon would say when he realised

I'd no sooner agreed to return to Bute than there'd been a murder.

I'm not involved in this, I told myself firmly. Besides, Simon worries too much. All I had to do was finish the interviews and head back to London to finish my research there and write up whatever information I'd found, little as that might be. There would be a lot of padding, if current results were anything to go by.

Yes, that was what I planned, but from previous experiences on Bute I'd a sneaking suspicion it wouldn't be as easy as that. And I kept thinking of what Susie had said about possible delays in returning to America. And how could I refuse to help her?

In the meantime, should I tell Simon about Max when I phoned him later that evening, or wait until there was some kind of development? In the end cowardice won and as I ran a comb through my hair and touched up my lipstick before re-joining the others, I decided I'd say nothing at the moment. Time enough to reveal all to Simon when there was some firm news.

Much heartened by the decision to put it to the back of my mind, I closed the bedroom door behind me and walked to the lift.

'Well, hiya, Alison.' I turned to see Margie coming up beside me. 'It's been another busy afternoon. Pretty hard on the feet.'

I smiled, recognising the reluctance to walk which characterised most of the group. On Bute and certainly in the town, there was little need for transport, but many of these people were unused to walking any distance.

'Yes, I'm hoping to finish the remainder of the preliminary interviews this evening,' I said. Then, mindful of Susie's request, I added, 'Though there may be a few more questions for those I talked to earlier.'

'Gee, wouldn't it be just swell if even one of us was related to someone from the early Stuarts? That'd be a story to tell the folks back home.' She fixed her gaze on me, making it difficult to look away. 'That Max kept on telling us he was on to a story about someone really famous, but I guess it was a load of baloney, huh?'

'I've no idea,' I replied, then to divert her, 'So what happened at the castle this afternoon? I thought Helena was going to have a researcher reveal some connection between a member of the group and Walter, the Steward?'

Margie laughed. 'That's what Helena believed would happen. Truth is, I was a mite surprised when she said there'd be a researcher.' She looked at me and raised her eyebrows. 'Thought you were the researcher.'

'Ancient Roots Discovered is nothing to do with me,' I protested. I didn't want everyone thinking I'd been hiding something, had been part of a scam. It was as well I hadn't made it to the castle.

Margie hesitated, eyed me warily. 'Anyway there was no time to talk about that. Not when we got the news that Max had been murdered. Stupid fellow.'

'To get himself murdered?'

'That and other things. I still don't believe it, no matter what the police might say. Not that I'd had much to do with him on this trip. I didn't realise he was one of the group when I signed up for this tour, else I might not have joined.'

Mmm. Here was someone else without a good word to say for Max. 'So you knew him before?'

Margie didn't reply. Instead she wagged her finger. 'So, what have you found out? Trying to keep us in suspense, Alison? We're all anxious to hear who might have a famous ancestor.'

There was no point in trying to explain again that one of the group having a 'famous ancestor' was highly unlikely. Ancient Roots Discovered had certainly muddied the waters.

The lift arrived, already almost full. Realising there was scarcely enough room for one other person, never mind two, I elected to take the stairs. This crush in the lift meant Margie and I separated, sparing me the tricky situation of disappointing her yet again about possible famous ancestry. I'd landed myself with a problem. Whatever the reality, I'd have to come up with something to placate them. Trouble was, at this moment I had no idea what that might be and I raced downstairs to beat the lift. I hurried through the lounge, waving briefly to Jerome and to Margie. Jerome had a kind of wild look on his face: he appeared to be trapped by Margie in the far corner of the room, but I'd no time to come to his rescue.

I'd other things on my mind. Perhaps it was time I went to see Mrs Halson, though I'd no intention of telling Susie until I had a clearer idea whether there was any truth in the story about Stuart not being Max's real name and the belief he wasn't American at all, but someone who'd been born on Bute. She and Dwayne had had so little time together on this trip and I could manage this perfectly well on my own.

And so it would seem that, much against my better judgement, I couldn't help but involve myself in the strange business of Max's death.

CHAPTER FIFTEEN

Firstly, I had to find out where Mrs Halson lived, but that proved much easier than expected. Remembering how the woman I'd met at the bank had said she was 'very elderly' which to a young person could mean anyone over fifty years old, and had told me she was a resident of one of the nursing homes on the island, I'd a bit of luck. When I phoned the second one (there were only four), it was to find she was indeed a resident at the Rullecheddan Nursing Home near Ardbeg. There was no time like the present and still unsure if I should be involved, I set off on the pretext of going to the chemist in Rothesay. 'To get something for my headaches,' I lied when Susie asked.

'You want to be careful,' Dwayne said, overhearing our conversation. 'You should get yourself checked out if you're having regular headaches.'

'No, I'll be fine. I usually have medication with me, but this time I forgot.'

I made a swift exit before I could be drawn into further discussions about my 'headaches' and walked down to the terminus at Guildford Square to catch the 490 bus to Ettrick Bay that called in at Ardbeg.

As the bus trundled off I tried to think of a cover story for my visit to Rullecheddan. At this rate I'd soon be an expert liar. All I'd said on the phone was that I wanted to visit Mrs Halson, but I knew that when I arrived I'd have to give an explanation for my visit. Surely I'd come up with a plausible excuse by the time I arrived.

The bus stop for the nursing home was only a few yards from the entrance. The home had once been a grand Victorian villa, and was now extended on both sides, giving it a rather dumpy look, but it was beautifully preserved and all the rooms at the front overlooked the expanse of well-tended garden and the waters of the Firth of Clyde.

It was a bright airy building, set only a little way back from the road, with a stone portico. The gravel path in front of the house made a crunching noise as I approached and I was glad I'd worn flat shoes.

Inside was quiet and calm, the walls of the grand foyer painted in a restful shade of blue that echoed the colour of the mosaic of the stained glass of the large window on the half landing, a faint smell of vanilla permeating the building.

'Can I help you?' A young woman dressed in a brilliant red skirt and matching top came up beside me, so silently I hadn't heard her approach.

'Oh, I've come to visit Mrs Halson,' I said, caught by surprise. I squinted at her badge and added, 'Diane'.

She frowned. 'Is she expecting you?'

'Not really.' Best to give a vague answer. 'I wanted to have a chat to her about someone she might know.'

She looked puzzled and I'd no option but to whip out one of my business cards. Unfortunately, it was rather tatty, as I don't use them much nowadays, but she didn't seem to notice the quality.

'So are you a researcher?'

'Of a kind,' I admitted. 'I'm researching the ancestry of a group of Americans who are currently on Bute.'

'Oh, the Stuart group! I've heard about them.' She laughed, displaying her prominent front teeth.

She stopped and looked more solemn. 'One of them had an accident in the castle.'

I didn't bother to contradict her. All I wanted to do was to find out if there was any truth in the story about Max being a Brandane.

At last she seemed convinced I was a bone fide visitor and motioned me to follow her as she began to climb the broad stairs, so thickly carpeted our feet made no sound. Half way up she stopped and turned back to me. 'How stupid. I forgot to ask you to sign in. Mrs Reever is very hot on that.'

I had to guess Mrs Reever was the person in charge and obediently followed Diane back down to the hallway where she produced a large visitors' book from one of the drawers in the old-fashioned bureau occupying most of the far wall.

As though she read my thoughts she said as I signed in, 'I know it's odd not to have a Reception desk, but the aim is to keep this place as much like a house as possible.' She indicated her skirt and top. 'We don't have a uniform, but are encouraged to wear something simple like this.'

As I replaced the pen she said, 'Is Helena Gibson still with the group?'

'Yes. Do you know her?'

Diane smiled. 'I know of her. There was a piece about her in The Buteman a few weeks ago, about her mother dying and…'

Before she could finish, the door across the hallway opened and a woman attired in an outfit similar to Diane's, but topped with a large white apron, wandered out.

Diane nodded a greeting. 'That's Fenella, the head cook,' she said as we began to climb the stairs once more. A savoury smell wafted up towards me and I realised how hungry I was. Hopefully, having missed lunch, I'd make it back to the hotel in time for dinner.

We stopped outside the last door on the first floor. 'If you could wait a minute, I'll check she's awake.' She sighed. 'Most of the residents sleep a lot.'

She knocked loudly and then went in. 'Una, there's a visitor for you.'

She beckoned me in. Mrs Halson was sitting up in bed, watching the television set into the wall in front of her.

'What did you say?'

'I said there's someone to see you,' said Diane, lifting the control and deftly turning down the sound on the set.

It was hard to tell how old Mrs Halson was. She was a small, thin, shrunken woman, her pale face heavily lined, but there was still a sparkle in her bright blue eyes behind her thick, pebble glasses.

I sat down on the chair beside the bed and introduced myself as briefly as I could. She seemed less than impressed by my credentials. 'So why did you want to come and see me?'

Diane hovered in the background, but Mrs Halson said sharply, 'There's no need to buzz around like a bluebottle, Diane. I'm sure I'll be perfectly fine. And before you ask, yes, I'll get up soon for dinner.' She might be old, but her voice was strong enough.

Diane slid out of the room and Mrs Halson pulled herself up. 'If you'd pull that pillow up behind me, my dear,' and I did as she requested.

She settled back. 'So how can I help you?'

'I'm sure you've heard the story about one of the party of Americans staying in the Stuart Hotel in Rothesay. He was called Max Stuart and he had an unfortunate accident in Rothesay Castle. Perhaps you know something about him?'

Her eyes glittered. 'And why would you be interested?'

This required a few more minutes of explanation, without giving too much away.

She sniffed and turned her head to gaze out of the window. For a moment I thought this might have been a wasted trip, but she settled herself, saying, 'Well, I was surprised when Diane told me about the death at the castle and even more surprised when I saw his photo in The Buteman. "That's not Max Stuart," I said to her. He's one of the Colpins.'

She stopped and gave a long sigh.

'And you knew the family well?'

'Yes, I used to live next door to them in Port Bannatyne. There were two of them, twins, you know. Like peas in a pod. Did everything together.'

This was becoming more interesting by the minute. 'So what was the other one called?'

She bit her lip. 'I'm trying to recall. It was also something beginning with …'She stopped. 'No, I can't recall.'

'So what happened?'

Mrs Halson shook her head. 'It's a long story.'

'So how are you sure the photo in The Buteman was of Max?'

She giggled, a girlish sound quite out of keeping with her looks. 'Oh, my dear, no one could mistake that nose, that long pointed nose and that high forehead. Their father had it and the twins inherited it. Caused them no end of bother. The other children made fun of them. I suppose nowadays you would say they were bullied and perhaps that's why they kept to themselves so much. It wasn't a happy home. Their father was always in trouble with the law.' She pursed her lips, apparently unwilling to elaborate.

While all of this might be interesting, it didn't take me much further forward. Perhaps I wasn't asking the right questions.

'So why would he have been interested in exploring the dungeon at Rothesay Castle?'

'I don't know anything about that, dear.' She stopped and peered at me over her glasses. 'Why are you so curious about all of this? Are you a relative?'

'No.' Once again I explained my interest in the case, but I wasn't sure she believed me. 'You'd think people would have enough to do without involving themselves in stuff which doesn't concern them.'

'I'm doing it as a favour,' I said, trying to encourage her to continue, though there might not be much else she could tell me. When Max left the island, there

118

might not have been any further contact with the family.

She lay back on her pillow and closed her eyes, to all appearances fast asleep. I stood up, ready to tiptoe out so as not to disturb her when she suddenly sprang into life. 'Where are you going?'

'You've been very kind and I didn't want to take up more of your time.'

'It's not a bother. I get very few visitors. That's one of the problems of living for a long time. There's no one left to come and see you. Make sure you come back.'

I muttered something in reply, knowing with my limited time on the island I was unlikely to find time for a return visit.

She lapsed into a doze again and I left the room quietly, closing the door behind me.

As I was about to cross the road for the bus back to Rothesay, the bus for Ettrick Bay came trundling along and on impulse I decided to jump on. It was a beautiful evening and a walk along the shore road would help clear my head and give me time to think over what Mrs Halson had said.

The tearoom at Ettrick Bay was busier than usual, so I bought some coffee and cake and headed out on the Kirkmichael Road. Past several houses, clustered together as if for cosiness, I went down on to the beach and found the little inlet I remembered from previous visits. I sheltered in the lee of a circle of large rocks and sat drinking my coffee and watching the noisy oyster catchers strutting about at the water's edge. In the distance, near the tiny island of Inchmarnock, the sails of a yacht fluttered in the wind as it made steady progress towards Arran, but it was sheltered enough in this snug cove.

This would never do. I had to go over what had happened, what I'd learned and consider whether it was worthwhile telling Susie about my visit to Mrs Halson. Trouble was, she'd want to know why I hadn't taken her with me, in spite of any protests I might make about not wanting to spoil her anniversary trip. And my instinct had been correct. I'd learned almost nothing, other than confirmation Max was a Colpin. But there could have been any number of reasons why he'd changed his name.

Time to be more methodical about this. What had I learned from my visit to the home at Rullecheddan? I took a notebook from my bag and began to jot down the essentials.

Firstly, I now knew a bit more about Max and his family. He had a brother. Was the brother still alive? If so, had the police managed to trace him? None of the Heritage Adventurers had mentioned a relative.

Secondly, what was the truth behind his name? Had he changed it for some particular reason? Was Max a criminal by any chance, on the run from justice? That seemed far-fetched. Perhaps his mother was a Stuart and he thought that would be a better name for living in America? I'd have to check that out.

Thirdly, what was his purpose in coming back to the Isle of Bute in this way? As someone who was originally from the island, surely he didn't have to come with the others? And why keep his Bute connections hidden?

I sighed and drained the last of my coffee, throwing the crumbs from my cake to the robin who'd decided to keep me company and had been perched patiently on a nearby bush during my scribblings.

I sat back, leaning my head against one of the larger rocks and turned my face to catch the afternoon sun, watching the light sparkle on the water. This was all such a muddle and I could think of no reason why Max might have decided to return to the island in this way and after all this time, bragging about his inheritance.

It was warm in this sheltered spot, the heat intensified by the rocks, and I closed my eyes, letting my thoughts drift. I was no further forward, had no idea why Max should have been killed. And if Susie was correct and it was one of his fellow travellers, who could it be? I really didn't see Connie or Margie in the role of murderer somehow. Wesley might just be strong enough, but even then the belief was that the body had been pushed down into the dungeon to make it appear he'd fallen down the steps.

Margie had said something about knowing Max before she came on the trip. She might have information that would help, but if so, I couldn't think why she wouldn't have told the police.

I ran through the others, excluding Susie and Dwayne, but there was no way I could see any of them having a motive to kill Max.

But someone had, and Max had some purpose in coming back to the island. In spite of my reservations, the answer had to lie in the history of the Stuarts and in the castle. A picture of Ricky flashed into my mind, his sly grin, his new-found wealth. Was it possible he'd taken something from the corpse?

Of course, that explained his strange behaviour. Instead of wasting time trying to find out from Mrs Halson, I should have been quizzing Ricky.

I stood up, stretching and yawning. There was no need to involve my friend in the business of Mrs Halson. There had been quite enough interruptions to her holiday already: best not to complicate the situation further. Nothing much had come of my visit to the nursing home. I'd head back to the hotel and once I'd told her of my suspicions about him we could do what I'd originally planned - tackle Ricky.

CHAPTER SIXTEEN

Dinner was a subdued affair. Susie and Dwayne were sitting with Lloyd at a table two removed from mine and there'd been no opportunity to speak to her before going in to the dining room. I wasn't sorry. In spite of my earlier resolution a worm of doubt gnawed at me: should I tell her of my visit to Mrs Halson? I couldn't make up my mind. But there was no choice about voicing my suspicions of Ricky. I could have gone directly to Lloyd, but assumed he would be even less sympathetic than Susie.

I ate little, conscious of the knot in my stomach at the discussion to come. Or perhaps it was more to do with the large slice of cake and the coffee I'd had at Ettrick Bay. I'd made one decision. If I could be brave enough, I'd make an excuse to finish up earlier than planned. I'd tell Simon I was coming straight home and once back in London, I'd put together some kind of general booklet for the group. I'd have to lessen my payment, but somehow even the thought of another trip to Canada to see Alastair wasn't enough to tempt me. At least that was my intention.

As soon as the meal was over, I jumped up and hurried over to grab her before she could disappear again.

'Susie, I absolutely have to speak to you…alone.' In case she'd any ideas about involving Lloyd, or even Dwayne.

If she was surprised at the urgency of my appeal, she didn't show it. 'Fine, Alison, do you want to go into the bar?'

'No, not there.' I suspected that was where most of the group would head before the planned entertainment of Scottish traditional songs taking place that evening in the lounge. 'Let's head out. The Ghillie Bar at the Victoria Hotel should still be open.'

'I'll fetch my coat. I won't be…'

I grabbed her arm. 'No, it's a lovely evening and it's not far.' I was concerned she might be way-laid by one of the other guests and now I'd made up my mind to discuss my concerns about staying on, I didn't want my resolution to fail.

She made no protest and with a quick 'Back soon,' to Dwayne, she joined me at the front entrance to the hotel.

We walked briskly in silence down towards Guildford Square and along Victoria Road towards the Ghillie's Bar. At this time of the evening the town was quiet, a few cars lined up for the last ferry off the island, several people queuing at the Fish and Chip shop, the tempting aroma wafting over the street, enticing the squawking seagulls competing for a tasty titbit.

'The council are trying to dissuade people from feeding them,' said Susie. 'They can be a real pest and vicious if you go too near where they nest.'

'Yet they are so much the sound of summer holidays on an island.'

It was a beautiful evening, the sky fading to pink and purple as the sun set over Rothesay Bay, a whisper of a warm breeze sending the rigging of the boats in the harbour faintly tinkling.

We reached our destination, chatting in a desultory way and 'Let's go through to the back,' I said. 'It will be quieter there.'

A few diners were lingering over coffee at the tables at the front window and it was better our conversation wasn't overheard, though I suspected they were holidaymakers with no interest in us.

The overhead lighting here was dim, the flickering candles on the table smelling faintly of ginger.

'Coffee, black, for me,' said Susie and I opted for a cappuccino.

As we waited for the waitress to return, Susie leaned across the table. 'So what's this about, Alison? Why all the secrecy?' Her face lit up. 'You've made a great discovery. That's it. You've come up with some connection, some important connection for one of the group.' She sat back, her eyes shining with anticipation.

I shook my head. 'Hmm. Sorry to disappoint you, Susie. It's something quite different. I'd like to head back to London earlier than planned. I can finish the rest of the booklet there.'

She looked horrified. 'You can't do that. You can't let us all down.'

'Let's be honest. This isn't turning out the way either of us anticipated. I've a fair amount of material and I've recorded the interviews.' I paused and fidgeted with the drinks mat on the table, avoiding looking at her. 'Max persuaded you he'd some illustrious connection, didn't he? That's why you sought me out, asked me to take this on? It was nothing to do with the others.'

I stopped talking as the waitress came over and set out our coffee in front of us.

Susie rooted in her bag and pulled out a packet of sweeteners, deftly popping a couple into the coffee before lifting her cup and cradling it in her hands. She looked shamefaced for a moment. 'Not exactly. Yes, Max did keep on about some connection, something that would make him famous. He was keen to stress this at the pre-meeting we had a month before we set off. Given we were having time on Bute, all his boasting probably gave the others an interest in the history of the early Stuarts.'

I sighed. 'It's not like that, Susie. Do you know how many people there are in the world with the surname Stuart?'

'No – how many?'

'Oh, for goodness' sake, I've no idea either, but there must be thousands, if not millions.'

'Yes, but some of them must be descendants of Mary, Queen of Scots or Bonnie Prince Charlie.'

'Only in the same way that we're all descendants of Adam,' I replied loudly enough to make the couple at the far end of the lounge turn around to see what the commotion was about.

I leaned forward, lowering my voice to a whisper, 'Honestly, Susie, it's not what I thought it was. The people in this group have such high expectations…all fuelled by Max no doubt, talking up his "inheritance".'

'It's nothing to do with the project, is it? It's about Max's unexplained death, isn't it? You're worried about that. Don't. It's nothing to do with you. The police will handle it. It happened before you came to the island so you won't even be called as a witness. For heaven's sake, Alison, if you abandon us now, what will I tell them?'

'No, it's not that.' I concentrated on drinking my coffee, staring into my cup.

She laughed. 'Got it! Why didn't I realise sooner? You're fretting about what Simon will say when he finds out you're on the island when another murder has taken place.'

There was a pause, stretching to a longer silence as I tried to rationalise my reasons for wanting to leave the island. What's more, I'd a niggle of doubt there was more truth in her words than I wanted to admit.

'There is something I want to talk to you about and I don't want you to be upset.' Scarcely pausing for breath, I rushed through the story of meeting the girl at the bank, the possibility Max wasn't a Stuart, the visit to Mrs Halson and my concerns about Ricky's possible involvement. There was no point in leaving out any of the details.

'Why didn't you tell me this before?' She frowned. 'I thought you didn't want anything to do with the problem of Max's death?'

'Because it might have been a lot of nonsense – the business about Max, I mean. I'm still not convinced

127

Mrs Halson was right. Besides, you and Dwayne are supposed to be here on an anniversary trip,' I finished, aware how lame an excuse that sounded.

Instead of calming her, my story seemed to fire her up. 'I knew something happened at the dungeon that day Max was found. We'll have to find a way of talking to Ricky, without alarming him.'

'I guess so, but honestly, I can't be involved in this.'

'In spite of all you've said you are involved, Alison, else why did you pursue that lead about Mrs Halson?'

I'd no answer, but I did want to make my intentions clear. 'I don't want to let you down, Susie, especially as you set up the project. I can still write a history, try to make it more individual to the people in your group, but my impression is there will be little of real interest and it's much better that I go home early. Surely we can explain to the others.'

'What makes you say that?'

'I've tried interviewing them, but unless I can come up with a direct link to Bonnie Prince Charlie or someone equally famous I've a feeling they'll be disappointed.'

Susie began tapping her fingers on the table and sighed as I put my hand over hers to stop the noise.

'We can come up with some excuse, some reason for cutting it short,' I pressed her.

'I suppose so.' She drained the remainder of her coffee and set the cup on the saucer with a loud clink.

Her reluctance to argue was a sign she understood how I felt. 'And I will make a good job of the historical booklet, include all their names in the dedication and such like,' I rushed on, eager to take advantage of this chink in her armour.

'Okay, Alison, I can go with that. But there's a favour I want to ask before you leave. It would be a great help and you'd be gone before there were any consequences. Especially as you've now told me about Mrs Halson's suspicions.'

Relief at her calm acceptance of my argument about leaving early made me careless. 'Of course I'll help you, as long as it's nothing dangerous,' I joked.

'No, but it would be…'

Before she could finish, a voice said, 'Well, well, look who's here.'

Susie and I turned to see Zachary coming towards us.

He threw himself into the remaining chair, without asking if he could join us. He winked. 'Playing hooky, ladies? Had enough of the Heritage Adventurers?' He leaned close. 'Well, I can show you the sights of the town, make no mistake.' He moved restlessly in his chair, twisting this way and that.

Susie visibly bristled as I blurted out, 'The way you did with Ricky, do you mean?'

He laughed. 'Every young guy has to start sometime. That mother of his smothers him. Time for him to spread his wings.'

Susie jumped in. 'This is a party of Americans, none of whom has been out of the States before. It's all strange and a bit scary for them.'

But Zachary wasn't in the least upset by her angry tone. 'All the more reason to show the youngsters what the island is really like.' He leaned back, letting his t-shirt ride up, exposing an expanse of flesh.

This was turning into a very difficult situation. 'How are the rehearsals coming along?' I said in an attempt to defuse the tense atmosphere.

Fortunately, this had the desired effect. 'Well enough,' he said, sitting up and crossing, then uncrossing his legs. He frowned. 'The only problem is that we've lost Felicity, who was playing the mother of King William. She's had to leave for a new job in Edinburgh sooner than expected. It leaves us at a bit of a loss. She's kind of vital to the story. I'm not sure what we'll do.'

He stopped fidgeting and stared at Susie. 'You look about the right age. How about stepping in? You don't have to do much. There's only one scene and you'd have no more than three lines of dialogue.'

'I don't think so,' replied Susie curtly, but whether it was because she was annoyed at the suggestion she could play someone's mother I couldn't tell.

Zachary smiled. 'No need to be shy. I'm sure you'd do very well. And,' leaning forward to deliver a final entreaty, 'if someone doesn't take on the role, the whole production might be in jeopardy. Now that wouldn't go down well, especially as it's planned for the last night as the highlight of your trip.'

'I'm sure you could do it, Susie.' Part of my eagerness to persuade her was relief I hadn't been asked. My one venture into acting had been more than enough.

'I'll think about it,' Susie said grudgingly, but the change in her tone made it clear a little more persuasion was all that was needed.

Zachary stood up, gripping the back of the chair tightly. 'I hope I can count on you. You'd be ideal.

Don't take too long. We have to have a replacement for the rehearsal tomorrow. You can get me on my mobile.' He passed her a card and from a brief glimpse I could see the space on it was mostly taken up by a very flattering photo of himself, much doctored.

With a wave and a 'Now don't let me down, Susie,' he was off, adding, 'In case you're wondering, I'm checking out the hotel for a friend who's coming over for the Pageant.'

We sat in silence for a moment or two after his departure, then looked at each other and burst out laughing.

'There's no way I'm going to do it,' said Susie, wiping the tears from her eyes. 'He'll have to find someone else.'

'Oh, it isn't much to ask, Susie, and be honest, you'd love the chance to be on the stage.'

'Yes, but I can't afford lots of time for rehearsals. Lloyd will be upset if he's left alone with the group. I'm supposed to be one of the leaders, after all.' She didn't mention poor Dwayne.

'From what he said, it's a minor part. Surely one or two rehearsals will suffice.'

'Suppose so.'

I could sense she was relenting and not only because she thought she'd some duty to make sure this final extravaganza of the holiday would be successful. And if what Zachary said was true, they had to find someone quickly.

'You heard Zachary's plea: it's not a big part, but one essential to the story.'

She smiled. 'Okay, okay. I'll do it.'

Much relieved the decision had been made, 'Now, 'I said. 'What was it you wanted to ask me?'

CHAPTER SEVENTEEN

Later, much later, I tried to rationalise what madness had made me agree to Susie's request. Was it because she was a good friend? Or because I felt guilty at wanting to cut short my time on the island, in spite of my suggestion of doing the rest of the research from home being perfectly sensible? Or perhaps a lingering fear that she would take fright and refuse to take on the role of Walter's mother, leaving Zachary with the problem of having to replace her?

Whatever the reason, all I did was land myself in another mess. I couldn't even comfort myself that I hadn't agreed immediately, but had demurred while trying to come up with a reason as to why I didn't think it a good idea to go to Rothesay castle, when she said, 'We need to make sure nothing's been missed, Alison. There must have been some important reason for Max being there on his own.'

Why Susie thought we might spot something that the police had overlooked I'd no idea, but what with her pleading and my feeling guilty, at last I said, 'Fine, but it will have to be no more than a quick look. I'm sure the police have searched every last corner of the castle and then some.'

Knowing my friend as I did, I should have guessed her plan wasn't straightforward. I'd envisaged a short walk from the hotel across to the castle to pay our entrance fee with the other tourists, followed by a quick reconnoitre of the Gatehouse and the Courtyard, perhaps scouring the remains of the chapel dedicated to St Michael the Archangel. It shouldn't take long. The castle was almost empty of furniture, and even in those buildings still standing there were few corners where anything could be hidden. Susie had other ideas.

'There's no point in going over when the place is teeming with visitors. We have to go at a time when the castle is closed to the public and there's no chance of us being seen. We must have time to go through the place properly.'

As the evenings were becoming lighter with every day that passed, I was immediately filled with alarm. 'When exactly would that be?'

Susie looked down at her empty coffee cup. 'I thought if we waited till it was dark, we could slip in unnoticed and take only a little time.'

'Excuse me. Slip in? You mean indulge in a spot of breaking and entering.' I could imagine the reaction if we were to be caught and hauled up before the local sheriff. 'I don't think so, somehow. Forgive me for saying so, but that's a mad idea, Susie. You'll have to come up with a better plan than that, I'm afraid.' My sarcasm failed to deter her.

She grabbed my arm as I stood up to leave. 'Alison, there's no other way to do it and if we start asking permission we'll start all sort of rumours.'

As though there aren't enough rumours already, I thought, but all I said was, 'This is a crazy idea and while I'm more than willing to help you as best I can, I can't go along with this.' Then I had a brainwave. 'The castle will be locked up at night so how could we possibly get in? And even if we do, there are floodlights around it. We'd be spotted at once.'

She smiled. 'Ah, there is a way in. I've checked it out.' A shrug of her shoulders. 'But if you don't want to come along, don't want to help me, then that's fine. If you won't come with me, I'll go alone.' The determined set of her jaw was indication enough she wasn't to be dissuaded from this crazy venture no matter how hard I tried.

I attempted a different strategy. 'If we do go, we'll have to know what it is we're looking for. There's no point in taking a risk like this on the chance we might find something of interest. What do you have in mind?'

Her face lit up. 'I knew you'd understand. I'm convinced there was something in that dungeon where Max was found. He wouldn't go down there on a whim. I didn't know him well, only met him as part of the group, but he struck me as someone who had something to hide. There's no other way he'd have left the rest of the group and gone off exploring on his own.' She stopped. 'I don't know why, but I'm sure you're right and Ricky knows something. He's been decidedly shifty and I don't for a minute believe that story about having a lock-in with Zachary. There's more to that story than either of them is telling us.'

I'd a sudden flashback, an image of Ricky poring over his Tablet. Ricky, who claimed to have no interest in the history of the Stuarts, whose only wish was to leave the island as soon as possible and return to his comfortable American lifestyle. But he was only a teenager. What possible connection could he have with Max's death? The very idea was ridiculous.

'Susie, what age would you say Ricky is?'

She looked puzzled, then closed her eyes.

'I know that seems a strange question, but I'm trying to work out if he might have had some involvement.'

'No, it's only that I'm trying to visualise his form, his application. Everyone had to fill in a questionnaire at the beginning of the trip, giving details about themselves, their interests in the tour and so on. From what I remember, his form had little on it apart from the barest personal details.'

I waited in silence, almost able to hear her brain whirring as she tried to recall the details.

She clapped her hands. 'Got it. I remember now. From his date of birth on the form I guess he's seventeen or perhaps eighteen, that's it. Wait – he must be eighteen if Zachary let him drink with them in the pub. The legal age for drinking in his part of the world is twenty-one.'

'No matter,' I interrupted. 'That's near enough. Are you sure? He looks a lot younger than that.'

'Yes, yes. At the time that was my thinking and we didn't want anyone coming on the trip who might prove a problem. Most of those who sign up for these holidays are, shall we say, of a more mature age.'

That explained a lot, but not everything. If Ricky was indeed in his late teens and not, as I'd originally guessed, much younger, it put a whole new perspective on his actions and the way his mother treated him.

A tingle of excitement ran through me. I convinced myself I owed it to Susie to help her with this mystery. Once we'd explored the castle under cover of darkness, I would feel I'd totally discharged any obligation. The thought of getting back on the ferry and heading for home added to my excitement. The sooner this was over with, the better.

'Okay, I'll come along with you,' I said, adding in a warning voice as I saw her smile, 'but only if you promise the visit will be short. And if we find nothing that will be the last time you'll mention it.' I was convinced it would be a fruitless trip.

'Of course, of course. I've no more desire to linger in that spooky place after dark than you have.'

Now the decision was made, I was determined we'd have a plan and not go charging in haphazardly as was Susie's usual method.

'We'll have to agree exactly what we'll do. We can't go bumbling about. So tell me, how will we get in if the place is locked up? What do you know?'

'I've thought of that. There's a gate in the railings in Castle Street and a set of steps leads onto the grassy area around the moat.'

This seemed highly improbable as a solution. 'But surely the gate will be locked?'

'It does have a padlock,' Susie said, 'but the padlock is rusty and gives easily - I've tried it,' she added seeing the look of disbelief on my face.

'So how do we get across the moat? Swim perhaps? Ride on the back of one of the swans?'

'Oh, don't be silly. We walk towards the ticket booth, move aside the portable barrier and we're at the bridge.'

Still unconvinced, I said, 'And then what?'

But she was ready with an answer. 'There's a little entrance by the curtain wall near the Gatehouse that isn't secured. I guess most people don't know it's there. We can slip in that way and head for the dungeon. If there's anything to be found, I'm sure that's where it will be.'

It all sounded easy. Slide into the castle under cover of darkness, head for the dungeon for a quick look (I was sure there was nothing to be found), then out the way we'd come in.

'Oh, very well, then. But once we've been in and had a look, promise me that'll be the end of the matter.'

She raised her hand in mock salute. 'I promise, Alison.'

I should have known that with Susie nothing is as easy as it seems and, as usual, I was landing myself in a whole heap of trouble.

CHAPTER EIGHTEEN

With the planned visit to Rothesay Castle occupying all my thoughts, the next day seemed to drag and evening couldn't come quickly enough. I couldn't settle: I went for a walk along the shore, then tried reading my book in the quiet of the lounge, decided to go into Rothesay and wandered around the Factory Shop, had a cup of tea in the Electric Bakery cafe, but in vain. All I wanted to do now was get this ridiculous escapade over with, spend the remaining time tidying up the interviews, then pack my bags to head for Glasgow to meet up with Simon. Just before I left, I'd tell Susie there had been a change of plan and I wasn't going straight back to London.

His latest call found him in a more cheerful mood. 'I'm looking forward to having a break, but let's make it in Glasgow. We could meet with the McDermotts. We haven't seen them since we moved to London and we'll still have time to see Deborah.'

The weather had turned cool and wet, something the Americans found strange. Here on an island, Atlantic weather made any season unpredictable as I tried to explain to Connie who was sitting in the lounge, gazing out over the window where the mainland across the bay could scarcely be seen through the fine mist of rain.

'It can change quite suddenly,' I said. 'Wait and see. By early evening the sun will have come out and you'll find it's pleasant enough for a walk. It's just unpredictable.'

'I don't know why you should say it's unforgiveable. It's only rain.'

'No, I mean it will probably stop soon,' I said in a louder voice.

'Perhaps so, but I ain't going to risk the trip to Scalpsie Bay. Think I'll jest make myself comfortable here with a book. Went down to the bookstore in town this morning - the Print Point, I think it's called and got a romance or two to keep me busy.'

Connie made it sound as if the trip to the bookshop had been a major expedition rather than a short walk from the hotel.

'Pity to miss out a place like Scalpsie. At this time of year, you might be lucky enough to see the seals.'

She looked at me over her glasses. 'Honey, even for the seals I ain't gonna venture out in that.'

'Are you enjoying the tour? Apart from this morning's weather?'

'Of course I am. It's a pity about Max, but it's Margie I feel sorry for. Imagine turning up and finding someone you detested was one of the group.'

'Margie didn't mention that.'

Connie smiled. 'Of course she wouldn't. I think they were related in some way.' She laughed, clearly finding the idea highly amusing. 'Besides, she's got other concerns. You'll have noticed the way she

140

shadows Jerome. She only told me because I happened to overhear her phone call to her daughter in the U.S.'

I left her engrossed in her book, trying to decide if this information about Margie was relevant. Probably not. It was no more than a co-incidence or else the police would have picked up on anything important.

Susie was nowhere to be seen and we hadn't yet agreed a time to meet so I left a message on her voicemail, then instantly regretted it. If I hadn't done so, perhaps she'd have forgotten about the mad idea of venturing into the castle after dark.

Glad of some time to myself, I went up to my room, intending to put my latest notes in order, but I lay down on the bed for a 'few moments' before switching on my laptop and promptly fell sound asleep. I couldn't remember when I'd last felt so tired, though the fresh air of Bute might have had something to do with it.

The sound of my mobile ringing startled me into wakefulness and I sat up, trying to shake off the sleepiness. I groped for the phone on the bedside table, wondering why it was so dark. The rain must be torrential.

'Hello,' I said glancing at the number. It was Simon not, as I'd expected, Susie returning my earlier call.

'Are you okay?' He sounded concerned. 'You sound very groggy.'

'Fine.' I sat up and pulled a pillow behind my head to support me. 'I was asleep. Just as well you phoned.' I yawned. 'What time is it?'

'After six o'clock.'

'What!' I leapt up. 'Thank goodness you phoned. I might else have missed dinner.'

'So I suppose you'll have no time to chat?'

141

My heart sank, with a sudden realisation this was more than a friendly phone call. 'Is there a problem?' Now wide awake, I was aware he was speaking more slowly than usual.

'Not really, least not immediately.'

A thousand possibilities raced through my mind, but I determined to remain calm. 'Go on. Tell me what's the problem. Dinner can wait. I'm probably eating too much anyhow.'

There was a moment's hesitation. 'I don't want to worry you, but…' He stopped.

'Oh, for goodness sake, Simon, what is it? Don't keep me in suspense like this.'

He cleared his throat, a habit he has when there's bad news. 'You may as well know. I had intended to wait till we met up, but everything is moving so fast.' Another pause, during which I could hear my quickening breathing. Then he said, 'There's to be a reshuffle in the company and talk of moving the Head Office to a different location.'

Well, that was a relief. 'That doesn't affect you in Training.'

'Ah, there's another difficulty. London has become so expensive that renting premises isn't sustainable. The firm's lease is up for renewal and the Board have decided it would be better to relocate.'

I waited for him to continue, becoming more and more puzzled. Did this mean he was about to be made redundant? Was that the reason behind his hesitation?

At last he said, 'Some of the sections of the company are being relocated to save money and it looks as if the Training division might be one of them.'

My mind was racing, going through all the possibilities. Where would British Alignment Ltd want to relocate to? Canada? India? Darkest Peru?

He went on, speaking more quickly, 'They're looking for ways to save money, as you can guess they might in the present economic climate.'

'Don't keep me guessing. Where are they going?'

'That's it. They're talking about relocating all the relevant divisions to join up with those already in Scotland. You know they kept a base there.'

'What?' I was about to add, 'We've not long left Scotland for London,' then thought better of it. He sounded as upset as I was, if not more so. The decision to move south had been traumatic with much soul searching and now it looked as if we would be back where we started. Moreover, it might be a sign the company was in more trouble than Simon was willing to admit.

Whatever was going on, it looked as if we were on the move again. And I suspected that he wasn't telling me the whole story. I was more anxious than ever to leave Bute and meet up with him in Glasgow.

CHAPTER NINETEEN

By the time my phone call with Simon ended, it was too late for dinner. The waiting staff were busy clearing the tables when I eventually made it to the dining room, having taken some time to mull over Simon's surprising news. There was so much to think about, I hardly noticed the time slipping past. If we were to move back to Scotland, it might not be Glasgow. To think of all the nights we'd sat up late before the move south, agonising about whether to sell our house. Now it appeared selling had been the wrong decision. True, since our house in London was rented, it would avoid the problem of selling up, but there were other difficulties.

One of the waitresses took pity on me and brought a plate of cold meat and salad. 'There's still time for dessert,' she said helpfully, indicating the buffet bar. 'That won't be cleared for a good half hour yet.'

Susie was sitting chatting to Lloyd and Dwayne, oblivious to the activity around her and Ricky and his mother appeared again to be engaged in some kind of altercation in the far corner.

Margie was sitting at a table on her own. What happened to Max must have been a shock, but any time I saw her she gave no outward sign of being upset.

I could scarcely swallow a mouthful of the salad. Most unlike me, but the knot in my stomach was growing tighter and tighter, thinking of what lay ahead. Not helped by Simon's news. Of course in many ways I'd be pleased to return north, but the thought of trying to find somewhere to buy, all that hassle wasn't helping my mood. And we'd miss seeing Connor grow up. Maura and Alan were firmly established in London and Deborah showed no signs of settling down. In fact, I was hard-pressed to keep track of her boyfriends, frequently getting their names wrong. And as for my son, Alastair, his latest research taking up all of his time, it would be a brave woman indeed who became involved with him.

Susie laughed loudly at some joke Lloyd made, seemingly not the slightest bit concerned about the plans for later that night. A little sliver of optimism crept in. Perhaps she had, after all, realised breaking into the castle wasn't such a good idea, but my hopes were to be dashed as she spotted me, waved and came over to join me.

'Ready, Alison?' Her eyes gleamed with excitement, though she glanced around as she spoke. Susie was clearly looking on this as an adventure, something to enjoy.

'Are you certain about this?' I made one last gallant effort to change her mind.

'Don't tell me you're afraid?' Her mocking tone irked me.

'Of course not, though goodness knows what excuse we'll come up with if we're caught.'

She grinned. 'Oh, you'll come up with something, Alison.'

This didn't merit a response and I shook my head in disbelief.

Susie stood up. 'We'll meet outside, in front of the Musiker café, at midnight sharp. It's better if we're not seen to leave together. Wear something dark.'

She said all this in a low tone of voice, as though to make sure we weren't being overheard. If the situation hadn't been so serious I'd have laughed.

How I passed the time that evening, I've little recollection. At one point I wandered into the lounge where a very young, very earnest man was giving a talk on the birds of Bute, but what he said is a blur, though the rest of the audience seemed intrigued judging by the rapturous applause when he finished. In little groups they headed for the bar, Lloyd in the lead as usual.

All I could think about was what would happen if we were caught breaking into Rothesay Castle. Featuring on the front page of The Buteman would be the least of our worries. Possibly Susie had some good excuse in hand. I certainly hoped so.

I kept going over the plan Susie had come up with to get into the castle, thinking of all the things that could go wrong – and there were plenty, from the padlock being more secure than she supposed to the barrier at the bridge being too heavy to move. My best hope was that we'd find the padlock wasn't as easy to open as Susie believed. Then we could abandon the project, comforted by the fact that we'd at least tried.

At last the appointed hour arrived. In spite of Susie's admonition to wear dark clothing, the best I could come up with was navy trousers and a dark red jumper, packed in case of emergencies.

I crept downstairs from my room and slipped through the lounge, averting my gaze in case anyone stopped me. But I needn't have worried. The few late night revellers in the bar were too busy laughing loudly at some story Lloyd was recounting to notice me.

Susie was already waiting for me outside the café, moving restlessly from one foot to the other, gazing in the window of Musiker's, though the café had long since closed for the night.

'Good, you made it,' she murmured. 'I thought you might decide not to come along.'

'I almost did,' I said, taking the torch she offered me. Then I thought about Dwayne. 'What did you tell him?'

'I said I was going to your room for a chat and a catch up. We haven't had many opportunities on this trip, or not as many as I'd have liked. We always seem to be in the company of other people.'

That much was true and I nodded as she added, 'He said he'd be glad of an early night. All this gadding about is exhausting him.'

He's not the only one, I thought grimly as together we crossed the road towards the castle. As predicted, the rain had cleared, leaving a few clouds scudding across the starry sky. The street lights seemed distant, dimmed by the bulk of the building looming up in front of us. But that wasn't the problem that faced us.

'Wait a minute.' I pulled her back. 'How could we have been so stupid? Look! The castle is floodlit. We'll

147

be spotted immediately.' A wave of relief surged over me. We'd have to abandon this nonsense.

Susie grinned. 'No need to worry. Haven't you noticed? They're renovating part of the castle on the other side and over by the scaffolding the floodlight is switched off. The gate is on that side of the castle. Don't you trust me? I told you I'd checked it out before I suggested it.'

Foiled in my final attempt to persuade her to call off this crazy idea, I'd no choice but to follow her meekly as she marched purposefully round to Castle Street, keeping close to the iron railings. 'There's a little gate here, seldom used. We can get in that way and then double back, staying on the grass and then going over the bridge.'

'I hope you're right,' I muttered, but if she heard me she didn't acknowledge it.

We arrived in front of the gate and to my relief there was a chain firmly fixed across it, well secured by a rusty padlock.

'That settles that,' I said, trying to sound disappointed. I pulled at the padlock, but it remained firmly stuck. 'There's no way we can get in, unless you've brought a pair of pliers.'

Susie laughed, then stopped suddenly, aware even the lowest sound would carry in the silence. 'Ah, it's not as difficult as it seems,' she whispered. 'The padlock doesn't work. It's probably been there so long everyone's forgotten about it. Didn't you believe me when I said I'd checked it out earlier?'

To prove her point, she put her hand under the chain at the back of the gate and gave it a hard tug. It fell away, together with the padlock, rattling and clattering to ground with a loud bang.

We stood stock-still, expecting someone to come running up at any moment, ask us what we thought we were doing. But nothing. The silence descended again, the only effect being on one of the swans which raised its head from under its wing as though cross at having its sleep disturbed.

'Oh, I forgot about the swans,' said Susie. 'They can be pretty fierce if disturbed.'

'We'll make sure we go nowhere near them, then,' I replied. 'Let's get on with it.'

Having secured entry, I was anxious to hurry to the Gatehouse and have a look at the old dungeon before making a swift exit. This was not a place to linger. The sooner we were back in the safety of the hotel the better.

We opened the iron gate cautiously, trying to ignore the creaking, and Susie closed it behind us, securing the chain again. 'Just in case,' she whispered. 'We don't want anyone to notice that it's unlocked.'

We made our way carefully down the steps, avoiding the cracks and broken edges. We were the first to use this way in goodness knows how long. At the bottom we ducked around what seemed to be a wooden hut used for storage and stood together in silence for a few moments, listening for any sounds of life. But there was nothing. No one came rushing out of the shadows to ask what we were up to and a few seconds later, Susie once again beckoned me to follow her.

Keeping close together, we crept along the grass towards the ticket booth and arrived at the wooden bridge over the moat, stopping only to push the metal barrier aside with some difficulty. Thankfully it wasn't as heavy as I'd feared. Susie was right. This side of the castle was under renovation, the white plastic sheets covering the scaffolding dancing like so many ghosts in the wind that had sprung up. Grudgingly, I had to admit she'd investigated the possibilities thoroughly: the floodlight in that part of the castle had indeed been switched off.

Another panic as the bridge creaked and groaned in spite of our best attempts at tiptoeing over it, but after an initial hesitation we threw caution to the winds and ran across, not stopping until we were safe inside the cover of the Gatehouse.

I leaned against the damp stone wall, trying to breathe normally. 'You've got me into some scrapes in the time I've known you, Susie, but this one surely beats them all.'

It was pitch dark. The overhead lights usually illuminating that part of the castle had been switched off and I was glad of the light from my torch.

'Keep the beam low,' she hissed. 'We don't want anyone to see us.'

'I have to see where I'm going. I don't want to have an accident.' But I did as she said.

She wasn't listening, but had gone on towards the dungeon, leaning over the railing and shining her torch into the murky depths. 'I think we'll need the torches on full beam for this.'

'Are you serious about going down there?' Although I'd suspected that was the plan, she hadn't actually said so and I was hoping she'd be happy with a quick look. 'There's no light at all inside the castle. I don't think a couple of torches will be enough to see our way clearly.'

'Of course. What else should we do now that we've come this far?'

Though I was anxious to make a hasty retreat, Susie refused to be moved as she muttered, 'These are pretty powerful torches. We could shine both of them down into the dungeon: that should give us enough light to see by.'

Then, a moment of inspiration. I said, 'We could take a few photos on our phones and have them enhanced later rather than actually going down there.'

Susie turned and stared at me. 'That's ridiculous, Alison. Why would we want to do that?'

She leaned over the railing again and peered down into the depths, the beam from her torch making shadowy outlines on the stone. 'Look how the stairway goes straight down. It's only a series of iron rungs. There's a very limited view from up here, even with a good torch. You can't see into the far corners.'

'Okay.' She was right. Having come this far, it would be foolish to leave without examining the place properly. I most certainly didn't intend to pay another night-time visit. 'As long as we have a quick look and then head back.' I was becoming more and more concerned that someone might spot us. We hadn't had time to find out whether there was a night watchman on patrol in the castle. It would be just our luck if there were.

'I'll go first,' said Susie, grasping her torch tightly and ducking under the blue and white tape that indicated the dungeon was still out of bounds.

I didn't argue, but I did follow close behind her as we negotiated the shallow iron steps leading down into the dungeon, using our torches to pierce the gloom below.

At the rung half way down, I almost slipped and my torch slithered from my hand to land with a clatter on the ground below. 'Damn,' I said, 'What do I do now?'

'Be more careful,' said Susie, turning and making a grab for me. 'We don't want any accidents here.'

'It's not the steps, it's these wretched shoes. When I packed to come to Bute I didn't take into account I'd need something suitable for climbing down into dungeons in the dark.'

'Oh, don't make such a fuss, Alison. It's perfectly okay. We'll have to make do with my torch. I'll shine it down in front of you.'

Very slowly and carefully we made our way to the bottom without further incident, though the light from Susie's torch continued to cast eerie shadows. Although I wouldn't admit it, I'd concerns about getting back up to the safety of the Gatehouse. What if we were trapped here?

At the bottom of the ladder we were in a square stone enclosure with a vaulted ceiling, too low at the far end to allow us to stand up. I retrieved my torch and switched it on again, relieved to find it was still working.

I shivered, more from fear than cold. 'There's nothing here. I told you the police would have made a clean sweep of every inch of the dungeon.'

But Susie wasn't paying attention. She was feeling her way around the walls, stopping every now and again.

152

'What are you looking for?' I said.

'Shh – I told you I'd done some investigation. I've read up on the history of several castles and in some of them the dungeon was used for important prisoners, but there were ways of getting messages out to supporters. Often there was a secret niche in one of the walls. It might be the same here. If we could only find it…'

By now I was becoming impatient. 'This is nonsense. Didn't Helena tell us that the high status prisoners were kept in the castle itself? Let's get out of here while we can. There's no secret recess. This is a solid stone wall.' I turned and had just placed my foot on the bottom rung, bracing myself for the journey upwards when Susie said, 'No, wait a minute, Alison. There's something here in the far corner.' She knelt down and ran her fingers along the ground.

Reluctant to turn back, but now curious, I said, 'Unless it's really important, I'm not stopping here a minute longer.'

Susie scrabbled about, before holding up a scrunched up piece of paper, shining her torch directly on it as she smoothed it out.

'It's only a piece of litter,' I said. 'And there's no secret niche.'

Susie shone her torch on the paper and I came up closer to peer at it, feeling my heart beginning to thump.

'So, what do we have here?' she said.

CHAPTER TWENTY

'How did the police miss this?' She held it up. 'Do you see what it is?'

'Let me have a look.'

Susie passed the find to me. 'It's a ticket for Mount Stuart House,' I said. 'It could have come from anywhere.' I was less than impressed. Breaking into the Castle in the dead of night to find an old entrance ticket to Mount Stuart House seemed a poor reward. I passed it back to her.

Susie said excitedly, 'Don't you understand?'

'Yes, it's an old admission ticket.'

Susie shook her head. 'Tut, tut, you're slipping, Alison. Look at the date on the ticket – the day Max was found down here dead. It was only because I shone my torch directly on it that it showed up.'

Less than convinced, I said, 'Let's get out of here.'

She turned the ticket over in her hand. 'I'm sure this is something to do with Max's death. It's too much of a coincidence, that he should have gone up to Mount Stuart House on his own, when there was a tour planned for the whole group.'

'Perhaps he was desperate to see the Shakespeare First Folio, couldn't wait a moment longer.'

My sarcasm was lost on her. 'You're wrong, Alison, there's…stop. What's this?' She peered more intently at the ticket, shining her torch this way and that. 'There's something written on it.'

'Fine. You can examine it properly when we get back to the hotel. Now, let's go.'

How we made it back to the hotel without being spotted, I'll never know. The journey back, up those thin metal rungs, then out of the Gatehouse across the wooden bridge to the grassy bank alongside the moat seemed to take forever. By the time we reached the bottom of the steps leading to the side gate I was exhausted. 'Wait a minute,' I said, stopping beside the wooden hut and leaning against it.

Susie paused. 'Keep going, Alison. It's not much further.'

'What's that?'

There was a sound of laughter, then a loud shout and together we crouched down at the side of the hut to hide. Had we been seen?

It was a false alarm. 'Only some visitors out late,' hissed Susie, but we stayed as we were until we were certain they had passed the gate and headed up the High Street.

'Are you sure they've gone?' I said as Susie peeped out from the corner of the hut.

'Yes, come on, before anyone else makes an appearance.'

We ran up the steps to the gate. Or rather Susie ran and I sprinted along behind her, trying to get rid of the cramp in my legs from being so long in one position.

Susie fiddled with the lock on the gate, but it wouldn't budge.

'Don't say you've accidentally locked it.' I could feel the fear beginning to rise again and my heart thumped painfully against my ribs. If we couldn't get through this way, there was no other way out.

'No, no,' hissed Susie as she continued to wrestle with the lock.

Minutes, seeming like hours, passed but still the lock refused to budge.

'Are you sure there isn't another way out of here?' I tried to speak in a normal voice, but my words came out as a squeak. I knew the answer to my question, but hoped I was wrong.

'No, not without getting someone to let us out. Stop worrying.' With a final effort she dislodged the chain, muttering as she broke a nail in this final attempt. The padlock fell off, making a loud clang on the pavement and we dashed through the gate.

Susie was unexpectedly cautious. 'Give me a minute.' Deftly, she replaced the chain and the padlock and making a final check said, 'Now, let's try to act as though we're out for a stroll.'

A stroll, at this time of the morning, I thought, but I saved my breath to walk slowly over to the hotel as Susie suggested, though my inclination was to run.

To my horror, Lloyd came ambling towards us.

'Hi, ladies. Out on the town?'

I was too troubled to think of a reply, but Susie came in quickly, 'You too?'

'Couldn't sleep,' said Lloyd, but as he came nearer I detected a strong whiff of whisky. Was he out for a walk or heading towards one of the late night venues because the hotel bar had closed? None of our business, really.

'We're going back in now,' I said, firmly catching Susie by the elbow. 'It's beginning to feel chilly.'

Lloyd waved as he headed off. 'See you in the morning.'

Inside the hotel, Susie motioned me to a chair in the hotel bar, now closed for the night, though I could have done with a large glass of wine.

She pulled out the ticket and together we pored over it. On the ticket where the details of entry were printed, there was a drawing, a series of squiggles and some numbers.

'Don't you think that's strange?' whispered Susie.

'Might be no more than someone doodling,' I replied, 'while waiting for the minibus that takes people from the Visitors' Centre up to Mount Stuart House.'

'You're wrong, Alison. This was to remind Max about something, of that I'm certain. I told you he was convinced he had some important link, something that would make his fortune.'

'It couldn't be anything to do with the Stuarts of Mount Stuart? That seems very unlikely.'

A sudden vision of Ricky came to mind and I recalled Susie's suspicions about his behaviour, but I was in no mood to remind her of that at the moment. All I wanted to do was go up to my room and crawl into bed. Anything else could wait until the morning.

'What are you going to do about this ticket?' I said, standing up and yawning. 'Are you going to take it to the police?'

Susie shook her head. 'I might, but not yet.'

'Susie,' I started to say loudly, before remembering how late it was. I lowered my voice to a whisper. 'This is not a problem for us. You know that. If this is a piece of evidence, then it should go immediately to the police.'

'Yes, but evidence of what? That's the question.'

'It doesn't matter. I don't want anything more to do with this and I don't think you do either.' I paused. 'You must remember what can happen.'

Susie laughed softly. 'I know what you mean, but think about it logically, Alison.'

'That's exactly what I'm doing and logic tells me you have to stop this immediately.'

'Ah, but what are we going to say?'

'Susie, get rid of it, hand it over to the police.'

A triumphant look on her face told me my pleas were falling on deaf ears. 'So, we're going to take it to the police station in the morning and when they ask us where we found it, we're going to say that we broke into the castle after dark, went down into the dungeon which is still sealed off and rummaged around and found an old ticket for entry to Mount Stuart?' She smiled, knowing this was her trump card. 'I don't think so somehow.'

There was no answer to that.

CHAPTER TWENTY-ONE

Susie was being unusually secretive. Having involved me in the night escapade at Rothesay Castle, it now appeared she was trying to exclude me from any follow up.

Any time next day I broached the subject of the ticket she put her finger to her lips. 'Let's discuss it later.'

As if, given my level of curiosity, I'd be able to pretend nothing had happened. What's more, I was more than a little annoyed at the way she was stone-walling me.

In the meantime, there was a distraction in the shape of Zachary's rehearsal for the Pageant.

'We need a couple of rehearsals,' he insisted. 'Only of the scene that concerns you, Susie.'

'Come with me,' Susie pleaded. 'I've never done anything like this before and you've so much experience. 'I was tempted to refuse, still being cross with her, but in the end friendship won.

'I don't think a bit part in a film that didn't make it past the cutting room floor counts,' was my reply, but with nothing in particular lined up for the rest of the morning and the remainder of the party of guests off to Kilchattan Bay now that the weather had changed, I could think of no excuse.

'Great. Zachary says it won't take more than an hour – I've checked. And the walk up to the college will be good for both of us.'

We set off at a brisk pace. Though uphill, the incline wasn't steep, but all the time I was aware of the presence of the castle, brooding behind us, as we left the High Street and went past the Police Station. The entrance doors swung open and a young constable came out, talking to his companion, a much older man. I didn't recognise either of them, but then it had been some time since I'd had any dealings with the Rothesay police. And if I kept my head down, no need to change that, though I admit to a slight feeling of guilt when I thought about our breaking into the castle.

'Don't say a word.' Susie glared at me as if anticipating my request, yet again, that she hand the ticket we'd found over to the authorities.

I sighed. If that was her decision, I wasn't going to say anything. No doubt she had some kind of plan and as long as it didn't involve me, that was fine. Or so I told myself as we passed the swimming pool on our right, close by the playing fields, host to many outdoor events including the Highland Games and Bute Fest. We slowed down near St Mary's Church. 'I must take time to have a look in there,' I said to Susie. 'There's lots to see, including the tombs. One is said to be of Alice, the wife of Walter Steward, the other is a knight.' Yet another place of interest on the island that I hadn't managed to explore.

At the Rothesay Joint Campus, the college was busy with students going to and fro, their youthful calls echoing in the still air, though many of them seemed to be talking to their phones rather than to one other.

'Zachary said to go straight through to the theatre. He's expecting you.' The receptionist smiled at us. 'If you'd sign in…and remember to sign out.' Without Zachary there to vouch for us, we had to obey the rules and after doing as instructed, we walked slowly towards the theatre, Susie dragging her heels.

'You don't need to go through with this,' I said. 'No one can make you and if necessary, they'll have to change the script.'

'Oh, I've committed myself now.' She quickened her pace as we reached the entrance to the theatre.

'Come in, come in.' Zachary leapt down from the stage to greet us. He was even more fidgety than previously, but then the performance was fast approaching. 'I promise this won't take long. No need to worry about the costume. We can sort that out for the dress rehearsal.' I stared at him, then quickly looked away. Once again he was wearing a strange kind of make-up.

He thrust a piece of paper into Susie's hands. 'Here's the revised script. You shouldn't find it difficult to memorise. If you would follow me.' And with that he hurried off again, leaving Susie trailing in his wake.

Suddenly noticing I was there, he added, waving his hand vaguely in the direction of the auditorium, 'Have a seat anywhere, Alison. You can be the audience.' He grinned. 'Make sure you applaud at the right bits.'

I chose a seat in the middle of the hall and settled down to watch Susie become King William's mother.

After a shaky start she acquitted herself well and Zachary seemed pleased, judging by the way he kept saying 'Well done,' and 'That's great,' though I wasn't too sure about the youth who had the role of her son, the King.

'Do we have to do it again, Zachary?' he complained. 'I'm supposed to be playing in the football tournament at lunchtime. We've a big game coming up on Saturday against the Gourock Greats and we need all the practice we can fit in.'

'What! No way. What on earth will we do if you get injured? I absolutely forbid it till the Pageant's over with. Then you can play football every day if you want.'

The boy shrugged. 'It's a friendly. Nothing will happen.'

Zachary wagged his finger. 'I've known people injure themselves badly even in a friendly game. No football till the Pageant is over. Do you understand?'

The boy glowered, but didn't reply, turning on his heel and heading off towards the exit. I'd the feeling Zachary's ban would go unheeded.

Zachary turned to us and smiled. 'Young people, eh?' as Susie came down the steps leading from the stage.

'Sure that was okay, Zachary?'

'Great, Susie. You're a natural.' He ran forward and grasped her hands. 'You'll be superb. The audience will love you.'

An overstatement, given how minor a part Susie was playing, but then I suspected Zachary was the kind of person whose life was characterised by exaggeration.

We opted not to stay for the lunch Zachary offered us. I've had enough of canteen food during my time teaching at Strathelder High and besides, the rehearsal had taken much longer than the hour we'd been promised.

I could see Susie swithering, uncertain whether refusing might be taken as rudeness, but I was determined. 'We have to be back for lunch at the Stuart Hotel. There's a trip to Mount Stuart this afternoon, if you remember?'

She nodded in agreement. 'Thanks for the offer, Zachary. Another time.'

'Make sure you learn your lines, Susie. We have someone to prompt you but it's a difficult thing to do if you're in the open air. Words tend to get lost.' He smiled as he said this, but there was no mistaking the underlying seriousness of his tone.

'Absolutely. I'm looking forward to it now.'

'The dress rehearsal will be on tomorrow afternoon at two o'clock. And if you could arrange with Terri here…'he pointed to a mousy woman standing in the shadows '…about a fitting for your costume, then we're all set.'

Aware that time was going on, I caught Susie by the elbow. 'We have to go. The bus for Mount Stuart will be arriving promptly and we don't want to miss the chance of seeing Shakespeare's First Folio.'

A student appeared in the doorway and Zachary rushed off, calling, 'Just coming, Darren. You weren't due for the audition till after lunch.' He turned back to us. 'We're doing Romeo and Juliet at the end of term.' And with that he and the student disappeared from sight.

'No wonder he's so manic,' I said, gazing after them. 'Come on, Susie, we have to hurry.'

This jolted her into action and she followed me out, grinning broadly. 'I did honestly enjoy that, Alison. I didn't realise acting could be such fun.'

I didn't think three lines in the Pageant constituted acting, not in any proper sense, but I didn't want to dampen her enthusiasm, nor to appear envious, so I kept quiet.

The boy playing the part of King William was standing by the outside door, smoking and scrolling through his phone. As we passed I heard him say, 'I think that's a rotten idea. Far too easy – it's bound to go wrong.'

He noticed us and stopped, nodding as we left.

'Always on their phones,' sighed Susie. 'I think future generations might be born with one in place of a hand.'

Half way down High Street, a little past the newsagents, she suddenly stopped. 'Damn. I can't believe it.'

'What's wrong?'

'How could I have been so stupid? I've think I left the script next to where you were sitting. I left it there for a minute, meaning to put it in my bag.'

'Are you sure?' It would take good ten minutes to walk back to the college if she was right.

She began to rummage in her bag. 'Nope. It's definitely not here.'

'Could Zachary drop it off?'

'I don't think so. It won't take long to go back for it…not if I walk quickly.'

'I'll come with you,' I said and we turned to head back up the High Street. 'I'll give Lloyd a ring, see if they could hold the bus for a couple of extra minutes.'

Now I was regretting refusing Zachary's offer of lunch. Had we stayed, Susie might have remembered her script and what's more, I'd have had some lunch. As it was the meal would be over by the time we got back to the hotel. We'd only just be in time to join the party heading for Mount Stuart. The attraction of Shakespeare's recently authenticated First Folio was too good an opportunity to miss.

Once again we went into the college, having to sign in, though we tried to explain we were only there to pick something up and had no intention of staying for long.

The receptionist was firm. 'Something could happen in the few minutes you're inside and I'd have to make sure everyone was accounted for.'

The theatre was quiet and Susie hurried down the aisle. 'Ah, here it is,' she said. 'Where I left it.'

As she went to put it in her bag, there was a noise from the side of the stage and we looked over to see Zachary in animated conversation on his phone.

'I can't do it,' he was muttering. 'I've told you before. It's not possible, not at short notice.'

In the gloom of the wings we couldn't see the expression on Zachary's face, but he sounded very cross indeed. Even so, Zachary's quarrel was no business of ours.

'Come on, Susie. Let's go. Lloyd has said they'll hold up the bus for a few minutes, but there will be a guide at Mount Stuart House waiting for us so we can't be too late.'

As we left, Susie said, 'I wonder what that was all about, who Zachary was talking to? It sounded serious. I hope it's not anything to do with the Pageant. We wouldn't want anything to go wrong at this stage.'

I shook my head. 'No, don't worry: it won't be anything to do with us. You won't lose your part.'

Susie made no answer, but I could sense her curiosity. Worse still, in spite of what I said, in spite of the way I tried to dissuade her from getting involved, I had to admit I was equally intrigued about what had made Zachary so upset.

CHAPTER TWENTY-TWO

Travelling by local bus was a novelty for many of the Heritage Adventurers and the West Coast Transport with its retro style livery of black and red caused quite stir. Fortunately, the driver was a patient man, well used to such passengers and he was unfailingly courteous as he helped them board.

'Be careful of the step, it's rather high,' he said to Connie as she grasped the rail at the side to get on.

'Yes, I can see that, young man,' she replied, though Jimmy, the driver, must have been on the wrong side of fifty.

I'd been to Mount Stuart on several occasions, but never failed to have a sense of anticipation as we drove through Montford with its stout redbrick villas before passing the curve of the little bay at Ascog. The picture postcard village of Kerrycroy drew gasps of admiration and Helena explained, 'It was built by the Marquess of Bute for his estate workers.'

Jerome said, 'Gee, they must have been prized workers to deserve this. I remember when I was appearing in The Architect's Dilemma we had to build a set very like this.'

He'd chosen a window seat at the back of the bus, but Margie had managed to slip into the seat beside him, effectively trapping him. He gazed steadfastly out of the window, ignoring her chatter.

The journey to Mount Stuart was short: more time was spent getting people on and off the bus than travelling, though I held on tightly to the back of the seat in front a few times as the driver accelerated and negotiated the sharp bend past Kerrycroy with a skill born of long practice.

The bus crunched to a stop on the gravel in the car park a short distance from the entrance to the house and Jimmy scarcely had time to open the doors before the passengers almost tumbled out in their enthusiasm to start the tour.

'If you go through the Visitor Centre the minibus will be waiting to take you up to the House,' said Jimmy.

A few minutes were spent arranging the group on the minibus as the driver, who introduced himself as Eric, cheerfully accommodated everyone.

'Gee, does someone live here?' said Wanda.

'Surely the family don't live here now?' Connie piped up.

'No, they live elsewhere,' replied Eric, who had been regaling us with stories about the Stuart branch of the family that once lived in the property. 'The house was built by the Third Marquess of Bute, but the present Marquess decided it was too big for his needs and it's been open to the public for some years.'

Even Ricky seemed to be impressed. To be fair, he'd said very little since setting off. I'd the feeling his mother had warned him to be on his best behaviour. At any rate, he was silent, contenting himself with occasionally replacing the wad of gum he was chewing.

Eric was a mine of information about the house: there seemed to be no question he couldn't answer, but then he'd probably heard most of them over the years and he answered all ours patiently as we drove through the acres of woodland, past the walled kitchen garden, and alongside the Pinetum.

'Yes,' he said in reply to Connie, 'It's Victorian – Victorian Gothic, to be accurate. The interiors show the Marquess had an interest in a wide range of subjects: art, astrology, heraldry, mythology and even religion.'

'Gee, he must have enjoyed living here.' Wesley spoke quietly.

'Sadly when he died in 1900, the house was unfinished. Ah, here we are everyone. Now you can see for yourselves.'

There was an intake of breath from several of the party as we reached the end of the drive and the gothic majesty of the house loomed in front of us, the red sandstone glinting in the sunshine.

We disembarked at the entrance and walked under the stone portico, the gravel noisy under our feet, to climb the broad stone steps to the Marble Hall, though one or two lingered at the entrance to take photos in front of the ornamental rock garden.

Lloyd backtracked to find them. 'Keep together, everyone,' he said, trying to sound calm, but the way he gritted his teeth as he spoke made me aware that here was a man on a short fuse.

'Now,' he continued, 'if you gather round the fireplace, our guide should be with us in a moment.'

Ricky sidled up beside him. I was too far away to hear what was being said, but Lloyd looked furious and Ricky moved away, grinning.

'That boy has a great knack of annoying people,' I said to Susie, but she was too busy marvelling at the huge tapestries adorning the walls of the Marble Hall to pay attention.

Lloyd looked around, as though beginning to doubt that a guide would appear, but a door in the far corner opened and, to everyone's surprise, Helena came bustling over.

'Hope I haven't kept you,' she said.

Lloyd looked perplexed. 'I thought we were having a guide for the tour of the house, someone from Mount Stuart.'

Helena arched her brows and drew herself up, pointing to the badge on the lapel of her jacket. 'I'm one of the official guides for the House. I do this as well as being a guide for the castle.'

Lloyd raised his hands. 'Fine, fine. I guess there ain't too many people on the island to choose from.' Then suddenly aware he'd said the wrong thing, he hastily added, 'People with the right experience who know the historic places on the island well, I mean.'

Helena bristled. 'I won't have to do this much longer,' she said.

'Are you going to another job?' said Wesley.

She grimaced. 'No, I'm about to come into some money, thanks to my mother who died recently. I'll be able to give this up.'

She clapped her hands. 'If I could have your attention, everyone. If you follow me, we'll begin the tour of the house. There are a number of rooms and areas open to the public, including some new ones such as the swimming pool. Be careful of your feet as we go down the stairs and if you've any concerns about your fitness, it's better if you keep to the main house.' She pointed over to the far corner of the hall. 'There's a lift, if you need it.'

The little group trotted dutifully behind her, though I did overhear Oscar saying, 'Hope those stairs won't be like those in the dungeon at Rothesay Castle.'

The tour left the members of the group spellbound, mesmerised by the marble Chapel and by the Dining room with its elaborately carved fireplace, reduced to silence at the Horoscope bedroom with the constellations magnificently painted on the ceiling above the bed.

Even when Helena stopped with, 'Any questions? Feel free to ask if you want more information,' they were too captivated by the craftsmanship all around them to pass any comment, far less ask questions.

The entrance to the swimming pool was down a series of narrow winding steps and some of the group elected to remain in the seating area in the centre of the marble hall.

'This was the first indoor heated swimming pool in Britain,' explained Helena.

Ricky leaned forward, but his mother pulled him back. 'Ain't a very big pool,' he sniffed. 'My friend Marvin has a much bigger one at his house.'

'Oh, be quiet,' his mother said. 'Ain't no possibility he has a house like this, does he?'

Helena didn't comment, merely saying as we followed her up into the main part of the house, 'And now, this is one of the most important parts of the tour.

171

You may know the Shakespeare First Folio has been in the library at Mount Stuart house for hundreds of years, but it has only recently been authenticated.' She paused for dramatic effect. 'And now it is on public display in the library, where we are heading next.'

Ricky dragged his feet as we all moved in procession at Helena's bidding.

'How long is this gonna take. Who wants to see some mouldy ole book?'

His mother grabbed him and hissed. 'If you don't stop complaining you ain't gonna get your allowance next month. I'll tell your dad what you've been up to.'

This threat of a monetary punishment had the desired effect and Ricky subsided into a morose silence. He might not be impressed but the rest of us couldn't wait to see the First Folio.

Helena was clearly relishing every moment of this part of the tour. She raised her arm, sweeping us behind her as she set off at a brisk place. She stopped and with a dramatic flourish, saying, 'Is everyone ready?' she threw open the doors. 'And now you can see the First Folio, printed in 1624, lying all this time in the library unrecognised for the important document it is.'

'Did no one know it was there?' Margie seemed to find this puzzling.

'Oh, yes, they did know about it, but the binding was much later than the Folio itself, which is why it took so long to confirm it was an original. Recent scientific developments have made it much easier to date it accurately.'

We crowded behind her, hardly daring to breathe as we followed her in.

CHAPTER TWENTY-THREE

If the opportunity to view this important historical document, this collection of Shakespeare's plays, was exciting, it was every bit as inspiring to be in the Mount Stuart library itself. Solid wooden bookcases on three sides stretched high, with ancestral portraits above them, the volumes tightly packed to make best use of space. Many of these books looked to be as old as the Shakespeare Folio we'd come to see. How long had it taken to amass a collection such as this, I wondered? It wasn't surprising it had taken so many years to authenticate the First Folio. There must be any number of precious volumes on these bookshelves.

Several pieces of dark furniture crowded the room and a model of a stately galleon on one of the tables looked particularly interesting, but there was no time to explore as Helena firmly called us to concentrate on the First Folio, three books in total, secure within glass cases.

'Do you think that's what Shakespeare really looked like, Alison?' whispered Margie, coming up beside me to peer at the title page with its portrait of the writer.

I shook my head. 'There's a lot of doubt about his appearance,' I said. 'There are a number of possibilities.'

'Why didn't they just take a photo?' Ricky hung back.

'Don't be silly – there weren't no photos in those days.'

'Only joking.' Ricky looked pleased that at least one person had risen to the bait.

'Lookee here,' said Jerome, commanding the attention of the group. 'Ain't that good. This one's open at Macbeth. I remember that was the very first play I appeared in at High School.' He sighed. 'My, that takes me back.'

'And what was your role in that?' said Lloyd waspishly. 'One of the witches?'

Jerome didn't reply. By now he'd moved over to the third case to peer at the first page of the script of The Tempest and the rest of us, reduced to a respectful silence, clustered around the glass cases.

'If you'd come earlier, you'd have had to queue,' the guide on duty said, rising from his chair in the corner to greet us. 'It's been really busy here since this went on display.'

As Connie said, 'Think I'll rest my feet,' and moved over to the wooden high backed seat beside the ornate marble fireplace, there was a commotion, a scuffle in the corner. As one, we turned to see Lloyd and the guide engaged in some kind of dispute and Shakespeare's First Folio, fascinating as it was, hadn't the appeal of what was happening over by one of the bookcases.

'Gee, I was only looking,' Lloyd protested as the guide clutched him by the elbow, almost causing him to drop the leather-bound book he was holding.

Helena stood beside him, hands on hips, her face suffused with anger.

'I'm sorry, Sir, but visitors aren't allowed to take those books from the shelves. All these books are valuable and strictly out of bounds to visitors except by prior permission.' The guide was polite, but firm.

'That's a bit mean. It wasn't as though I was going to do anything except look.'

The guide wasn't to be swayed by this appeal. 'Even so, please don't touch anything here.'

Lloyd shrugged and came over to join the rest of us, muttering, 'I was only looking at the books: some of them are very rare. When will we get this kind of opportunity again?' I noticed him hastily pushing something into his pocket, but I was too far away to be able to see what it was. Surely Lloyd wasn't stealing from Mount Stuart House? Of course not: no more than my overactive imagination at work again.

Ricky came up beside him. 'So what's so important about those ole books? They don't look very interesting to me.'He blew a large bubble with the gum in his mouth, oblivious to his mother saying, 'Stop that.'

'What would you know?' Lloyd glared at the youngster.

Ricky shrugged and sauntered away to stand by the door, muttering, 'Only trying to help.'

There was little sympathy for Lloyd and Helena said curtly, 'You have to remember all these books are valuable. If ANYTHING in this room is damaged, we'll be held responsible. Now please do keep with the rest of the party.'

Connie pursed her lips. 'Would be a nice headline in the local paper if we were all thrown out,' but Lloyd ignored her and stood at the back of the group, sulking at being chastised in this manner, like a child.

Ricky, on the other hand, appeared to find this reprimand a subject for mirth. He moved to stand beside Lloyd and I heard him say, 'Got what you wanted,' but Lloyd glared at him and turned away without answering.

Helena continued with her description of the printing process for the Folio. 'You have to consider how new the printing press was, what a lot of effort went into making even one copy of the book.'

Everyone was duly impressed, but out of the corner of my eye I could see Lloyd, edging again towards the table where the guide had temporarily placed the disputed volume. In spite of myself, I wondered what it was that so intrigued him, but I didn't want to draw attention to him, get him into more trouble.

The guide was talking to a couple who had just come in to the library, explaining why it wasn't allowed to use flash to take photos.

'But we've come all the way from London to see this,' the man was saying, reaching into his pocket. 'I can make it worth your while.'

The guide smiled, but again the response was firm. 'Sorry, Sir.'

This momentary distraction gave Lloyd another opportunity. I saw him sneak out his mobile and quickly flicking through the book on the table, he took several photos before creeping over to join us.

No one else had noticed him flouting the guide's strict instructions, but now he stood at the back of the group and said in a loud voice, 'Can you tell us a little more about the discovery of the Folio?'

Delighted to have this positive reaction, Helena began explaining how the Folio had been authenticated.

The door to the library opened and a troupe of schoolchildren came spilling in, led by a harassed teacher, whose stringy hair and slight frame gave her the appearance of being not much older than the children in her charge.

'Gather round,' she shouted. 'No, don't go wandering off. Especially you, Danny. It was bad enough that you almost fell into the swimming pool downstairs.'

There were a few giggles from some of the girls and Danny swaggered a little, clearly pleased to be the centre of attention, whatever the reason.

This distraction seemed to be what Lloyd required and with a swiftness that was surprising, he slipped another of the books off the shelf and snuck it round to the side table, replacing it a few moments later before the guide had an opportunity to realise what had happened. If he sensed I'd noticed him, he gave no sign.

The children gathered around the first glass case, after several warnings about 'having to find your own way home,' from the teacher, but they were more interested in one another than in the First Folio, pushing and jostling as the teacher tried to explain why it was so important.

'I think we've seen enough,' said Helena frowning at this interruption. 'There will be an opportunity to have another visit before you leave the island. If you could follow me out and we'll head to the restaurant for a cup of tea.'

'Will that be extra? And does it include a cookie or two?' said Kimberley, her face lighting up at the prospect.

'Yes, it's all included as part of the trip,' said Helena patiently.

A look of triumph crossed Kimberley's face as though she'd won a personal victory. 'That's just swell. Though I think I'd prefer a cup of coffee, as long as it's fresh.'

Ricky meanwhile had perked up considerably at the mention of food. For a moment I felt almost sorry for him. This wasn't much of a holiday for a youngster with no interest in history. He was so out of his comfort zone.

Helena opened her mouth as though to reply to Kimberley's comment, then closed it and turned to lead the way out of the library.

I'd have to follow them, but the café was at the back of the main entrance to Mount Stuart and it would take them a few minutes for the group to reach it and settle in. By now I was consumed with curiosity to know what Lloyd had been doing over at that bookcase. Why he had been so eager to examine the books in that particular bookcase and why had he been taking photos?

So as the Heritage Adventurers began to straggle out I deliberately hung back, pretending to be having a last look at the copy of The Tempest in the Folio. Fortunately, Susie was deep in conversation with Connie, discussing what we'd seen and Lloyd was

178

chatting to Helena, but by the smug expression on his face it was clear that whatever he'd been up to, he was pleased with the result.

The first book Lloyd had examined was no longer on the table and I went over to the bookcase and scanned the shelves, trying to pinpoint the books he'd selected. He and I were of a similar height and by positioning myself as best I could, I narrowed it down to one of two shelves. It had to be the second or third shelf up.

This section of the bookcase contained several series of leather-bound volumes, many with the spines faded, making them difficult to read. The second shelf appeared to be a collection of books of essays written by various Victorian worthies, but the shelf above was devoted to historical themes. Several bore an inscription or a title linking them to the history of the Stuarts, but although I quickly scanned them several times, conscious I didn't have much time before I had to join the others, I couldn't work out why any of these would be of special interest to Lloyd. Perhaps, like the First Folio, they were of particular value? But they weren't for sale and in spite of his furtive behaviour, I didn't see Lloyd as a thief somehow. Even had the security at Mount Stuart been lax – and it was quite the opposite - these volumes were enormous, much bigger than the heftiest hardback book published today. Hardly the kind of thing you could stuff into a bag without being noticed. What's more, I'd seen Lloyd replace the second one on the shelf.

This was something to ponder, but not at the moment and I hurried to join the others, catching up with them as they went down the stone steps and out

179

through the open wooden doors. I don't know what made me turn around when I did, but it was to see Ricky sneaking back into the library. Surely he wasn't interested in the books? Stranger and stranger.

But he didn't stay for more than a moment or two and came hurrying back to walk behind his mother through the Marble Hall and out into the courtyard.

I edged my way towards the front so that I could have a good look at Lloyd. But he was still talking animatedly to Helena, laughing at some comment she made, as though the event in the library had been of no consequence.

I was sure I hadn't imagined it. For some reason he'd been determined to examine some of the books. It must surely be to do with the Stuarts, with the purpose of the Heritage Adventurers' visit to Bute.

I glanced over at Ricky, still with a look of glee on his face. Had he found something of interest when he went back into the library? Impossible…he'd only been there for a few moments.

Then I remembered the entrance ticket Susie had found in the dungeon. Apart from the doodles, what had been written on it? I closed my eyes tightly, trying to visualise it, but all I could remember was '2nd opp fp, vol 3' or was it '3rd opp fp, vol 2'? I'd have to check with her as soon as we were alone.

In a moment of inspiration, it came to me. It had to be a reference to one of the books in the library. That's what Lloyd had been looking for, why he was taking photographs. Was there time to go back and check?

The rest of the group would by now be in the café, enjoying a snack, and if I returned to the library and started looking for these books, the guide would be suspicious. Yet when would I have another opportunity?

I hurried back, wondering how Lloyd had known what to look for. I'd thought of all possible ways to distract the guide and have a glimpse at the books, from fainting to shouting, 'Fire', but in the end I decided honesty was best and approached him directly.

'Would it be possible to have a look at a couple of the volumes on the bookshelf over there?' I pointed out the books I was interested in, noting with quickening excitement as the guide pulled them off the shelf that the title of the second volume Lloyd had examined was titled Excavation at Rothesay Castle.

'Can I have a look at that one?'

Perhaps surprised by my request, he held it up for my inspection, opening it at the title page showing the date of publication as 1970. I tried to remember exactly where Lloyd had opened it: there wasn't time to scan the several hundred pages of text the book contained. But 1970? There must surely be photographs?

The guide looked puzzled. 'Was there something in particular you wanted to see?'

'I'm looking for illustrations of the excavation?'

'Ah, those would be in the middle of the book,' and he quickly flicked through to stop at a collection of photos showing details of the excavation of the moat at Rothesay Castle.

What a bit of luck. I examined each page carefully and there on the fourth page I found what I wanted. It was much clearer than the doodled drawing on the ticket, but there was no doubt it was the same – some squiggly symbols on a sliver of stone. I peered at the information beneath the picture.

'Early stone artefact dated to c.1190 found in the moat at Rothesay Castle.'

I snapped this illustration on my phone and with a hurried, 'Thank you,' went off to find the others, leaving the guide staring after me, still clutching the open book. This excavation of the Rothesay Castle moat was clearly important, but why? I couldn't think why Lloyd would have an interest in this.

In spite of all my good resolutions, I had to find out what was going on – and consider how much I should tell Susie. Here we go again, Alison, I said to myself, now resigned to staying here on the island until the mystery was solved, in spite of my earlier decision. What had my friend got me in to when she'd asked me to explore any links this group of Americans might have to the Stuarts?

CHAPTER TWENTY-FOUR

When we arrived back at the hotel, all thoughts of Lloyd's strange behaviour were overtaken by other concerns.

Susie grabbed me and pulled me aside. 'Over here, Alison,' she hissed. Everyone else had collapsed into the various chairs dotted about the bar area.

'Coffee for me,' I heard Margie say, adding, 'Don't you think it's a bit early for a drink, Lloyd?'

Lloyd ignored her and I saw him lift his order of a large whisky before heading off to sit on his own. He whipped out his phone, doubtless to make it clear he'd no intention of engaging in conversation.

'Oh, my poor feet,' said Connie, wriggling out of her shoes as she collapsed into an easy chair. 'All this walking is making my corns ache.'

'Told you. You should have had the operation to sort them.' Margie showed no sympathy.

'I don't need an opinion,' replied Connie and Margie shook her head before turning her attention to Jerome.

As most of the excursions, even the short ones, had been by coach, I found it hard to believe Connie had done enough walking to cause her difficulty.

'What's wrong?' I said to Susie.

'Let's find somewhere quiet. Somewhere we won't be disturbed.'

This suited me. I had to tell her what I'd discovered at Mount Stuart. She might be able to throw some light on its significance, because I was confused.

She ushered me across to the dining room, empty at this time in the evening and motioned me to sit down at one of the end tables. 'We shouldn't be bothered here,' she said, drawing in her chair. 'They won't start serving for a while yet.' She pushed aside the cutlery and rested her arms on the table, ruffling the white tablecloth.

I put my phone on the table, ready to show her the photos I'd taken, but she fixed me with what could only be called a steely glare before I could speak. 'Now, Alison, I'm going to ask you a question and I want an honest answer. If you need time to think about it, that's fine.' She cleared her throat. 'You saw what happened up at Mount Stuart, in the library?'

I should have guessed nothing much escapes Susie. 'That's what I was going to discuss with you. Yes, Lloyd was intent on examining some of the books in the tall bookcase opposite the doorway.'

'Exactly!'

Everyone had witnessed what had happened, including Lloyd being reprimanded by the guide, but I'd the impression I was the only one who saw him sneak the second volume from the shelf. I started to say, 'Yes, but I've a good idea what…' but she wasn't finished yet. 'Yes, and did you notice anything else?'

184

Best to wait to hear what she had to say before I started telling her how I'd gone back to the library, about the illustration I'd found.

'Well, Lloyd wasn't very happy about being told not to go near the books.'

She shook her head. This clearly wasn't the answer she was after.

'And…what else?'

'Give me a clue,' I said.

'Don't you think there was someone else interested in what was going on?'

This took me by surprise. 'Oscar?' I hazarded. 'He was pretty upset.'

'No, I don't mean Oscar. I rely on you being observant and here, when there was something really important, you didn't notice. Don't you think Ricky was behaving very oddly?'

'Now that you mention it, yes I did think he looked very…' I searched for the right word, '…very…smug.'

'That's what I thought.' Susie sat back with a look of triumph on her face.

'Perhaps he was pleased that someone else was in trouble for a change. It can't be much fun for a youngster being on a trip like this. Surely you can't think it was anything more than that.'

Susie wagged her finger at me. 'That's where you're wrong. I've been watching him closely and my feeling is that he's up to no good. Something happened in that dungeon where he found Max.'

'But what?'

Susie glanced around, but we were alone in the dining room. She hesitated. 'You know that ticket we found? I've examined it closely and I think it's evidence of what Max was doing.'

'So you think there's another clue in the dungeon? But I thought we'd had a really good look.'

'No, there's nothing there, but I think Ricky has something else. And that's why he's been behaving so strangely, all that business in the library.'

'What could you possibly mean?' There were few opportunities for anything other than a mischievous prank or two on a trip like this.

Once again I was on the verge of telling her what I'd found, but she hurried on, 'I've been wondering about him ever since we began. I mean, why would a youngster come on this trip?'

'Because he couldn't be left at home on his own? It was his mother's turn to have him?' After all, she'd said as much during their quarrel the first evening I'd met them.

'That's where you're wrong. Keep an eye on how he behaves with Lloyd. I think both of them are up to no good and I was even more convinced when I saw what happened at Mount Stuart.'

'Lloyd and Ricky in some kind of league? I thought I had a vivid imagination, Susie, but this is way beyond anything I could picture. I don't doubt Ricky is up to something, but it can't be as suspicious as you imply. I saw him speak to Lloyd in the library, but that was only another example of how annoying he can be.' Susie was dreaming up all sorts of plots and schemes where there were none.

Now I re-considered my decision to mention the writing on the ticket, the link with the illustration in the book in the Mount Stuart library. What purpose would be served by telling her? I'd no proof of anything. Max might only have had an historian's interest in the excavations at the moat and with Susie in this edgy state, I wanted to calm her, not cause more excitement. Best to find out a bit more first. It was bad enough having been persuaded to break into Rothesay Castle: I'd no intention of attempting a similar break in at Mount Stuart.

'You mark my words.' She frowned, upset perhaps that I didn't appear to be taking her seriously. 'Then there's the business of Ricky suddenly being flush with money. What about that?'

I had to quash this silly idea once and for all. Susie is as likely as I am to get involved in events that don't concern her, but in the past there's been some real purpose behind her actions. 'So what do you think they are planning to do? Steal Shakespeare's First Folio? I think that's unlikely. And the books in the library are far too cumbersome to be smuggled out without being noticed.'

'Hmm…okay, even if they're not working together, I strongly suspect Lloyd is up to something and that Ricky has discovered what it is.'

This conversation wasn't going anywhere fast. I stood up. 'We've been friends for a long time, Susie and you know I'm only too happy to help you in any circumstances. But this is all a product of your imagination, I have to say. Why can't you relax and enjoy the rest of the time here with Dwayne? Let the police solve Max's murder. This trip is supposed to be a way of celebrating your anniversary. And now you're involved in the Pageant, you've plenty to concentrate on.' I put my phone back in my bag. I'd tell her about the moat excavations later.

Susie remained sitting at the table, but she looked up and said, as though I hadn't spoken, 'I hoped you'd have noticed one or two very odd things going on in the group. You've had a lot of experience of this kind of thing…much more than I've had. Perhaps it's unfair of me to involve you.' A moment's hesitation, then she said quietly, 'I do think Lloyd is up to something and what's more, I think Ricky knows what it is. It's all to do with Max, with what happened in the dungeon at Rothesay Castle.'

'How can that be?'

She hesitated for a moment. 'I should have told you before, but I wasn't sure what it might mean. When Ricky came back up that ladder after finding Max's body, I don't think he was empty-handed.'

Ah, so my suspicions were correct.

CHAPTER TWENTY-FIVE

'What on earth do you mean?' I could only guess Susie had a strong impression Ricky was hiding a secret, but didn't have the slightest idea what it might be.

She shook her head. 'I'm telling you, Alison. He had something in his hand when he came out of the dungeon. I was nearest the entrance, standing beside his mother and I could tell by the awkward way he came up, one of his hands tightly clenched, that he was clutching something. At one point he almost fell and only saved himself at the last minute. His mother noticed he was about to tumble, but I'm sure she didn't know why.'

'If Ricky found something down there beside Max's body, surely he would have handed it in to the police?'

'Or to Lloyd, as leader of the group?' Susie was determined to pursue this idea of hers that Ricky was involved with the death of Max. 'Or again, thinking he could gain something by keeping it, perhaps he decided to hang on to it, wait and see what happened.'

I couldn't begin to imagine what Ricky might have taken from Max, especially as he was dealing with a dead body. 'Someone would have noticed if it was important. If anything was missing.' I tried to recall what I'd heard about the discovery of Max's body.

'Ricky was down there for longer than you'd have thought necessary. If you'd found a dead body, wouldn't your first reaction be to come back up at once? There's a lapse of time that's unexplained. And what he brought up wouldn't have to be anything large.'

I didn't say I wouldn't have volunteered to go down into the dungeon in the first place. 'Isn't it possible he was giving Max first aid, not realising he was beyond help? Or that in the gloom of the dungeon, he didn't notice what had happened?'

'What? I don't think so, Alison. During the daytime, when visitors are allowed to go down, the dungeon is very well-lit to make sure there are no accidents. And as for Max, Ricky could tell he was dead.'

'What do you think we can do about it? We've been back to the castle and found nothing more than that old ticket for Mount Stuart. And without any evidence, it's only a guess that Ricky took something from Max's body. If he did, it might have been nothing to do with the ticket.'

'Such as…' Susie wasn't about to back down.

'Oh, I don't know. Money? Perhaps he stole Max's wallet …or his phone? That might explain his sudden wealth.'

'No – you're wrong about that. When the Police brought the body up there was nothing like that missing. It had to be something else.'

The memory of our night-time trip to the castle made me shiver. 'And,' I held up my hand, 'before you make a suggestion, let me tell you I've no intention of doing that again. Once was enough.'

'Of course not. I thought there might be something in the dungeon, something the police had missed, but clearly this was all. There was nothing else there. No, whatever it is, it's something Ricky has found, is keeping to himself. He's the one we have to tackle.'

Even if he had taken something, was up to no good, there was no way I could think of that we'd be able to persuade him to tell us. I'd have to check out that illustration quickly. I couldn't keep up this pretence that I knew nothing for much longer.

On the other hand, Susie was right about one thing. Ricky was acting oddly. Before she mentioned her suspicions about his finding Max, I'd noticed his behaviour, putting it down to no more than the antics of a bored teenager. What's more, in spite of all his complaints about lack of money, he seemed to have plenty. What was it he'd said to his mother when she'd asked about his new found wealth?

Before we could continue, the door to the dining room swung open and one of the waitresses came in, laden with a tray of starters.

She stopped suddenly when she saw us. 'Oh, I'm sorry,' she said, a look of surprise crossing her usually placid face. 'We won't be ready to serve for an hour yet. But if you're really hungry, you can get a snack at the bar.'

'No, we're going this very minute.' I moved away and Susie stood up to follow me out.

Thank goodness for the interruption, I thought, then I said as we went to join the others in the lounge, 'Let's talk about this later. I'm not sure there's any way we

191

could encourage Ricky to confide in us.' I added, 'If there is anything to confide. I still think you're going overboard with your story.'

She didn't reply, pursing her lips to show she was annoyed at my lack of enthusiasm for what she had, or thought she had, discovered, but in spite of all she'd said, it seemed too far-fetched to be true. If Ricky had taken something of value, what would be the point, unless he thought he could make money from it.

I left Susie and went over to sit down with the group of Margie, Connie and Oscar. With all that had been going on, not to mention Susie's attempts to involve me in what I still thought of as a non-event, I was in danger of neglecting the original purpose of my visit.

'I'd welcome the opportunity to have another chat, find out if you remember anything more about your ancestors.' I smiled encouragingly.

'Right now?' Margie looked perplexed and Connie leaned forward. 'What did you say, honey, about our ankles.'

'Ancestors, Connie, ancestors,' Margie shouted, causing Connie to draw back.

Pulling my notebook from my bag, I said, 'I'd like to interview each of you individually again, so if we could arrange a time that suits?' Once again I'd the distinct impression Connie's 'deafness' was selective.

After some discussion, we managed to agree a time for all three of them – immediately after breakfast the following day. I gave them a list of the questions I'd be asking, constructed from the information they'd given me previously. 'If you could have a look at these before we next meet?'

Margie frowned as she looked at the list then stared at me with apprehension. 'I'm not sure I can answer all of these, Alison. Not without help from other members of the family. And I don't know if I can get in touch with them before tomorrow morning. The time difference,' she added hastily.

'You don't have to answer every one,' I reassured her. 'The questions are only there to flesh out what you've already told me. I imagine there will be a lot of emailing once we all leave here.'

Instead of reassuring her, this made her all the more agitated. 'I don't think I can do this email stuff. I suppose I could get my grandson to help.'

'Yes, yes, that would be fine.'

The dinner gong sounded. 'Oh, dinner is ready, it would appear.'

Over by the door I spotted Susie. She was waving her arms up and down, hopping from foot to foot, beckoning me.

'What's wrong,' I hissed. 'Why are you behaving like this?'

'I had to get your attention. Didn't you see? Ricky has just left, looking most furtive.'

'Will you stop imagining things, Susie. He's probably had enough of us all and gone off to seek younger company.'

'Without dinner? You know how much he likes his food. Don't you think that's enough to make anyone suspicious?'

CHAPTER TWENTY-SIX

There was no sign of Ricky later that night, at least not before I went off to bed. This time his mother didn't appear worried, probably understanding he was weary of the company of the Heritage Adventurers and had sloped off to join some of his new-found friends in Rothesay. Whatever the reason, she was chatting happily in the lounge to Margie, their raucous laughter reaching me from time to time.

It made for an easier evening, almost a relaxing one, without Ricky sitting glowering in the background, his boredom plain for all to see. Perhaps his mother was relieved that he'd found friends nearer his own age.

One of the local folk groups had been booked to provide an evening of Scottish songs and that seemed to go down well, especially as, much to everyone's surprise, Margie knew several of the songs and not only joined in, but provided a solo performance of Ye Banks and Braes o' Bonnie Doon.

'My grandma was from that part of the world, from Ayrshire,' she explained when asked, 'And she taught us lots of Scots songs when I was a little girl. When you learn something as a child, you don't forget it. I remember well her stories of picnics by the banks of the River Doon. Some of my friends didn't believe it was a real place.'

It would be fair to say I was feeling buoyant. I'd managed to conduct further interviews with those most interested in their ancestry, without making too many promises about what I might find. Some of their stories did sound interesting and while there might be no direct links to the more famous Stuarts, there could be some fascinating tales: enough to satisfy them, give them a connection with their families who had once lived in Scotland. As for the others who were less interested and only concerned about enjoying the holiday, the proposal for a booklet about the history of the Stuarts seemed to meet with genuine approval. Perhaps remaining for the rest of the week wouldn't be so difficult after all.

A couple of hours of putting everything in order and pulling together the threads of the various stories further increased my satisfaction with the way the project was developing. My plan was to have a general outline of the history of the Stuarts, embellished with case studies and stories from those in the group who had been able to provide relevant information.

Even so, I was glad when the evening was over and refusing Dwayne's offer of a 'nightcap' in the form of another glass of wine, I headed to my room. I'd have to be up early to run through my notes before conducting the final interviews. There were a few details I wanted to check and the various excursions would occupy most of the time left.

Once in my room, I slipped out of my shoes and perched on the bed, pulling my notebook from my bag and reading through my draft. Yes, there were bits and pieces of research I still had to complete and some of the interviews were a bit muddled. Hopefully, once back home, I'd be able to sort them out.

I'd also managed to take a number of photos. If I could add to those from the various sites with Stuart connections on Bute, that would help fill out the pages, make the brochure more substantial. Truth was, this was turning out to be a more time-consuming commission than anticipated and sadly my idea about gossiping with Susie, catching up on her news, had to be curtailed. Each time we did have a moment together, the problem of Max's death seemed to be the only topic of interest. She was more convinced than ever that Ricky had something to do with it, though I couldn't see how. 'He's only a youngster,' I said. 'And what possible motive could he have for killing Max?'

The writing was beginning to blur in front of my eyes. It had been a long day. Sleep beckoned and I went over to put my notebook over on the table by the window, ready to make a good start in the morning. If I managed to get up early, I could go over the notes, identify what was missing and track down the relevant members of the party.

Of course, as sometimes happens, as soon as I lay down, exhausted as I was, I was suddenly wide awake. Something Susie had said came to mind and I began to reflect on all the possibilities, trying in vain to come to a conclusion. As a result, when I looked at the clock, it was almost two a.m. and I hadn't slept a wink.

Now, in spite of all my efforts, I couldn't drift off. Everything I did – counting sheep, trying the relaxation exercises I'd once learned – only made me more awake and eventually I gave in and got out of bed. If I made a cup of tea and had a biscuit that might solve the problem. Perhaps I was hungry.

Yawning, I plugged in the little kettle and as I waited for the water to boil, I went over to pull aside the curtain and look out of the window. Soon it would be dawn, that early lightening of the sky, a chorus of birds heralding a new day. At the moment, it was still dark. There were a few hours yet to grab some sleep, though I suspected my plans to get up early and work before breakfast would come to nothing.

My room gave a good view of the street below and of the castle, illuminated on this side by floodlights. At this time of the very early morning there was no sound, no one about. The silence was complete. In a little while, the first ferry of the day would set off, carrying commuters to work on the mainland and the town of Rothesay would come slowly to life.

I was about to turn away, make my cup of tea, when a light caught my eye on the far side of the castle. For a moment I thought it was part of the floodlighting around the building, then realised this particular part of the castle was under renovation, it was the way in Susie and I had used because there was no lighting.

In an attempt to convince myself it was my imagination at work, I closed my eyes, counted to ten, and when I opened them again the light had disappeared. I breathed a sigh of relief. But then it came again, from a different part of the castle and I suddenly recognised it for what it was. There was someone in the castle and the light was from a torch, swaying this way and that, then disappearing.

Remembering our recent visit, I knew whoever was there had to be up to no good.

Should I tell someone? Given Susie and I had done the same thing a couple of nights previously, could she have gone back, bent on trying to find more information? She'd tried to convince me often enough that there was some clue in the castle, something we'd missed.

As quickly as I had it, I dismissed the thought. If she had decided to have another look, she'd have told me, or more likely, tried to persuade me to go along with her.

One thing was for certain. Whoever it was, they weren't in the castle lawfully, to explore the building. Not at this time in the early morning. And how had they got in?

A chill ran through me. We'd been so careful, made sure to lock the gate, but someone must have been watching our every move. There was no other way into the castle at this time of the morning.

If I waited at the window long enough, perhaps he or she would make an appearance and come past the hotel…or even into the hotel. Susie's suspicions rang in my head. She was right. There was something going on.

Now, having seen the light in the castle, I was determined to remain by the window as long as it took for the person to emerge, but after an hour of peering intently into the darkness with no sign of the intruder, I decided this was a futile task.

Once in bed I found it impossible to sleep, in spite of, or perhaps because of, two cups of tea and the packet of biscuits. All kinds of possibilities went through my head. I tried to rationalise that it must have been a night watchman on his rounds, patrolling the grounds and the castle, but I recognised that was nonsense. If there had been anyone on duty, he'd have spotted Susie and me when we broke into the castle. Yes, 'broke in' was the correct way of describing it, no matter how I tried to convince myself otherwise. Every time I thought about our venture, I felt a cold chill run through me. Why on earth had I agreed? Still, no harm done. If we'd been seen, someone would surely have mentioned it by now.

I must have drifted off to sleep eventually and when the alarm went off I woke with a start to see the sun streaming in through a chink in the curtains where I hadn't closed them properly.

I couldn't linger a moment longer. I was already late for breakfast and I hadn't so much as glanced at my notes, in spite of all my good intentions. I'd have to reorganise my day.

After a quick shower, I dressed, threw my notebook and pens and Dictaphone into the capacious bag I carried for this purpose, promising yet again I'd try to master the phone app that would allow me to record and hurried down to the dining room, opting for the stairs rather than waiting for the lift.

Most people had finished breakfast, but Susie and Dwayne were sitting drinking coffee and I waved over before joining them. They'd had little time to themselves on this anniversary trip, but Susie beckoned to me to their table.

Dwayne raised his eyebrows. 'Late this morning, Alison.'

'Yes.' I wasn't in any frame of mind to come up with excuses, but as soon as I could get a word with Susie on her own, I'd tell her about the strange lights I'd seen at the castle.

This wasn't easy.

'We're going to take the local bus to Port Bannatyne and have a walk along the Tramway route out to Ettrick Bay,' said Dwayne. 'It's such a great morning, and we've been cooped up for so much of this holiday, we haven't had much of a chance to see the island. There's nothing on the itinerary until later this afternoon.'

Susie nodded, setting her curls dancing. This morning she was wearing her hair loose and to my surprise I noticed a few strands of grey among the dark brown.

'We might even stop off at the Ettrick Bay tearoom for some coffee and cake. My reward for all the exercise.'

'Enjoy it,' I said. 'I'll be working.' As they stood together to leave, I caught Susie by the arm. 'Could we meet up later?'

'Yes, we'll be back this afternoon. We'll see you then.'

'No, I want to meet you on your own.'

There must have been something in the urgency of my tone that caught her attention, because she glanced swiftly at Dwayne's retreating back, then put her finger to her lips. 'Shh, be careful. Dwayne knows nothing about this, about our trip to the castle. He'd be angry if he thought I was becoming so involved in the business of Max's death.'

'It's something about the castle I need to tell you…'

But now Dwayne had turned to say, 'Is there a problem, honey?'

'No, no,' said Susie, shaking off my hand. Then in a loud voice, 'See you later, Alison,' leaving me staring after them.

Against my better judgement Susie had persuaded me to go along with her concerns about the death of Max and I had to tell her what I'd found. The business of Lloyd and the photos in the book at Mount Stuart was one thing, but I was increasingly concerned about those lights I'd seen in the castle.

The waitress came over, 'Would you like some more coffee?' but I shook my head. I didn't want any more sleepless nights.

I wasn't on my own for long. Connie came over to the table and sat down opposite me. 'Well, now, Alison, Oscar and I've remembered something that might be of interest to you. That's one thing about my husband: we might be getting on in years, but he still has a great memory. He was no more than a teenager when he left Scotland, but he still feels Scottish.'

With great difficulty I turned my attention to what she was saying. Her story might be what I needed to fill a page or two. After all, this was the reason I'd come to Bute and no matter what else was happening, I'd a contract to fulfil.

CHAPTER TWENTY-SEVEN

There was something nagging away at the back of my mind, something I'd seen, but for the life of me I couldn't reach it. I tried thinking through all that had happened, hoping my subconscious would come into play, but nothing worked.

One good thing: I'd finished the interviews. As I'd suspected, there were a number of the party not too concerned about their family history and some who were real enthusiasts. Those with no interest in their ancestry seemed content with the promise of a booklet detailing the background to the Stewarts or Stuarts as they became known, others were genuinely intrigued by the way I could organise the information, even though there had been no sign of famous ancestors. Connie had provided me with some good data about her grandfather, something I could follow up during my post-Bute research.

The only person showing signs of nervousness as the trip was coming to an end was Susie, anxious about the Pageant.

'I'll never be able to do this, 'she wailed. 'Why did I say I'd do it?' though Dwayne tried his best to bolster her confidence.

'You'll be great, honey. You'll wow them.'

As Susie's lines had now been cut to no more than two short interjections, 'There's so much to cram into this, we need to make a few changes,' Zachary had said, Susie's concerns seemed somewhat over-dramatic.

Admittedly there had been more rehearsals than Susie had bargained for. 'We want to make sure it all goes well,' Zachary kept saying.

There had been no more word about the death of Max, or who might be responsible and I hoped Susie would be too preoccupied with the Pageant to try to involve me in any more attempts to investigate further. In the end I'd decided not to tell her about the photos of the archaeological dig at the Rothesay Castle moat in the book at Mount Stuart...nor about the lights I'd seen in the castle, at least not yet. She had enough on her mind at the moment and Dwayne, usually the most placid of men, had said once or twice, 'Pity this trip to celebrate our anniversary didn't work out as planned.' Besides, the police would be busy behind the scenes and I reminded myself it was best left to them. At least, that's what I tried to do.

Even worse, my confidence in the Pageant as a distraction for Susie was, I soon discovered, misplaced.

I was sitting in the lounge, writing up my notes from the final audio interviews when she came bursting in and flopped into one of the easy chairs opposite.

'Phew. Thank goodness, that's the last rehearsal and Saturday will be the finale.'

'And then you'll be going home.'

'Yep! Can't wait.'

'Haven't you enjoyed your time here?'

She shrugged. 'Yes…and no. Let's say it wasn't the kind of anniversary trip I was expecting.' She gazed around. 'Are the others not back yet?'

'No.' I looked at my watch. 'Lloyd said they'd be back about four.'

'It's a great day for a trip to Scalpsie. I hope the seals are out basking on the rocks, though it can be a bit of a trek down to see them.'

'The viewing platform above the bay is ideal for those who can't manage.'

'Yes, I'm sorry to have missed it, but Dwayne will enjoy it.'

I refrained from making a comment. What with the interest in the castle and the time taken up by the rehearsals for the Pageant, he hadn't seen much of his wife on what was supposed to be a celebratory visit to Bute.

I offered to fetch us some tea, anticipating settling down for a proper chat at long last.

Alas, Susie had other ideas. As I returned with tea and a selection of cakes, she wriggled in her chair and said, 'The police don't seem to be any further forward in finding out who killed Max.'

I concentrated on pouring the tea, not looking forward to what she might say next. I'd a funny feeling I wouldn't like it.

'It's strange that they haven't come back to us. I asked Lloyd, but he doesn't appear to be interested, in spite of the way he and Max were always together. Poor Max. He was a bit of a boaster, but still, murder? That's something else.'

'Look, Susie, the police will be working on it. They're not going to tell us about every step they take. I'm sure they'll brief Lloyd before you leave.'

She sniffed, leaning forward to sip her tea and recoiling at how hot it was. She slowly poured more milk into her cup, then gazed up at me. 'Don't you think I've some responsibility in all this?'

'I don't see why you think that. Max made the decision to meet up with whoever killed him. It was nothing to do with you or any of the Heritage Adventurers.'

She took a moment to select a cake, finally settling on a slice of fruit cake.

'I'm not so sure,' she said, nibbling at the edge of it. 'I can't think there would be anyone on the island who might want Max dead, so that only leaves someone from our party.'

My thoughts exactly, but I didn't want to encourage her. 'Can you see Connie, or Oscar or even Wesley, being fit enough, not only to kill Max, but to move him and get him down those narrow iron steps into the dungeon?'

'Even so, even so. I am one of the leaders of this party and as such do have some responsibility for what happens.'

She finished her fruit slice and leaned forward to reach for another cake, before drawing back. 'Better not have another one. I don't do all this sugar now.'

Then I made my big mistake, an error I could have kicked myself for as soon as the words were out.

'I've something to tell you,' I said and proceeded to relate the story of the illustration in the book at Mount Stuart and the lights I'd seen in the castle.

'Why didn't you mention this? Don't you see, this could be the missing piece of the jigsaw.'

'In what way?'

Now she was excited. She scrabbled in her bag for a pen and some paper. 'Look at what we've got so far.

- Lloyd and Max are constantly together
- Lloyd appears to be fed up with Max and his boasting
- Max is killed
- Ricky takes something from the body
- Ricky is suddenly flush with money, so it looks as if he's sold whatever it is he stole
- Lloyd shows a keen interest in that book at Mount Stuart
- You see lights in the castle, so someone else has managed to get in and is looking for something related to whatever it is Ricky stole.'

She sat back, a triumphant look on her face. 'So whatever happened, Lloyd has something to do with it. What information did you find in the book at Mount Stuart?'

'I took a photo and wrote down the details.' I took my notebook out and flicked through. 'Here it is. The castle was originally made of earth and timber, then the stone castle was built by Walter the Second. But in the 1970s a stone artefact with some runic writing was found in the moat. If it could be proved it was genuine, it would show the castle was built much earlier than currently believed.'

A look of disappointment flitted across Susie's face. 'That's it? That's all?'

'No, wait a minute. This artefact disappeared sometime in the late 1970s.' I tried to think through the implications of this. 'If Max was a history professor and could prove Rothesay Castle was built much earlier than previously believed, that would be worth a lot to him?'

Susie's eyes grew wide. 'Of course.' Then she slumped back. 'But who would be interested in that?'

'Any number of academic institutions. It would be a very important part of the history of Bute, of the history of castle building. Think of the book, the television programmes, the lecture tour.'

'But how would Max get hold of this? And who would want to kill him for it?'

That stumped me. 'I've no idea, but Lloyd must have something to do with it. Probably realised its value.'

'There must be something else, some other possibility. What did this artefact look like?'

I pulled out my mobile phone and showed her the pictures I'd taken. A lozenge shaped stone, clearly part of something larger and engraved with runic writing, was among the artefacts on display. Don't you think it looks as if it's only part of something? See how the edges are broken off.'

She continued to drink her tea, then lifted the teapot to pour herself another cup. She looked at me thoughtfully before replying, 'Well, I can't let it rest, Alison. And I'm convinced that the answer to the crime lies somewhere within Rothesay Castle.'

'Tell the police then.'

She shook her head. 'No, I think the only way to do this is to go back into Rothesay Castle. This time I've an idea what I'm looking for. If there's a match for this artefact anywhere in the castle that might have been what Max was after. Show me the photo again.'

She peered at the image on the screen then flicked to enlarge it. 'Don't you see – the shape shows it's part of something bigger. That's what Max was looking for – the fit for this artefact within the castle.' She pulled out her phone and snapped the photo.

Susie could go to the castle as often as she liked, looking, as far as I was concerned, for non-existent clues, but I'd no intention of going along with her and told her so in no uncertain terms. Which didn't do much for our friendship, but made me feel a whole lot better.

'Anyway, we examined every inch of the dungeon and there was nothing that could possibly be a fit.'

No matter what the story about the piece of stone, nor how Max had acquired it, there was still no explanation for his being found dead in the dungeon.

CHAPTER TWENTY-EIGHT

Of course, I didn't think Susie would really do it, go exploring the castle again on her own. Unfortunately, she was convinced the photo of the inscribed piece of stone was important enough to merit a return to the castle, that there was something we'd missed.

Wesley's news from the police confirmed her belief. 'They're saying very little, but my suspicion is that Max was lured into the dungeon before he was killed.'

'Why would anyone do that? And HOW would someone do that? Max was surely able to fight back if he was attacked.'

I hadn't intended to be party to this conversation between Susie and Wesley. I happened to be there, saying goodbye to Susie, and warning her yet again not to get any more involved, when he appeared from the street outside, a grim look on his face.

Wesley shook his head in answer to Susie's question. 'Ain't sure, but I'm guessing the idea was to give the impression of an accident. That he'd fallen down those steps into the dungeon and cracked his skull.'

Susie shivered. 'So what happens now?'

'Guess the police go on with their investigation. Ah hope they get to the bottom of it soon, very soon, or we jest might be stuck here.'

'Surely not,' I butted in.

Wesley turned as though suddenly noticing I was there. 'They have to be sure it ain't one of us, that's for certain. We have to do as they ask.'

'We all have to stay on here on Bute? For how long?' Susie sounded agitated. 'Dwayne is due back at work next week. He's already had extra time off as it was a special trip to celebrate our anniversary.'

'Can't be helped.' Wesley shrugged. 'Worse if we had to come back, or worse still, if the person responsible had to be extradited.'

'What is Lloyd saying?'

Wesley laughed, showing a set of highly-polished white teeth that brought to my mind a picture of a shark. 'He ain't pleased. No, indeed, you could say he's mighty put out by it, Ma'am.'

I wasn't surprised and I didn't imagine any of the others would be pleased either.

'But what will we do? Where will we stay?' Susie was suddenly aware of the practicalities of having to remain on the island.

'Guess Lloyd will have to sort that out. With your help of course,' he added acknowledging Susie's role as a leader of the Heritage Adventurers. And with a wave of his hand, 'Off to have a shower before our next event.'

I gazed at him as he headed for the lift, his long stride showing someone who was if nothing else, very fit. Was it possible Wesley had something to do with Max's death? Of all the Heritage Adventurers, he was

210

the one who was fittest and he must be about the same age as Dwayne. And then I recalled that conversation about Wesley being a member of the State basketball team when he was younger. But what could possibly be his motive for killing Max? And if he had one, why do it here? And I was sure the police wouldn't ask us all to remain on the island, not unless they had a definite lead.

I suddenly became aware that Susie was talking to me. '…and you see, Alison, that's why it's important I make another trip to the castle. I'm sure part of the answer is there. If we could wrap this up, we could all go home as planned, after the Pageant.'

I faced her, feeling my anger rising. 'Susie, this is madness. Leave it to the police. I'm sure they'll make some kind of arrangement and not have everyone left here for months on end. Be sensible for once.'

She looked astonished at this outburst, but I was determined not to give in. Friend or not, I wouldn't be accompanying her on another break-in to the castle. 'I won't be going with you.' I hoped my tone of voice was firm enough to put an end to this conversation.

She smiled. 'I didn't expect you would. Not after last time. But don't worry. I've no intention of breaking in, as you put it. This time I'll pay my entrance money like everyone else and go over in broad daylight. There's no need to go down into the dungeon again.' She began to head for the lift, then stopped and caught me by the arm. 'One thing I want to make sure of.'

'What's that?'

'I don't want you to tell anyone where I'm going.'

'Of course not. I understand you want to do this, but it would be difficult to explain why.'

211

'Yes,' looking more determined than I'd ever seen her, 'but I mean PROMISE. No matter what happens you mustn't tell anyone about this visit to the castle.'

'Why should anything go wrong?' Was there something she was keeping from me?

'Of course not. I'll be fine. There will be plenty of other people about at this time of day, so you don't have to worry.'

That was some consolation, but not enough to make me change my mind about going along with her.

CHAPTER TWENTY-NINE

I'd made it perfectly clear to Susie that I'd no intention of going back to Rothesay Castle with her, even if we did pay our entrance money this time. Why then did I feel so guilty?

She'd decided it would be best to go about four o'clock, which gave her an hour before the castle closed for the day.

'That way I'll have the chance to look around as if I was an ordinary visitor, but I'm sure it won't be too busy at that time.'

'Mmm,' was my only comment.

Just after five o'clock I came into the hotel. I'd been into Rothesay to buy a few bits and pieces and I peeped into the lounge as I came through, hoping Susie might be there, might have changed her mind about this mad idea.

There was no sign of her, though Dwayne was sitting chatting to Wesley and to Connie, the conversation made difficult by music which was being played at an unusually loud pitch.

Better not to join in given my promise to my friend, but before I could head for the lift Dwayne called over, 'Hi, Alison. Have you seen Susie?'

I glanced around as though she might suddenly appear before saying, 'Sorry, I haven't seen her since this morning.'

There was a puzzled expression on his face. 'She said she'd meet me here at five.'

'It's only ten past now,' I pointed out. 'Susie isn't best known for her timekeeping.' So she hadn't told Dwayne of her plan to visit the castle. I was beginning to regret my promise not to say where she'd gone.

'Yes, but we were heading for the Discovery Centre Cinema to see a film she was really keen on. The performance starts at five thirty.'

'What about dinner?'

'Oh, we intended having fish and chips out after the performance.' He grinned. 'Susie says no trip to the seaside is complete without at least one fish supper.'

'I'm sure she'll be here soon,' I reassured him and headed for the lift to my room, before he could ask any more questions.

But when I came back downstairs at six o'clock, in good time for dinner, Dwayne was sitting where I'd left him, though he looked very concerned. There was no way I could slip past him, so as I approached I said, 'Still waiting?'

He sighed. 'Yep. I've tried phoning her, but her phone appears to be switched off.'

He looked so anxious, a frown creasing his normally amiable features that I said hurriedly, 'I wouldn't worry about that. The reception can be very bad in some parts of the island and it's likely to be particularly poor in some areas of the castle.'

'The castle? What's she doing in the castle?'

Oh, no. I hadn't meant to say that. It had slipped out. Now I'd have to lie, if only I could think of something appropriate quickly. 'She said something about wanting to go over to the castle to have another look.'

He appeared more confused than ever. 'Why would she want to do that? We've had a couple of visits to the castle. Ain't that enough? And why would she want to go on her own? I'd have been happy to go with her.'

I made a non-committal response, trying hard to think of an answer that would satisfy him, without giving too much away. If Dwayne learned what we'd been up to, I suspected he'd be very cross. And with good reason. Why, oh why, had I not made a greater effort to stop her? Yes, she felt a certain degree of responsibility for the group, but catching a murderer wasn't included, surely?

The best I could come up with was, 'Don't worry, Dwayne. She's most likely forgotten all about the trip to the cinema. You know how scatter-brained she can be.'

'That's as maybe. But she was the one who wanted to go and see this film. It's not my kinda thing. I only agreed because she was so enthusiastic. What's more,' a hint of annoyance so unlike Dwayne, 'between her jaunts here and there and this involvement in the Pageant I've hardly seen her this holiday.'

'Yes, I understand. Why don't you come and have dinner? Then we can try her mobile again. I'm sure there's nothing to concern yourself about. Wait and see. She'll come breezing in as she usually does.'

Dwayne looked reluctant to take my advice, but after another try I succeeded in persuading him there was no point in hanging about waiting.

'Guess you're right, Alison. But I ain't happy about it.'

'The film will be on in the Discovery Centre again tomorrow and you can go then.'

He sighed deeply. 'I don't know Susie as well as I like to think. She's always surprising me.'

She's always surprising me, I thought, and I've known her for longer than you have. I followed Dwayne through to the dining room, trying to make cheerful conversation, but was unable to give him my full attention. Where was Susie? The castle had closed a good hour ago and even had she been doing an incredibly thorough search, there was no way she would still have places to explore. Apart from the Great Hall there were no complete buildings left, only ruins. An hour would have been more than enough time to investigate. I'd a horrible sinking feeling that something might have gone terribly wrong.

CHAPTER THIRTY

The evening wore on and there was still no sign of Susie. Dwayne paced the floor, refusing offers of a drink 'to calm his nerves'. Lloyd made up for his sobriety and by eleven o' clock, even he, with what seemed like a limitless capacity, was showing signs of having had enough.

'I'm sure she'll be fine, bro,' Wesley kept repeating, but every time he said it, he sounded less certain.

'You know how resilient she is,' I added, but Dwayne was by now ready to call the police.

'There ain't no way she'd have gone off like that, been away so long without telling me. What can have happened to her? The castle closed at five o'clock. She can't still be there.'

There I was, torn between telling Dwayne about Susie's plans and her swearing me to secrecy. In the end I decided to wait a little longer before mentioning to him, or to anyone else, the reason Susie had gone back to the castle. There was nothing to be gained. It was too late to gain entry legally and even if Dwayne went to the police to report Susie missing, they wouldn't take any action immediately.

'It's usually twenty-four hours before they follow up a missing person alert,' I persuaded him. 'Let's wait till morning and if she hasn't turned up, I'll come with you.'

An idea struck me. It wasn't the truth, but I convinced myself it wasn't exactly a lie. 'Perhaps she headed for the mainland and missed the last ferry back.' True she'd told me she was going to the castle, but she might have changed her mind for some reason.

Dwayne's face lit up. 'That would be so like her,' he said. 'She was saying something about an anniversary present. Maybe she wanted to surprise me.'

His look of relief suddenly vanished. 'If she did go to the mainland, why isn't she answering her cell phone? I've tried phoning her loads of times, but it goes to voicemail.'

'Oh, you know Susie,' I replied trying to sound more light-hearted than I felt. 'She's probably forgotten it, or it's run out of charge.'

Lie was piling on lie, but this suggestion did appear to calm him. 'If there's no word by early morning then you can inform the police, but I'm sure she'll turn up safe and sound.'

Dwayne yawned. 'Go off to bed,' I said. 'I'll wait up for a bit, but I'm sure she's safe.'

'Think I will have some shut-eye if I can. I'm feeling pretty wiped by all this.'

He uncoiled himself from the chair, stretched and yawned again. 'I'll only have an hour or so. Give me a call at once if there's any news.' I watched him walk slowly through the lounge towards the lift, pleased my

218

cover story about Susie's whereabouts had worked and equally pleased that Dwayne was too exhausted to question the more doubtful parts of it.

It was an eerie feeling being in the lounge where even the late night barman had gone to bed and my worries about Susie's safety grew. The lights were dim, those in the gantry behind the bar winking in the tinted mirror which ran its length. There was a vending machine at the entrance to the hotel which sold hot drinks and snacks, but the effort of rising from my chair was too much. I had to think through what Susie had told me and make a choice about the next step. In a way I regretted not telling Dwayne the truth, but what good would it have done? A lot of good, a little voice in my head kept whispering. A search of the castle could have been arranged pretty quickly and if Susie was there, had hurt herself, time could be of the essence. Yet she had sworn me to secrecy. These conflicting emotions were causing me to feel nauseous, the last thing I needed at the moment.

I'd have to make a decision. Trouble was, I had a good idea what I should do. I might have been able to lie to Dwayne, but I couldn't deceive myself. Susie had said she was going to the castle, that she had some notion there was evidence there to help with solving what had happened to Max.

If she'd followed through her plan, but hadn't returned to the hotel, she must still be somewhere in the castle. There was no other explanation: she must be in trouble.

I went over to sit beside Connie, relieved Oscar had decided to 'have an early night'.

'Are you sure Margie said nothing about Max's death?'

Connie shook her head. 'She doesn't want it spread about that Max was a relation. I shouldn't have told you, Alison, but I expect you can keep a secret.'

Mmm, the less said about that the better. 'But you did say she wasn't terribly upset about his death?'

'Well, that was the strange thing. When we all thought it was an accident, that it was his own fault, no one was terribly concerned, but when we discovered it weren't no accident, that someone had murdered him, she didn't seem upset at all. Odd that, don't you think?'

She stood up, clenching and unclenching her hand. 'Touch or arthritis – can't sit too long in one place,' she said. 'Anyhow, best get off to bed.'

She turned and moved stiffly towards the lift, leaving me staring after her. Was it possible Margie was involved in Max's death? That it was nothing to do with his boasting about his 'inheritance'? This put a new slant on what had happened, but if he was a relation I couldn't imagine what her motive might be.

In the meantime, I'd other business. Reluctant as I was, I owed it to Susie, and to Dwayne, to go over to Rothesay Castle and try to find out what had happened to her. And this was a task that wouldn't wait till morning.

CHAPTER THIRTY-ONE

Although it was by now almost two in the morning, I hurried to my room to change into the most comfortable clothes I'd brought with me, especially suitable shoes. This time I'd be breaking into the castle on my own and, if anything happened, if I tripped on the stairs, there would be no one with me to find help.

I slipped out of the hotel by the night door at the back of the building, conscious my heart was beating loud enough to burst. In my haste to get away I hadn't considered what to do if I found Susie was in trouble, had injured herself. I stopped to check my phone: thankfully it was fully charged.

Dismissing any fears, I crossed the road, all the time casting glances warily behind me, sure I'd be spotted by someone wondering what on earth I was doing out at this time of the morning.

But there was no one about. The street beside the castle was deserted. Not even a stray dog lurked in the shadows and fortunately the scaffolding was still up around the curtain wall, which meant the floodlight was still switched off.

At the gate where Susie and I had entered previously I'd a moment of panic as the padlock seemed much more secure. Perhaps one of the staff had discovered it had been tampered with and had it fixed? I pulled and pushed, trying not to panic, conscious of the clanging echoing in the still night air, but as I was about to give up it came away with a groan and a thump that made me almost lose my balance.

Down the mossy stone steps I scurried, at a pace foolish in the circumstances, but if I hesitated now, I knew I'd give up, forget my promise to Susie and persuade someone else to find out what had happened to her.

I snuck past the wooden hut, keeping to the railings along by the grassy bank surrounding the moat, until I reached the steel barrier shutting the bridge off from the rest of the castle. It was much more difficult to wrest it away on my own, but somehow I managed to move it enough to allow me to squeeze through the gap and, quickening my pace again, I ran across the bridge to reach the safety of the Gatehouse.

For a moment I was disorientated in the darkness surrounding me, not daring to switch on the torch I'd brought with me. There might be a benefit in the nearest floodlight being switched off, but the only other lights were from the street lamps and they were too distant to be of much help.

Suddenly the full moon peeked out from behind the scudding clouds, shining briefly along the length of the passageway, casting shadows on the damp stone walls. There was something menacing about it and I shivered, but not from cold. What on earth was I doing here on my own, when I should be safely tucked up in bed? I'd a choice: I could turn and head back to the safety of the hotel, or I could continue, hoping to find out what had happened to Susie. Much as my common sense told me the former would be the better thing to do, something drove me on, pushed me further into the castle.

Though I walked on tiptoe as I moved forward through the Gatehouse, my footsteps echoed in the silence and several times I stopped, listening for any movement, any indication I'd been spotted. Nothing. My temptation was to call out Susie's name as a way of locating her, but I decided against it, the memory of the lights I'd seen the night before still fresh in my memory.

The entrance to the dungeon was on my left, but I steadfastly ignored it. I'd only venture down as a last resort, if every other possibility failed. And I couldn't imagine Susie would have gone back there on her own. She'd explored every corner last time. No, she must have been interested in some other part of the castle, and there was no option but to work my way methodically round.

At the foot of the stairs leading to the Great Hall, I stopped again, listening intently. About to grasp the rope handrail, for some reason I looked in the direction of the set of stairs on the other side of the passageway. Helena had warned us in no uncertain terms to stay away from that part of the castle. 'The stone steps are crumbling and it's too risky.'

At first glance they looked in a state of poor repair, but they were secured with no more than a slack length of chain so surely they couldn't be that dangerous?

I tried to remember what Helena had said about this part of the castle, a vague recollection about the story of

223

a princess who had refused to marry her father's choice and on the night she'd arranged to elope with her lover had come down this set of stairs only to miss her footing and tumble to her death. But surely that was no more than a tale? There was nothing about it in the Guide Book, but it probably served to warn off more adventurous visitors who might be tempted to explore an unsafe section of the building.

Even so, I was certain there was a room at the top of the stairs. Could that have been where Susie had gone?

As I stood there, becoming more and more agitated as I tried to make up my mind whether or not to risk the climb, I heard a noise, so faint as to be almost undetectable. Aware of the loud beating of my heart, I took a deep breath as I stood motionless, trying to pinpoint the source of the noise. Yes, there it was again: a faint knocking sound. There was only one explanation. Someone had spotted me sneaking into the castle this time and was coming to find me. What excuse could I possibly give for being in the castle in the middle of the night? Another sound. This time I breathed a sigh of relief. It was only the hoot of a distant owl, somewhere in the trees around the moat, probably getting ready to hunt its prey. My nerves were so on edge I was imagining danger where there was none.

The set of steps in front of me was a different kind of problem. Be sensible, I told myself sternly. If you have an accident on these stairs, who will come and rescue you? I knew enough about the phone reception to realise there would be none through these thick walls.

The chain slipped off easily and cautiously I put my foot on the first step, then the second, then the third. There was a soft shushing sound and the edge of the step crumbled to dust beneath my foot. Just in time I managed to grab the rope handrail, struggling to regain my balance. This was madness. Even Susie wouldn't have risked this.

A moment or two later, I backed down the steps and stood at the bottom, annoyed I hadn't made more progress. The stairs up to the Great Hall loomed in front of me, scarcely visible in the darkness. There was no option: I'd have to use my torch and directing the beam downwards I made my way, step by careful step, up to the Great Hall. As I'd guessed, the doors were unlocked and opened with a gentle push.

Inside, the Hall looked spookier than ever, tiny shards of moonlight dancing on the wooden floor, illuminating the motes of dust I disturbed as I walked through, like countless fireflies. I switched on my torch, running the beam all over the room, picking up the outline of the fireplace. Slowly I inched my way around, looking in all the alcoves. But the room was empty and what's more, there was no place to hide. Susie wasn't here.

I shone my torch around the room again, picking out the elaborate carving of the empty fireplace. That was it. Perhaps there was some kind of secret passage, accessed by a hidden door. Convinced I might have found something significant, I headed over, almost tripping as I did so and my torch slipped from my hand, rolling on the floor. As I bent to pick it up, annoyed at my clumsiness, there was another sound, a slight clinking noise. I stopped and listened, but all I could hear now was my breathing.

My imagination fuelled by numerous stories I'd read as a child and scarcely unable to contain my excitement, I stretched out to grab hold of the mantelpiece and stepped under it, fingering my way over the smooth stone surfaces, expecting any minute to hear a loud click as part of the fireplace rolled back. There must be a button or a release mechanism here somewhere. But there was nothing. A few of the stones were rough in places, but there was no sign of an entrance to a secret passage.

More than disappointed, I ducked out of the fireplace and stood contemplating it for a moment, before scanning the remainder of the room with my torch, seeking inspiration. This had been my great hope, that Susie had found a passageway concealed somewhere in the fireplace, gone into it and become trapped. If that wasn't the case, where could she be? The rest of the castle was in ruins, with no obvious hiding place, except, except… That left the dungeon. There was no alternative. I'd have to go down there, reluctant as I was.

I walked across the wooden floor to the doorway, trying to make as little noise as possible, convincing myself any odd sounds were no more than the wind whistling through the ruins.

I came back down the spiral stairway, clutching the rope handrail tightly. It was much more difficult going down than going up and when I reached the foot of the stairs I considered for a moment if it might be better to go back to the hotel and summon help. I don't like enclosed spaces at the best of times and the dungeon, in the dark and on my own, was far from appealing.

Don't be such a coward, I told myself sternly. This is your friend Susie you're trying to help. And it was your fault for coming over here alone in the first place.

Steeling myself, determined to overcome my fear and head for the dungeon, I started towards the Gatehouse.What was that? I stopped and waited, straining to hear. Silence. No, wait, there it was again. A regular rhythm, just loud enough to be heard if I stayed absolutely still. Thump, drag, thump, drag. What was it?

What might be making that unearthly sound? This time it wasn't an owl, nor the soughing of the wind through the crevices of the ancient stones. Could it be footsteps? But it didn't sound like that. My heart began to pound again.

The noise had stopped. Calm yourself, I said aloud. It was no more than my imagination, brought on by fear. I'd have a quick look in the dungeon (if such a thing were possible) and then leave. I'd have to tell Dwayne what I'd been up to and why Susie had decided she had to pay another visit to the castle, but then if I'd been honest in the first place I wouldn't be in this position.

Another noise, more a distinct rapping sound, and this time I was sure it was coming from the top of the set of stairs beside those leading to the Great Hall. I shone my torch on the steps. Could Susie be trapped up there in the tiny room at the top? I remembered again the story about the princess. Stuff and nonsense I told myself firmly, but here, alone in the darkness, it was proving hard to be brave.

When the noise started again, there was no choice. Dangerous or not, I had to make it to the top of these stairs. Besides, it was probably slightly safer than going down into the dungeon. And if I was really careful, took it slowly, pausing after each step, surely I wouldn't come to any harm.

Decision made, I put my foot on the bottom step and, keeping the beam of my torch as low as possible, began to climb. Some of the steps were crumblier than others and halfway up, my courage almost failed me. Only the thought that my friend might be in serious trouble spurred me on. I'm never doing anything like this again, I repeated to myself. No matter who asks me or who is in danger.

So slow was my progress, it took much longer to reach the top than I'd anticipated, but at least I'd made it unscathed. Facing me was yet another heavy wooden door. If this was locked, I'd head straight back down. I didn't have the strength to force it.

I stopped again and listened. The rapping noise had stopped and I put my hands on the wooden door. To my surprise, after a couple of sharp pushes, it yielded easily to my touch. Warily, I opened it wide, as far back as it would go and shone my torch around the room. It was empty. Nothing here and nowhere for anyone to hide. No sign of Susie. Having braved the dangerous steps, I screwed up my courage. There was only one way to make sure and emboldened by my success, I strode over to the far wall.

Suddenly I felt a pair of hands grab me and, taken by surprise, the torch slipped from my hand. It rolled across the uneven floor to become wedged in the corner, leaving me in darkness.

I struggled to free myself, but I was choking, could scarcely breathe. I thought about Max. Was I to be another victim of Rothesay Castle? Of course. Susie had already been killed and this was her attacker about to do the same to me. All I could think of was that at last my foolishness was about to catch up with me.

Somehow, determined that I wasn't giving in, I found greater strength than I thought possible and writhed, pushed and pulled, managing with one last supreme effort to wrest myself free.

'Let me go,' I yelled, pulling my attacker's hands from my throat. 'What do you think you're doing?'

All of a sudden the grip on my neck was loosened and unable to regain control, I slid to the floor with a thump.

'Oh, Alison,' said Susie, 'Thank goodness it's you.'

CHAPTER THIRTY-TWO

It was a few minutes before I could get my breath back, recover from the assault. I was trembling all over and when I tried to stand up, my knees gave way. Susie caught me by the arm before I fell again.

'Sorry,' she said. 'I thought you were my attacker come back.'

'Never mind about that, though you gave me a terrible fright. What happened to you?' Only now did I notice she was walking with a limp as she moved towards the door and peered out.

'What?' She turned to face me. 'I came up here while I was checking out the castle. You'll remember this was the only place we weren't allowed to enter when we came with Helena last time.'

She made it sound as if we were no more than a pair of casual visitors. I'd almost recovered, but was still shaky and decided to remain sitting, though I edged over to lean against the wall, shivering as the coldness from the stones seeped into me.

'Yes, but why were you still here? Why didn't you return to the hotel? Everyone, especially Dwayne, was so worried about you.'

'You didn't tell him where I'd gone, did you?'

Avoiding answering her directly, I said, 'I only managed to stop him going to the police. If you're not back by morning that's what he'll do.'

She sighed. 'Thank goodness,' she replied, apparently unconcerned that when she did return she'd have to think up some plausible excuse for her absence.

'I heard a rapping noise. Was that you?'

She nodded. 'Yes, but then I thought how silly it was to be letting my attacker know.'

'And what happened to you? I can see you damaged your ankle, but you can still walk.'

She slid down the wall to rest beside me. 'I'd only just come in when I felt a great push and was thrown into the room before the door banged shut. I must have twisted my ankle as I tumbled in, but it's only a strain.' She grimaced. 'There must have been someone following me into the castle. Someone watching me.'

I was puzzled. This didn't make any sense. 'But you came over while the castle was open to visitors. How did you come to be here for so long?'

She had a guilty, furtive look as she turned to face me. 'The castle was busy and I knew I wouldn't be able to explore this part of it properly while it was open to the public, so I hid in the toilets a few minutes before closing time and waited till everyone had gone.'

'Even so. How were you going to get out without being seen? It's light at this time of year until well after nine o'clock.'

'Mmm, I didn't think about that. Guess I'm now so used to the Californian time where the darkness comes down suddenly, covering you like a blanket.'

'And then…' I prompted her.

'And then, when I was sure the coast was clear, I came out of the toilets and made my way up here. Problem was, there was someone else in the castle. I heard a noise, but thought I was imagining it. Or didn't pay it much attention.'

She coughed and sneezed as she inhaled the dusty air. 'But there was someone here and as I began to explore, I was attacked. At first I thought it might be a gust of wind, but I'm sure it wasn't. And then I managed to lose my torch. It's outside on the landing somewhere, but I don't think it's working. I heard the glass splinter as I dropped it.'

'Why didn't you just open the door?'

'That's the problem, it only opens from the outside. If you check the lock you'll see what I mean.'

Panic-stricken, I jumped to my feet. 'For goodness sake, Susie. Whoever locked you in might still be in the castle. Might be waiting to lock both of us in.' Energised by fear of being trapped in this turret room, I jumped up and went over to the door, peering out into the gloom, but there was nothing to be seen.

'Let's get out of here before it's too late, before whoever locked you in comes back.'

This idea seemed to astonish Susie. 'I don't think so. Whoever it was surely only meant to give me a fright, knowing I'd be rescued in the morning. I'm sure the whole castle is checked each day before visitors are allowed in.'

'I'm not so sure and we're not going to take any chances. This part of the castle is supposed to be out of bounds, if you remember. Come on. Can you walk down the steps if I help?'

I rescued my torch from the far corner where it had rolled and we left the room together, me supporting Susie as best I could. 'Lean on me and then I'll go down first. Take your time. We don't want any more accidents. Some of these steps are unsafe.'

I moved in front of her. 'Ready. Now hold on to the side wall as you come down.'

'Shh – what's that?'

I hesitated on the top step. 'What is it?'

'I can hear a noise,' said Susie.

We waited, scarcely daring to breath. Yes, there it was, the sound I'd heard earlier – thump, drag, thump, drag. Susie was right. There was someone else in the castle. It could only be whoever had attacked Susie earlier and we were trapped at the top of this flight of stairs, with only one torch between us for protection.

I flattened myself against the wall, motioning Susie to do the same, trying to think of a way out. Thump, drag, thump, drag.

The noise grew steadily louder, coming ever closer.

CHAPTER THIRTY-THREE

'I can't keep still for much longer,' hissed Susie. 'My leg's gone into a cramp.'

I clenched my fists, motioning her to be quiet, all the while listening intently for the noise.

Silence again. Whoever it was had stopped at the foot of the stairs. We were trapped here at the top of this narrow flight of stairs and I'd no notion what to do. At first I consoled myself with thinking it was two against one, but we didn't know what we were facing and as Susie had twisted her ankle, the odds might not be as good as I hoped.

Another few minutes passed, but there was no further sound.

'Perhaps he's gone?' Susie shifted uncomfortably on the spot. 'Whoever it is must be up to no good.'

I raised my eyebrows. We couldn't claim to be without blame. 'We have to make sure.' Another few minutes passed while we waited, scarcely daring to breathe until I said, sounding more courageous than I felt, 'I'll go down the stairs. You stay here.' I ferreted in my pocket. 'Take my mobile and if there's any problem, phone the police.'

She took the phone, but made a face. 'We're not supposed to be here. How will I explain?'

'Don't let's worry about that just yet.' I didn't want to add that the mobile was more to give her comfort. There was unlikely to be a Wi-Fi signal in the turret room.

It wasn't that I was feeling particularly brave: my hands were shaking as I passed the phone to her, but we couldn't stay on this ledge for much longer.

Susie grabbed my arm. 'Do you think it might be the ghost? You remember, that story we heard about the princess who fell to her death down these stairs?'

'Oh, don't be silly,' I muttered, neglecting the fact that the same thought had occurred to me earlier. 'Now, keep as still as you can and listen. I'll yell if I get into trouble.'

Taking a deep breath, I began the descent, picking my way down carefully, placing my foot on one step, then stopping before continuing. The stairway was tricky to negotiate at any time, but more so in the dark and I didn't want to alert whoever else was here by switching on my torch.

The nearer I got to the bottom, the slower my progress, mindful of how unprepared I was for any real danger.

The area at the foot of the steps was empty. There was no one in sight. Nothing that could have been making that noise – and yet something or someone had. Susie and I had both heard it clearly.

I peeped around the corner at the other stair, the one leading to the Great Hall, but it too was empty.

I breathed a sigh of relief and for a moment was tempted to believe it might indeed have been the ghost of the Princess, before dismissing the idea as ridiculous. As experience had taught me, any 'ghosts' were likely to be attributable to humans in some way or other.

I almost ran back up the flight of stairs, ignoring the crumbling stone giving way under my feet. Susie was standing in the spot where I'd left her, clutching my mobile as if her life depended on it.

'Well?' Her eyes were as wide as saucers.

I shook my head. 'Nothing to be seen. I'm sure it's safe to come down. I'll help you. We can switch on the torch to guide us. These steps are treacherous.' Which is why they're out of bounds and you shouldn't have come up them in the first place, I thought, but didn't say so aloud.

She passed me back my phone.

'I'll go first. Keep an arm on my shoulder and feel your way down using the wall.'

'Yes, of course,' she said in a meek voice that was so unlike her it made me appreciate how much her ankle was paining her.

Slowly, step by difficult step, we made our way down to the bottom, letting out an audible sigh of relief as we found ourselves once again in the Gatehouse.

'Let's get out of here as quickly as we can.' I didn't want to hang around a moment longer than necessary. There was no one in sight, but whoever had locked Susie in the room might decide to return and we didn't want to be around when he did. This was not the place to start berating her for her fool-hardy behaviour. I'd been pretty reckless myself.

'What are you going to tell the others? We'll have to agree on a story.'

This problem hadn't occurred to her. 'What do you suggest? Maybe they'll be so glad to see me safe, no one will ask.'

Very doubtful, but I didn't want to waste time discussing it. 'I'll go along with whatever you decide to say.'

A spasm of pain gripped her and she grabbed the wall for support.

'Can you manage? If you take my arm, you could perhaps hop?'

'No, no, I'll be fine.'

I wasn't sure about that and we still had to negotiate the bridge and the grassy slope beside the moat before climbing the set of steps up to the street. 'Let's take it slowly. If you need to stop at any time, say so.'

With that we set off, Susie making a valiant attempt not to let the pain from her ankle hinder her progress, though why she should be concerned about the time we would take to get back to the hotel after what had happened I'd no idea.

The first light of dawn was beginning to streak the sky with a rosy glow as we reached the steps below the side gate. A melody of chirps and tweets signalled the start of the dawn chorus and very soon the early morning workers would be making their way to the first ferry. We had to get out of here before we were spotted.

But it was evident Susie couldn't go any faster and stood looking at this final flight of steps with trepidation.

'Let's rest a while in the shelter of the shed,' I said. 'Give yourself a couple of minutes and then we can do the last bit.' I scanned the immediate area, but we were alone.

Susie sank down, her back against the wooden shed and rubbed her ankle. 'So stupid of me to end up like this,' she said. 'Sorry to give you all this trouble.'

'Never mind that now. The main thing is to get you back to the hotel and then think of a cover story. Here, let me give you a hand up.'

I pulled her to her feet and she hopped a few yards to the first of the steps.

'Have you dropped something?'

'What?' She turned to look at me.

I bent down and lifted what seemed to be a piece of cloth, sodden by the early morning dew.

'No,' she said in a puzzled voice. 'What is it?'

I examined it more closely and whispered, 'I recognise this. It's Ricky's baseball cap. I'm sure it wasn't here when I came over earlier.'

'What's it doing here? He's never parted from it.'

'Exactly. And if this is his, it means he must have been here and dropped it. Could it have been Ricky who locked you in?'

'But why would he do that?'

'No idea. But he has been behaving very strangely. And this is proof he was here.' I twirled the baseball cap in the air, checking it carefully. There was no doubt it was Ricky's: the logo of the Los Angeles Dodgers clearly identified it.

Susie watched, looking thoughtful. 'Yes, but why did he leave it here?'

That was the question neither of us could answer.

CHAPTER THIRTY-FOUR

We arrived back at the hotel, slightly out of breath, having covered the last part of the journey more quickly than I'd have thought possible, given the problem of Susie's ankle. Fear can be a great motivator.

We'd decided we'd be better to say as little as possible. Susie agreed Dwayne would have to know the truth, but there was no need for anyone else to have the full story.

Ricky's soggy baseball cap was stuffed into my coat pocket, but we'd been unable to decide what we should do with it. Confront him? Was it possible he was the person we'd heard in the castle and that he'd followed Susie over there? No matter which way we tried to spin it, there was no answer that made sense.

We had only a couple of hours left before we were due downstairs for breakfast. I very much doubted if I'd make it. The only appealing thing at the moment was bed.

'Will you manage?' I said. 'How is your ankle?'

'I'll think of something. It's still painful, but I'm sure it's no more than a strain.'

At the corner by the lift, my mind focused on the reason for Susie's visit to the castle.

'So it was a waste of time?'

She hesitated, her finger poised above the lift button. 'What gave you that idea?'

'Well, you didn't mention anything.'

'I was too concerned about getting out of the place before whoever it was came back to find me.'

She sniffed. 'Besides, you gave me the impression you weren't interested.'

'What made you think that? Because I wasn't willing to come with you? You know me better than that.'

A wicked grin. 'This isn't the time to be discussing it. I'll tell you later.'

'Good luck,' I whispered as the lift doors opened at her floor, while Susie's heartfelt, 'I can't tell you how grateful I am you came to look for me,' made me feel a whole lot better about the incident. Sure, she would have been found eventually, but this way there was far less explaining to do.

And with that she was gone, leaving me more frustrated than ever. I'd tried so hard not to become involved in this and yet here I was whether I wanted to be or not.

The lift doors opened with a loud ping and I stumbled out at the top floor, exhausted by the early morning misadventure. I almost crawled down the corridor to my room to flop down on the bed without stopping to take off my clothes.

I dozed, rather than slept. Outside, the sun was up, shining through into the room and I pulled the thick curtains tight shut, blocking out the light.

There were so many loose ends. Someone must know what had happened to Max and had discovered Susie's determination to find an answer. But the idea it could be Ricky seemed far-fetched. He was only a sulky teenager, more pleased by the fact he'd made friends with some of Zachary's students than anything the island had to offer. And yet there was the tricky question of finding his baseball cap in the castle. He must have been there.

What had Susie found out? She'd promised to update me later, but that meant finding a time to speak to her on her own, not an easy matter, given my strong suspicion Dwayne would be reluctant to let her out of his sight, and with good reason, whatever story she came up with to explain her absence.

It was all too much. Better to put the mystery surrounding the death of Max out of my mind, use the remaining time to concentrate on chasing up any outstanding questions for the Stuart booklet and re-order my notes as best I could. Saturday would be the end of the tour, taken up with the medieval festival at the castle during the day and the grand Pageant in the evening in the grounds. And on Sunday we would all be heading for home.

Surely nothing more could go wrong now?

CHAPTER THIRTY-FIVE

Zachary arrived immediately after breakfast. I'd struggled downstairs, but all I could face was coffee. I felt terrible and it wouldn't have taken much to persuade me to go back to bed. The lack of sleep, or sleeping at odd hours, was beginning to tell. What's more, as there was no sign of Susie, nor of Dwayne, all my concerns of the previous night began to surface.

I was desperate to see her, find out if she'd managed to spin a plausible tale to convince Dwayne there was a good reason for her escapade the previous evening, but I didn't want to phone her in case she might still be trying to concoct a story.

In the dining room, Kimberley was sitting chatting to Connie and to Wesley, the remains of breakfast scattered over their table. The staff were one short today. Someone had gone down with 'flu and everything was well behind - the reason not everything had been cleared away. On the plus side, I'd managed to get a full pot of fresh coffee.

Kimberley waved over to Zachary. 'Hiya. Come and join us. Ricky not with you?'

Zachary looked puzzled. 'No, why should he be?'

'Because he said he was going out last night to meet you and some of your students. Guess he's become real pals with one or two of them.' She chuckled. Ricky was clearly back in her good books.

Zachary scratched his head. 'I haven't seen him. You must have been mistaken.'

'No mistake,' shrieked Kimberly, rising to her feet and holding on to the corner of the table. 'He said he was to meet up with y'all, make a bit of a night of it.'

Zachary shook his head. 'No, honestly, I haven't seen him. I came over to have a quick word with Susie.' He cast his eyes restlessly around the room, his face registering disappointment when he realised she wasn't there. 'What?' he said vaguely, turning back to Kimberley, his mind clearly elsewhere.

She came up beside him and shook his arm. 'Where is he? Where's my boy?'

'Oh, for goodness sake, woman, I've no idea.' Zachary shook her off impatiently.

Kimberley began to wail, putting her hands up to her face. 'What's happened to him? Where are you, Ricky?'

Wesley came up and put his arm on her shoulder. 'He'll be fine; he'll have gone off somewhere. You know what he's like.'

'A damn nuisance,' said Oscar who'd been listening in from the side. 'That boy's been nothing but trouble since he came. You should have realised that before you brought him along.'

This criticism only had the effect of making Kimberley wail even louder and all eyes in the room were now fixed on her.

At last Zachary appreciated the seriousness of the situation and a look of horror crossed his face. 'It's nothing to do with me.' He chewed at his fingernails. 'I'm here to find Susie, to tell here there have been a couple of changes to her role in the Pageant.'

'Tell Susie what?' Unnoticed, so intent were we all on Kimberley and her altercation with Zachary, we failed to notice Dwayne and Susie had come into the room.

I spun around, expecting to see…what was I expecting to see? A furious Dwayne, a contrite Susie? But the couple standing before me were wreathed in smiles and though I was aware Susie was still walking with a slight limp, it wouldn't be detectable to anyone who didn't know about the previous evening's incident.

I sidled over to her. 'How are you?' I kept my voice low, but everyone was still concentrating on Kimberley and her wailing and had no interest in our conversation.

'Okay,' she hissed and I realised that close up she was a lot paler than usual, her lack of sleep well-disguised by her make-up. 'I'll catch up with you later this morning. Dwayne wants to buy me an anniversary present, something to remind me of our time on Bute, and he'll be off for an hour or so.'

I didn't say that it would be likely she'd remember this visit to Bute without Dwayne's present.

Meanwhile, Zachary was determined to speak to Susie, tell her about the changes to the Pageant and I left the room, in need of some fresh air.

I walked down to Guildford Square to buy a morning paper and a copy of the Buteman. The ferry, the MV Bute, had docked at the pier and was disgorging her passengers, some on foot, but most in cars. Holidaymakers to the island. The season had begun in earnest.

In the harbour a few new boats had arrived overnight and there was scarcely a free berth. Others would have headed further up the coast to the Marina at Port Bannatyne for shelter. It was good to see the island so busy and I stood idly watching, leaning over the railings, savouring the warm breeze on my face.

I found a seat and scanned through my copy of the newspaper. The story about Max was now relegated to Page 4 – with no additional news other items had taken priority. I stared at the photo of Max again. There was something familiar about his face. Nonsense. It was probably no more than I'd seen him in that earlier edition of the paper.

Reluctantly I pulled myself away from the tranquil scene in front of me to head back to the hotel. Susie hadn't said when Dwayne would be going shopping, but I suspected it would be soon. There was a walk along the shore at Kilchattan Bay planned for the afternoon and then, weather permitting, a barbeque to be held on the shore at Port Bannatyne.

As I reached the main door, Zachary came tearing out, even more agitated than usual. 'The woman's mad,' he said, his voice shaking. 'She thinks I've kidnapped her stupid son. I wish I'd never got involved in this Pageant, never been persuaded…' still muttering to himself he sprinted off up the High Street towards the college.

Suddenly I remembered that Ricky's soggy baseball cap was still in the pocket of my coat, now hanging on the back of my bedroom door. Damn! I'd have to decide what to do with it and I cursed myself for not bringing it down this morning. I'd been so tired; it had completely slipped my mind.

I decided to wait for a bit, see if Ricky turned up any time soon. I wanted to ask him how his baseball cap had come to be in the castle, but I'd have to think of a way of questioning him without giving too much away. Guiltily I thought I should probably tell his mother about it, but that would mean revealing Susie had been in the castle. I sighed. What a tangled web this was.

Inside the hotel all was quiet. This was a 'free' morning so I guessed some of the Heritage Adventurers had decided to follow Dwayne's example and head into town. Or perhaps return to their rooms in preparation for the long day ahead. At the moment the sun was shining from a clear blue sky, a good omen for the barbeque, though on an island the weather could change with little warning.

I phoned Susie's mobile. Sure enough Dwayne had left and we agreed to meet in the foyer and head out to one of the cafés where we were unlikely to be disturbed.

This was easier said than done as the first couple of places we tried had already been commandeered by some of the Heritage Adventurers.

'Oh, hi,' said Connie who was happily ensconced in the Blethers Tearoom with Oscar. 'We shouldn't really be having this after such a huge breakfast, but it looked so tempting.'

She pointed to the very large slice of gateau sitting in front of her. 'Do come and join us.'

'I think it's rather busy,' I said, beating a hasty retreat. Outside I ventured, 'We can take the bus from

Guildford Square and head out to the tearoom at Ettrick Bay.'

'Won't that also be busy? It always is,' said Susie doubtfully.

'It may be, but none of the customers are likely to be Heritage Adventurers'.

The bus to Ettrick Bay was sitting at the terminus, ready to depart, and we hurried to catch it, throwing ourselves somewhat breathlessly into the seats at the front once we'd paid our fare. We were the only passengers but that soon changed as others joined us at the stops in Ardbeg and Port Bannatyne.

Conscious we might be overheard, we said very little, but contented ourselves with gazing out the window, from time to time exclaiming as we identified familiar landmarks we hadn't seen for some time.

The bus sped up as it turned at the Lodge House at Kames Castle, heading past the ruined church at Cnoc an Rath and the old Blacksmith's house to come to a sudden halt at the terminus overlooking Ettrick Bay.

We left the bus and stood together for a moment, gazing past Inchmarnock towards Goat Fell on the Isle of Arran.

'When you come here, you feel nothing has changed,' I said.

'Yes, well, now's not the time to be reminiscing,' replied Susie abruptly and I turned away from the view to follow her into the tearoom.

As I'd hoped, there were a few empty tables and we secured a seat by the window.

'It's a bit of a lull at the moment,' said the waitress. 'It'll be busy in an hour or so as people begin to arrive for lunch.'

We ordered coffee, resisting the luscious home-made cakes resplendent on ornate glass plates in the chiller cabinet, though I was tempted, remembering my breakfast of no more than coffee.

We waited in silence for our order to arrive, each preoccupied with our thoughts.

When it arrived, Susie stirred her coffee, spooning the froth into her mouth.

'So, are you going to tell me what this is all about? What you discovered in the castle?'

She took a deep breath and laid the spoon down on the saucer. 'It was all to do with that ticket for Mount Stuart I found earlier. I was convinced the doodles must have some meaning, but I couldn't think what it might be. Then when we were at Mount Stuart and you found that photo of the artefact and the allusion to the excavation at Rothesay Castle...'

'Yes, yes.' My impatience was beginning to show. Would Susie never get to the point?

'I realised that's what Max must have done. He must have visited Mount Stuart house and sketched what he saw on the ticket. That's what he was looking for in the castle.'

'In the dungeon? He thought the answer lay in the dungeon?' This sounded very far-fetched.

Susie shook her head. 'No, I don't know why he was there. But he was after something in the castle that was for sure. So I tried all sorts of possibilities and finally found the answer in that room at the top of the stairs.'

She sipped her coffee. 'I didn't tell you last night, because I wanted to check online to make sure I was right.'

'And…?'

'And then I felt an enormous shove and fell headlong as someone locked me in. With my torch out of action, I wasn't in a position to explore further.'

She leaned forward, her face alive with excitement. 'But I've a good idea what it was. What's more, it's certainly something to do with Max's death. The only problem is I'm no nearer finding who is responsible.'

CHAPTER THIRTY-SIX

'In the corner of that room at the top of the stairs, there's a carving on the far wall. I looked closely and I'm sure there's a piece missing from it. What's more, the so-called 'doodles' on the ticket were very similar to some on the wall in the turret. There must be a connection.'

I stopped, my coffee cup poised in mid-air as I tried to understand.

'So that was what Max was looking for?'

'Possibly. I checked it out on the internet. There was a description about the excavation of the Rothesay Castle moat and the artefacts they found. Many of them are in the museum, but some of them went missing soon after the dig was over.'

'Stolen?'

'No idea, but I guess so.'

'But how could Max have any of them if they went missing in 1970?'

We discussed all kinds of options: we'd no idea why Susie's discovery might be important. We were sure it had some bearing on Max's death. But why would he be keeping this information to himself? I recalled the tales of his boasting, about how he was about to make a great discovery that would ensure wealth for him.

'Remember we found Ricky's baseball cap? Do you think it could be blackmail?'

'Ricky?' Susie looked astonished at this suggestion. 'I can't believe he's got the brains to blackmail anyone.'

'I'm not so sure. Do you remember his mother asking where he got the money?'

'Yes, I do. Anyway he said his father gave him money to spend on his holiday.'

'His mother wasn't sure that was the truth, judging by her reaction. He seemed to have plenty of money to splash about.'

'Wait a minute. You think Ricky might have got money by blackmailing someone, someone who was involved with Max's death?'

'Yes, I do. I think he's known about it since he went down into the dungeon and found Max's body.'

Susie shuddered and pushed aside her empty coffee cup. 'He's only a youngster. How would he get involved in that kind of thing?'

'Quite easily. He saw an opportunity and took it. And he's not such a youngster – didn't we find out he must be around eighteen?'

Still Susie looked sceptical. 'Well, if you're right, we have to go back and question him. What pretext could we possibly use?'

'I still have his baseball cap. We can start by asking him how it came to be in the castle.'

'That means letting him know we were also in the castle.'

'Yes, but who is he going to tell? He'd be in as much trouble as we would.'

'It seems ridiculous at our age to be fretting about dealing with a teenager. We've had enough practice during our time as teachers at Strathelder High.'

'Exactly. When we go back we'll confront him together, as long as Kimberley isn't anywhere near.'

Resolute about our plan, we paid our very modest bill and headed out.

I consulted the bus timetable on display at the stop. 'The next bus isn't due for half an hour. Do you fancy having a walk along the Kirkmichael Road or do you want to head along the Tramway into Port Bannatyne? We can catch the bus that comes from the ferry at Colintraive there.'

Susie hesitated for a moment then said, 'Let's go into Port Bannatyne. Take advantage of the decent weather and forget this business of Max for a while. Once I'm back home there won't be much opportunity for walking. Being on the island has given me the taste for it again.'

'But what about your ankle?'

'I'm fine,' she said dismissively. 'The exercise will do me good.'

We set off in good spirits, pleased at last to have an opportunity to catch up on all that had been happening in our lives over the past couple of years before the conversation turned inevitably to the Pageant.

'What did Zachary want? He mentioned something about changes to the script.'

'Oh, that. Nothing major, thank goodness. He wants to cut one of my lines. Seems the show will go overrunning and he's got to save time. I'd have been more worried if he'd wanted to add in lines.'

By now we'd reached the ruined church beside the graveyard at Croc-an-rath. There was a funeral taking place, the mourners standing respectfully beside the graveside. A fine place to lie, with the view of Kames castle and the Bay in the distance and I thought again about Max. 'Will they release Max's body?' I asked.

She shrugged. 'Lloyd said it's been decided we don't have to hang around past our flight date, though we may be asked to return at some point. A big relief to all of us.'

'I can imagine.'

We joined the queue at the bus stop beside the Marina in Port Bannatyne in time to see the bus from Rhubodach come speeding around the bend in the road.

Now we had to put our plan into action. We must confront Ricky and find out exactly what he knew and what his involvement was in the mystery surrounding Max's death.

Then I'd do my best to persuade Susie to go to the police with her suspicions.

CHAPTER THIRTY-SEVEN

It wasn't as easy as that, of course and it looked as if the time we'd spent concocting a plan to confront Ricky had been for nothing.

As we entered the hotel, there was a great commotion, people going to and fro. 'What's happening here?' Susie said to the Receptionist.

The Receptionist looked wild-eyed. 'Haven't you heard?'

'No, else we wouldn't be asking,' replied Susie, a little abruptly, I thought.

'It's Lloyd…'

'Is there a problem? He shouldn't drink so much.' As one of the leaders of the group of Heritage Adventurers, I guessed Susie felt some responsibility.

The Receptionist gasped. 'I think that's rather harsh in the circumstances.'

By now I'd guessed that something awful had happened. 'Just a minute, Susie.' I grasped her by the elbow to indicate she should be quiet. 'What is going on? We were worried about Ricky.'

'Oh, Ricky's back. He's fine. But it's Lloyd - he's had an accident.' Her words were almost a whisper so that I had to strain to hear what she was saying.

'What do you mean? He was out last night, but he's done that before and we all thought he'd gone out on the town.'

'You're right, he didn't turn up last night for dinner, but everyone assumed that's where he was.'

'Yes, yes,' said Susie impatiently, 'we're aware of that. So who found him and where?'

'That's the thing. He was found in the castle, at the foot of the stairs on the far side of the open space. One of the attendants found him. Well, not immediately, but they always check everywhere before they allow people in. Apparently he fell and broke his leg. He was lying there all night and was barely conscious.'

'The Police are here,' she added, pointing to the far corner. For the first time we noticed the high-viz jackets and the cluster of guests around two burly police officers.

Of Ricky there was no sign.

'Let's move,' I said, but the Receptionist called after us as we walked away, 'The police will want to question everyone.'

'What do we do now?' asked Susie as soon as we were out of earshot. 'What do we tell the police?'

'We have to tell them the truth,' I said firmly, not relishing the prospect of admitting what we'd been up to, breaking into the castle. 'And you have to tell them what you discovered about the ticket you found in the dungeon…and what you think the inscription might mean.'

Susie looked unhappy at this suggestion. 'I think that's a very bad idea, Alison. Should we not wait and see what happens?'

I was beginning to lose patience. 'Don't you understand what this means, Susie? Yes, we were in the castle last night and if I'm correct, so was Ricky. The baseball cap – remember? And Lloyd must also have been in the castle last night.'

'Lloyd? Of course. I didn't make the connection; I was so focused on Ricky.'

'Wait a minute. Perhaps it was Lloyd who locked you in? It was nothing to do with Ricky?'

'I don't see what good it will do to tell them we were there and it will only put us under suspicion.'

'That's not the problem, Susie. Someone locked you in to that turret room. We made a mistake about Ricky. It could only have been Lloyd.'

She stared at me, uncomprehending, then the awful truth struck her. 'Of course,' she whispered. 'I thought Ricky was responsible after you found that baseball cap, but he might not have been.'

'No, that's just it.' I shivered, recollecting being in the castle and that dreadful sound coming nearer. Thump, drag. Thump, drag.

We had to find out for sure. We would have to find Ricky and question him before the situation became more muddled, but in spite of our bravado, we were at a loss as to what to do next.

As anticipated, the police did want to question us and while we didn't exactly lie, we decided to be economical with the truth. We made a pact to answer all their questions truthfully, but not to volunteer any additional information. So, when asked when we'd last seen Lloyd we could answer honestly, but I didn't mention finding Ricky's baseball cap in the castle.

Even so, feelings of guilt persisted and I shifted uncomfortably in my seat as I answered the fresh-faced young constable's questions, sure the look on my face would give me away. But he seemed to notice nothing out of order, or if he did he made no comment. It was perfectly possible they had a lead already, nothing to do with us, and this questioning was a formality.

'Right,' he said shutting his notebook. 'If you think of anything else that might be relevant, give us a call.'

I re-joined Susie who was sitting in the bar, nursing a large glass of fresh orange juice. 'I think I could do with a glass of wine,' I said, pulling up a chair beside her.

'Tut, tut, a bit early for that, isn't it?'

'No – you might be on a health kick, but I'm not.' And ignoring her disapproving glance, I headed over to order a glass of white wine, though I made do with a small one.

'What do we do now?' I put my glass down on the table.

Susie slumped back in her chair and looked at me thoughtfully, twirling a lock of her hair. 'There must be someone who knows about Max.'

Now was the time to tell her about my visit to Mrs Halson. 'There is someone on the island who has something to say about Max. Who believes he wasn't who he said he was.'

'Oh?' She sat up, now interested.

'Yes. I think another visit to Mrs Halson might be worthwhile.' And I admitted I'd been to see Mrs Halson and how she'd said she didn't believe he was Max

257

Stuart, but Max Colpin, someone who had been born on Bute.

Susie looked more and more astonished as I went through my tale, finally saying as I ended, 'So that's why I think it would be worthwhile going along to see her once more.'

'Why didn't you tell me about your visit before now? I can't believe you didn't see it might be important.'

I shrugged and muttered something about 'not being relevant' but it was clear from her expression that she didn't believe me.

To be honest, I'd no idea why I hadn't confided in her. I suppose I didn't want to interfere with her holiday, her celebration of her anniversary, foolish as that was. A bit of me hoped it would all go away. I should have known better.

'Right, let's make an arrangement to go back to see this Mrs Halson as soon as possible.'

Until the police left, it would be difficult to get information from Ricky, so Mrs Halson was our only hope. 'She did say Max had a brother, so perhaps if we could get in touch with him.'

'Won't the police have questioned him already?'

'Yes, but perhaps Mrs Halson might know some of the family gossip the brother is unwilling to disclose. If it were that simple, the case would be solved by now.' Now I realised I should have been more precise in my questioning of the old lady. I wouldn't make that mistake again.

Dwayne had returned from his shopping trip to be greeted with the news of Lloyd's accident. 'Gee, Susie, the sooner we're on that plane back to L.A. the better,' he said, putting an arm protectively around his wife's shoulders.

He didn't actually admit it, but I was beginning to have the impression he thought I was in some way to blame for all this disruption, if not the death of Max, judging by the way he frowned at me over Susie's head. I know I've been involved in similar events before, but this was one I'd really wanted to steer clear of.

'There's no point in all of us sitting here,' said Jerome a bit abruptly, appearing from nowhere to join in the conversation, Margie trailing behind him. Fortunately, there were only a few of us in the room at the time or his comments would have seemed a little heartless.

'Don't worry,' said Susie to me in a quiet voice as Dwayne went over to have a word with the police officer. 'We can go and visit Mrs Halson tomorrow morning. It's the dress rehearsal for the Pageant – I can slip away by telling Dwayne that we have to be at the college a bit earlier than planned.'

So, now as well as lying by omission to the police, I'm part of lying to Dwayne was my immediate thought, but I said nothing, merely nodded in agreement. I'd no better solution to the problem and there was no way Dwayne should be involved, least not until we'd worked out the importance of what Mrs Halson had to tell us.

'Are you coming along to Kilchattan Bay with the rest of us?' said Dwayne, approaching me.

'No, I've some work to do. I want to write up the rest of my notes in case I've missed anything and have to ask some of the party more questions before you leave for home.'

'Yep. Understood. Connie is pretty excited about what you've told her so far. Come on, honey, lunch is ready and then the bus will be here.'

Susie took his hand and they headed into the dining room, leaving me staring after them, thinking how much people were preoccupied with their own concerns.

Still, I'd promised Susie I'd sort out the visit to Mrs Halson. I'd have to phone the nursing home and make arrangements.

It was all such a mess, I could only hope she'd finally managed to remember the name of Max's twin and help us solve the puzzle.

CHAPTER THIRTY-EIGHT

The next morning a drizzle of rain greeted me as I pulled back the curtains in my room. It was one of those fine mists of rain that occur from time to time on the West Coast and although for the moment the mainland was obscured from view, I was confident by lunchtime it would have lifted and we'd have a sunny afternoon.

I'd arranged to meet Susie in the dining room at eight o'clock for a quick breakfast. A phone call to the nursing home where Mrs Halson was staying had given us the opportunity to go along there at nine o'clock, plenty of time to do what we wanted before the rehearsal at the college.

'Zachary said to be there at ten thirty,' muttered Susie, 'but I think he's the kind of person who's never on time for anything.'

Breakfast over, we set off. Susie suggested taking a taxi.

'I don't think that's a good idea. The fewer people who know about this visit the better.'

Reluctantly she agreed that we should take the bus from Guildford Square, though it was clear she thought this an unnecessary precaution.

There was an air of bustle as we signed in at the home after an uneventful journey, though Susie did say a couple of times as we walked up the long driveway, 'Oh, my poor feet,' but then as I pointed out, she should have worn more suitable shoes.

This criticism only resulted in a loud, 'Hmm,' but there were no further complaints as we reached the sturdy wooden doors of the nursing home.

Mrs Halson was sitting in the residents' lounge, a little apart from several other residents, apparently transfixed by a report on the news about the cost of foreign holidays, but as we approached her, we saw she was in fact, dozing.

One of the carers approached. 'Don't worry, she often does this.'

She shook her gently. 'You have visitors, Una.'

Mrs Halson came to with a start, but her face lit up when she saw us. 'So early in the day? Or have I been asleep for a long time?'

'No, no,' Susie hastened to assure her as we sat down on the couch opposite her chair. 'This was the only time we could manage.'

Best to get straight to the point. After I introduced Susie I said, 'We thought you might be able to help us, Mrs Halson. We've a question about someone who was born on the island.'

She shook her head and adjusted her spectacles which had fallen down over her nose. 'I'm not sure about that, dear. My memory isn't what it was.'

'Oh, I think you'll remember this.' I prompted her. 'Last time I was here, you told me about Max Stuart. You said his real name was Max Colpin and that he had a brother?'

262

For a moment she looked perplexed, as though struggling to remember the conversation. 'Who did you say you were again?'

Patiently I explained who I was, why Susie was with me and the reason for our coming along to see her at such short notice.

She laughed, displaying a set of teeth that were clearly her own, slightly yellowed with age. 'Short notice isn't a problem for me, dear. I've all the time I need at my disposal. I'm pleased to see visitors at any time of the day…'

Fearing she would wander off into some other subject I gently tried to bring her back to the matter in hand. 'Max Stuart, or rather Max Colpin…what do you remember about him? About the family?'

'Of course. You may as well know the whole story. They were quite a family. Now let me see.' She began to count on her fingers. 'There was Millie, she was the eldest, but she died young. The year she died there was an outbreak of whooping cough on the island. She was only four, it was a terrible tragedy, but then it was a calamity for a number of folk who lost children in that way. The McConnells, who lived next door to me, lost two children in quick succession…'

Once again I tried to nudge her back to the main story. 'The other Colpin children?'

'Ah, then there were the twins, Max and…now what was the other one called?'

She stopped speaking and stared out of the window, closing her eyes. For a minute I thought she'd drifted off to sleep again, but as Susie leaned forward to touch her lightly on the arm, she opened her eyes. 'They were twins, you know, that was why it was so cruel to separate them like that.'

I caught Susie glancing covertly at her watch, no doubt concerned that with the slow progress we were making, she'd be late for the rehearsal.

'Yes,' Mrs Halson resumed. 'The parents split up. It wasn't the done thing in those days, but I'm sure the death of Millie had a lot to do with it. That's when Max and his father left the island. Left before the police caught up with him, that was the story. He was light-fingered.'

She pursed her lips to make sure we understood before continuing, 'She was a Stuart and went back to her maiden name. He'd relatives in America somewhere, which was about as far away as you could get from the Isle of Bute. The other twin stayed with the mother. I wish I could remember the name.' She furrowed her brow in concentration, then shook her head again. 'It will come back to me, at some point. Just not now.'

I suddenly realised she looked exhausted. 'That's been very helpful,' I said, indicating to Susie that I thought it was time to leave. 'If you remember any other details, we'd be pleased if someone could contact us.' I rummaged in my bag for one of my cards and found a rather crumpled one at the bottom. I smoothed it out as best I could and circled the phone number in black pen. I'd no confidence that Mrs Halson would contact me, but hopefully she'd ask one of the carers to do so if anything else came to mind.

We said goodbye, leaving with promises of returning soon, but by the time we reached the door I looked back to see she was once more sound asleep.

'What did we learn from that?' Susie asked as we walked back down the corridor to the entrance.

'So far we know Max was a Brandane originally, that when his mother and father split up he went to America with his father and later in life he took his mother's name and that he has a twin brother, who may well still be on the island.'

Susie raised her eyebrows. 'Do you think that's likely?'

'It'll be easy to find out. We could check out all the people with the surname Colpin on the island, but didn't the father come from Glasgow originally? Still, there might be a relation who can point us in the right direction.'

'But the police will have already done this, surely?'

I shrugged. 'Possibly. But if we can track some member of the family down, we may be able to help. There's more to this than a straightforward murder, for sure.' I hesitated. 'Wait. I'm sure Margie is some relation to Max.' Yet again, in spite of all my good resolutions I'd become embroiled in something that didn't concern me.

'I'd no idea. How do you know that? We'll have to speak to her, then,' said Susie, raising her eyebrows in surprise. She glanced at her watch. 'Help! That will have to wait. I'm running late for rehearsal.'

'We can get a taxi up to the college,' I said. 'You sign us out, while I phone.'

I moved outside on to the gravel path to make the phone call to the taxi rank in Rothesay. As I finished, having been assured we would have 'to wait no more than five minutes' I tried to get over my disappointment at the outcome of the visit. What we needed was the

265

name of Max's twin brother. Margie might be our way of finding out.

Susie moved over to look at the carefully tended flower beds by the side of the path, but as I stood waiting for the taxi, I spied a familiar figure coming out of the side entrance to the Nursing Home. I blinked twice to make sure my eyes weren't deceiving me.

There was no doubt about it. It was Zachary, but before I could alert Susie, he had disappeared from view. If Zachary was visiting here, it must mean he had some connection to the island. But how could we find out what that might be?

CHAPTER THIRTY-NINE

There was no time to discuss our visit to the Nursing Home and the sudden appearance of Zachary, as the taxi arrived to take us up to the college. I say we, because Susie had persuaded me to go with her. 'You've nothing else on at the moment, have you?' she pleaded. 'It won't take long.' And I was happy to give her moral support.

The students who were acting in the Pageant were milling around in the theatre, while one of the teachers from the primary school tried to keep her charges in order. This was proving a difficult task as the Viking costumes for the boys included imitation swords and the temptation to engage in a contest was proving too much for some of them.

'Will you stop that,' she was saying, trying to separate a pair who were intent on fighting the battle well before it started.

She turned to us as we came in. 'Where's Zachary? I can't keep these children in order for much longer.'

No sooner had she finished speaking than Zachary came hurrying down the aisle, waving his arms to announce his presence.

He clapped his hands. 'Now if you could all take your places.' There was a hubbub of noise as the actors shifted here and there, one or two of the younger boys using it as an excuse to jostle each other.

The rehearsal, after a slow start, with Zachary becoming increasingly agitated, finally settled into a rhythm, though there were several blips in the performance, not least the King who kept forgetting his lines.

Zachary jumped up out of his seat in the front row and leapt on to the stage. 'No, I told you. You have to give it emphasis, like this. You're a King, about to lead your followers into battle. Mumbling like that wouldn't inspire anyone.'

He began to declaim, 'Listen, my knights, to the words of your King. Today you will show your mettle, repel the invaders and once more claim the castle for the rightful King.'

The members of the cast appeared suitably impressed by this bravura performance, all except the boy who had the role of the King. What's more, as Zachary was in full flow, I spied the boy sneaking his phone from under his cloak and scrolling through.

I was sitting at the back of the theatre, but I wasn't paying attention to what was happening on stage. As though in a flash, what had been nagging away at the back of my mind came to me. That poster of Zachary as a young man showed his face clearly before he'd grown a beard and his features reminded me so much of the photo of Max that I'd seen.

Was that the answer? Was it possible that Zachary was Max's twin? I was sure I could detect the same aquiline nose, the same broad forehead. And he must have some connection to the island if he was visiting someone in the Rullecheddan Nursing Home.

What was it Susie had mentioned Max as saying? Something about claiming his inheritance? I'd dismissed it as yet another of the group assuming a link to one of the more famous Stuarts, but supposing it was nothing to do with that? Suppose it was a different kind of inheritance, one Max's twin also had an interest in?

Over on the stage, Zachary was bouncing up and down, pulling here, moving someone else there, never satisfied with the results.

'No, no, no,' he shouted. 'This will never do. You have to have more energy. This is important. If you don't win, you'll be DEAD!'

And so the preparations continued, Susie was eventually called to perform her part, Zachary ran backwards and forwards, filling in the pauses and at last, the final rehearsal came to an end.

'Let's hope it all goes according to plan tomorrow,' he said, flopping down in a seat in the front row.

'Make sure you're all on time. Remember we need extra time for the make-up.'

The students sauntered off, the teacher gathered the children together and Susie and I were left alone in the theatre with Zachary.

By now I had convinced myself that Max and Zachary were related, and unable to contain my excitement or consider pursuing Margie or any other Colpins on the island, I leaned over and said to Susie, 'I think I may have a lead here. I'm going to speak to Zachary.'

'What do you mean?' she said in a loud voice and I put my finger to my lips as Zachary came up the aisle towards us.

'Let's hope the real thing is better than this?'

'I'm sure it will be fine. You know what they say about a bad dress rehearsal.'

He didn't appear convinced, and rubbed his hand over his beard. 'I should have realised the problems of working with amateurs.'

'Oh, come, it won't be that bad. Everyone's looking forward to the day and the Pageant will only be one part of it,' said Susie. 'A very important part,' she added hastily, seeing the frown on Zachary's face.

I had to seize the moment while Susie was here. If Zachary was Max's twin, could he have had something to do with his death?

I took a deep breath. 'Are you related to Max Stuart by any chance?' Put like that it sounded harsh, but I hadn't had time to consider a form of words.

Susie's mouth opened in astonishment and Zachary was completely taken aback. 'The guy who was found dead in the dungeon in Rothesay Castle? What makes you think that?'

No time for hesitation. 'You look very alike and we know Max had a twin, a twin who might still be on the island.'

Susie interrupted before Zachary could respond, perhaps concerned about my use of the word 'we'. 'I don't think so, Alison. It's Colpins we're looking for and Zachary's second name is Benford.'

I wasn't so easily put off. 'Is that right, is that your real name?'

Zachary looked at me and then at Susie as though weighing up what to say. He muttered, 'I guessed you'd find out sooner or later. I don't like people finding out. It spoils the illusion. No, Zachary Benford isn't my real name – it's my stage name.'

So I was right, I thought triumphantly. We might at last be about to solve the mystery.

CHAPTER FORTY

So, it was true. I waited, scarcely able to breathe, trying not to feel smug at having finally discovered the answer, as Susie continued to look from me to Zachary and back again.

'Why shouldn't I have a stage name,' said Zachary defiantly. 'It's common practice. You have to have something that makes you stand out from the crowd.'

'No reason. Except you misled everyone by using it.' I adopted my school teacher voice, though it had been some time since I'd used it.

'I don't see how you reach that conclusion. Who's bothered about my stage name? Who's bothered about me, full stop?'

He waved his hand around the theatre. 'You've seen the posters on the way in. At one time I had a golden future in front of me and now I'm reduced to this – directing a two-bit Pageant with a bunch of incompetents, having to involve kids from a primary school in order to get some funding.' He was now on a roll and all his frustrations spilled out. 'Don't you think I realise how ridiculous it is to have these half-sized Vikings, having to justify it?'

While I was pleased I'd managed to make some progress in the mystery, I still didn't have a clear idea of Zacharay's motive. It was now or never. I had to confront him, but perhaps I shouldn't have been quite so abrupt.

'And was it to do with a family inheritance? Was that why you killed your twin?'

He stared at me as though I'd been speaking a foreign language. 'What are you talking about? What twin? What family inheritance?'

This response took me aback, but I calculated he'd been taken by surprise by my accusation, my discovery of the truth. 'Come, come, it's too late to pretend. The police will be here soon and it will all be over.' If I hoped this would persuade him to confess, I was wrong. The look on his face was of confusion, not fear.

'Why are the police coming? I've no idea what you're talking about.'

'Yes, 'said Susie. 'What is this to do with Zachary? And who called the police?' She looked as dumbfounded as Zachary was.

'Because,' I said, whirling round to face her, 'Zachary isn't who he says he is. He's Max's twin brother, he's a Colpin. And he killed his twin because of the inheritance.'

Zachary burst into loud peals of laughter. 'Oh, Alison, where did you get this from?' He sat down and clutched his sides, tears rolling down his face.

'You can act all you like, but I know the truth and so will everyone else soon.' I tried to disguise the note of uncertainty in my voice.

He stopped laughing and wiped away his tears. 'This is ridiculous. I really don't know how you came to this conclusion, but it's a load of nonsense.'

'Yes,' said Susie, 'it sounds perfectly ridiculous.'

'It's not ridiculous,' I shouted, angry that she didn't believe me, refusing to back me. 'You heard him. Zachary Benford isn't his real name.'

'Yes,' said Zachary, 'but my real name is Robertson Sidebottom. Not too inspiring as a stage name is it? And what's more, I'm no relation to any of the Colpin family.'

'But you were born on Bute?'

'No, I was born in Stirling, actually, where the rest of my family still live. What's all this about an inheritance and this Max guy?'

I could feel my courage seeping away. Was it possible I was wrong? How could I have made a mistake like this?

'So what were you doing at the Rullecheddan Nursing Home? You must be related to someone there, must have a family connection to Bute.'

'My grandparents retired to Bute and my gran is in the nursing home. I'd a phone call yesterday, she gets confused, but I'd so much to do that going this morning when I'd a bit of free time was fine.'

I remembered the phone call Zachary had been making when we'd returned to collect Susie's script. How could I have jumped to conclusions like that?

'So what are we going to tell the police when they arrive?' Susie sounded worried, looking to me for reassurance.

'There are no police,' I had to admit. 'I was trying to frighten Zachary into making a confession.'

Zachary and Susie exchanged a glance.

'Stick to what you do best, Alison,' sniffed Zachary. 'You might be a good writer, but you'd make a lousy detective.'

Thankfully, he stood up and headed towards the exit to the dressing rooms, still shaking his head and chortling.

'How could you, Alison?' said Susie.

'Anyone can make a mistake,' I replied defiantly, 'and all the signs were that he was a Colpin, the one responsible for Max's death. Why, he even looks like Max.'

'I didn't mean that, Alison. How could you have accused him in that way? And I don't see why you think he looks like Max. How can you tell under all that facial hair?'

She looked over towards the exit. 'I hope he doesn't decide to sue, that's all I can say. You'll have to apologise…properly.'

There was nothing more to say. What a terrible mistake to make. Yet I'd been so certain, so sure. But if Zachary wasn't a Colpin, wasn't Max's twin, who on earth was?

Margie was my only hope of finding out.

CHAPTER FORTY-ONE

Discovering Zachary wasn't responsible for Max's death in this way left me sick with embarrassment. I slunk off to find a seat at the back of the auditorium, trying to avoid further conversation with Zachary, though he seemed to find the idea he might be a murderer highly amusing.

From time to time he'd look over in my direction and I'd see his shoulders shaking with laughter.

As soon as the final fitting for Susie's costume was over, I was in no mood to linger and persuaded her to walk back to the hotel. Or rather, I insisted. I needed time to recover.

'What I can't understand is why you would have thought Zachary was the murderer. And even if he was, why you would have accused him like that? Didn't you think it might be dangerous?'

How could I explain my motive to Susie? 'There were two of us and it was a public place,' but she shook her head. I was tired and overwrought, frustrated by the whole business. If we could wind this up, we could all leave the island.

We walked the rest of the way in silence, each preoccupied by our own thoughts. Susie was right. I'd have to leave it to the police. Behind the scenes there would be a flurry of activity: they had no need to involve us directly.

Back at the hotel, there were more problems to deal with. As we came in through the foyer it was to see Oscar and Wesley standing there, apparently having an argument.

'You ain't got a clue about this,' Oscar was saying. 'Why it's so important to me. You ain't got any Stuart ancestry, that's for sure.' Connie hovered in the background, visibly upset by this spat.

'You don't know that, bro, not for sure. Though that wasn't the reason I came on this trip.' He spied Susie and me. 'Here's the very woman who can help us.'

'Help with what?'

'Oscar seems to think he's got a claim to the Stuart throne, that he might be the next king of Scotland.' Wesley threw back his head and laughed uproariously, but Oscar's expression showed he wasn't amused.

Oscar pointed at me. 'I was depending on you coming up with the information,' he said accusingly.

Still upset about what had happened with Zachary at the college it took me a moment to focus as I tried to get my head around this idea. 'You think you're descended from the Stuart kings?'

'Yes. My mother told me all about it. She was convinced we were of the Royal Stuart bloodline. I left Scotland for America when I was a teenager. Like all kids, I didn't pay much attention to those old family stories. It was only later, when I became interested in my family history that I understood what my mother

277

had told me. You were supposed to investigate that, Alison, but you haven't come up with much. I've had to try to sort it out for myself.'

I laughed, then quickly turned it into a cough. Oh dear, I'd no idea when I took on the commission that there was this underlying current.

'Did you know about this?' I said to Susie as Oscar continued to glower at me.

'Not exactly.' She sounded evasive. 'One or two of the party were particularly keen, but I didn't know Oscar had this in mind.'

'Don't talk about me as if I wasn't here,' shouted Oscar and Wesley put a restraining hand on his arm. The usually mild-mannered Oscar was red with rage.

'Calm down. I'm sure Alison knows as much as there is to about any Stuart ancestry.'

Now I was in a fix. Sure, I'd interviewed those with an interest, but there was still a lot of research to do and I'd planned that part for when I was back home. After a moment's thought, trying to sound as positive as I could, I came up with, 'It's not as simple as that, Oscar. There are all kinds of branches of the family Stuart and not all of them are of royal blood. The direct line died out, as I tried to explain.'

Oscar breathed deeply and close up I could see how bloodshot his eyes were. 'I know I'm right.'

'How come?' Susie stepped into the discussion.

'Because I had the story from my mother.'

All this seemed very unlikely and before I could stop myself I said, 'But if that was the case, surely your mother would have employed a qualified genealogist to investigate the claim?'

A look of cunning came over his face. 'She didn't have the money to do that, we were dirt poor when I was growing up, but I made money in America, had my own construction business. And when I sold the business, I decided this would be the time to stake my claim. But I needed the proof.' He glared at me again.

'And…?'

'And it was all a conspiracy. The guy I employed didn't want to find the information …or else he was bribed not to. What an upset it would cause if a claimant to the Scottish throne turned up.'

'Well, yes, that's true,' I replied, adding, 'but not likely.'

But Oscar wasn't to be persuaded. He reached into the bag he was carrying and pulled out the sheaf of papers he'd been carrying with him during the tour. 'I ended up doing the research myself.'

'And did you find what you were looking for?'

'No, I didn't have long enough, didn't have the skill. That's why I was depending on you.'

This conversation was becoming more and more bizarre, but Oscar had had enough for the present. He shoved the papers back in his bag. 'But I won't be defeated,' he said. 'And if you can't help, Alison, I'll have to take steps to find out on my own.'

He turned on his heel, leaving us staring after him.

'Wow, ain't that something?' Wesley looked astonished. 'Do you think he is of Royal blood? That he could be the legal King of Scotland.'

'Don't be ridiculous.' I tried to soften my words by adding, 'I've explained to everyone that the original line died out. Oh, he'll have Stuart connections, but not those particular ones.'

279

Jerome came strolling over from the lounge. 'What was that all about.'

Wesley grinned. 'Oscar got some idea he's the King of Scotland.'

'What? How ridiculous. Mind you when I had a part in The Uncrowned a bit of the plot was about someone who …'

Luckily, as Jerome was about to launch into a long explanation of the plot of yet another obscure film, Dwayne came in. 'How did the rehearsal go?' he asked as Wesley raised his hand in farewell saying, 'Time I phoned my folks at home to let them know what the arrangements are.'

Jerome turned on his heel and headed out of the hotel, making no attempt to disguise his disappointment at our lack of interest.

Susie made a face at me before saying, 'Fine. A few hitches, but you expect that with a dress rehearsal, don't you?'

Fingers crossed she wouldn't tell Dwayne about what happened with Zachary. The fewer people who knew about that the better. It would be difficult enough to face Zachary at the Pageant, but then he'd be so busy I'd surely be able to avoid him.

'Are you coming along this afternoon, Alison? This may be our last trip on Bute.'

'Mmm…we might yet be asked to stay on.' I wasn't too sure about Susie's information.

'Why should that be?' Dwayne frowned.

'Well, because of the death of Max and this latest problem with Lloyd, of course.'

'Oh, I see. No need to worry about that, Alison. The police have decided we can leave. If there are any developments later on, those can be dealt with.'

While this was good news, it made my accusation of Zachary all the more cringe worthy. We were free to go, to leave Bute as arranged. But all I said was, 'I'm glad about that. It would have caused a lot of problems.'

'So, are you coming with us?' Susie returned to the original question.

'I'm not sure. I might be better working on my notes and transcribing some of the interviews in case there's anything I've missed. This evening will be my last opportunity to check up on any details.'

'Like Oscar having Royal blood, being King of Scotland,' she said, a wicked gleam in her eye.

But I was too upset by what had happened with Zachary to respond and with a cheerful, 'Perhaps we'll see you later,' she and Dwayne headed off.

Undecided about my next move, I went over to sit at one of the tables in the far corner of the empty lounge. In the quiet I'd have the opportunity to review everything that had happened during the past few days. I'd heard Ricky had returned, surlier than ever. We'd have to make questioning him a priority. Had he disappeared because he'd witnessed Lloyd's accident? Or had something to do with it? There could be no other explanation if they were both in the castle last night.

Meanwhile, there was talk of a bus tour of the island and I was tempted to join them. It would be the last opportunity to explore and goodness knew when I'd be back. If I did return, it wouldn't be for work. It was such a lovely place, with its secluded beaches and long woodland walks, the tranquil town of Rothesay, the friendly people. Yes, all the things I like about Bute were still here and if I'd had any sense I'd have arranged to come here on holiday to meet up with Susie and refuse all opportunities for working.

Too late now. I'd committed myself and I didn't want to let Susie or any of the other members of Heritage Adventurers down. Except for Oscar. No matter how much research I did, no matter how I tried to gild the story, there wasn't the slightest possibility Oscar had royal blood running through his veins. I didn't blame his mother. Such stories about inheritances are often passed down through generations and get muddled in the telling: no doubt that's what had happened in Oscar's case. I'd have to find a way of making sure he understood the truth.

No sooner had I reached into my bag to find the notebook where I'd summarised my information than I felt a shadow fall across the table. I looked up, expecting to see Oscar, still consumed by anger at my inability to find out the truth, as he saw it, about his royal connections. But it was Wesley. 'You okay, Alison? Don't pay no attention to Oscar. We all know he came here on a wild goose chase, thinking he was the king of Scotland.'

'You all knew about it?'

'Oh, yeah. He told us, talked about claiming his inheritance, but no one paid the least bit of attention. We realised you'd be able to talk him out of it.'

This last observation left me speechless. It would appear I was the only one who didn't know about

Oscar's belief in his royal ancestry. Surely Susie should have warned me?

'Anyway, I can see you're working. I won't disturb you anymore, Ma'am.' And with that he was off, leaving me gazing after him, all sorts of thoughts going through my head. I put my notebook down on the table and gazed into the far distance. If Oscar was as obsessed as Wesley suggested, could he have had anything to do with the murder?

I felt a shiver run down my spine as I tried to recall the details of our conversation.

What was it exactly Oscar had said about his parents? His mother was Scottish, a Stuart and he'd gone to America as a teenager to seek employment. This wasn't exactly the story Mrs Halson had told us, but it had all been a long time ago. Possibly she'd mixed up events. That meant Oscar must be a Brandane as well…and Max's twin. But they didn't look in the least alike. I tried to remember what I knew about twins. They could of course be fraternal twins – born at the same time, but from different eggs. That was something else to be checked out.

There still remained the question about the killing. Would Oscar have a good enough reason to kill Max, his twin? He was such a small nervous man. I couldn't see him having the strength to overcome Max, though sometimes even the weakest of people could acquire superhuman force if the motivation was enough. That was the answer. If he believed he'd a claim to the Scottish throne, he would have had to be the twin born first. Was Oscar mad enough to have killed Max for this? I'd been wrong once before and yet this time everything seemed to fit so well.

But then if I believed Oscar was guilty, what was I going to do about it? Would Margie be able to help?

CHAPTER FORTY-TWO

I'd forgotten my phone was on silent. I'd set it to mute when we'd gone up to the rehearsal at the college, aware nothing is more annoying and more distracting for those on stage than a phone going off in the middle of a performance.

'Missed call' flashed up on the screen. I was tempted to ignore it, assuming it would be Simon, asking for details of my plans for leaving the island, but something made me check. It wasn't my husband, it was the carer, Diane, from the nursing home. She'd left a message, asking me to call her as soon as convenient. I'd have to abandon the bus tour.

She was brisk, business-like when I phoned back. 'Mrs Halson has asked to see you. She says she's remembered something that may be important.'

This was intriguing. At last this might be a way of confirming my suspicions about Oscar. Mrs Halson must have remembered the name of the other twin and if not I could prompt her. I'd no intention of delaying, though Susie would be cross she hadn't been included. No sense in interrupting her last outing on Bute, I told myself. She'd only want to come with me, which would mean telling Dwayne the whole story. I could see a long string of consequences unfolding, which was exactly what I didn't need. And given the mess I'd made of things by accusing Zachary, I didn't want to voice my suspicions about Oscar yet.

'I'll be along in about half an hour,' I arranged.

This time, I'd no intention of travelling by bus, but headed down the High Street to the taxi rank at Guildford Square.

There was one taxi left in the rank, a sign how busy the island was becoming as the tourist season arrived, and in no time I'd arrived at the nursing home to see Mrs Halson.

Luckily, Diane was still on duty and she ushered me through to Mrs Halson's room with no comment beyond a brief, 'Great to see the weather has turned sunny again.'

Mrs Halson was sitting by the window. I suspected she'd been looking out for me.

'Sit down. No, a bit closer,' and she motioned me to the upright chair next to hers.

She smiled. 'I knew I'd remember eventually about that family of Max Colpin.'

'I'm glad you did,' I encouraged her.

'Yes, it was quite a story and there was a lot of fuss and gossip on the island when it happened. But I suppose things are different now and it takes a great deal to get people upset about the difficulties in a marriage.' She stopped and gazed out of the window.

Anxious as I was for her to get to the heart of the story, I understood she wasn't to be rushed. She wanted to tell me all about it in her own good time. Now having recollected the sequence of events, I supposed she was eager to make sure I had a complete understanding of the story.

She turned back to me. 'You see, a lot of it was to do with him, with Ernie Colpin. He was a drinker and she was from a good family on the island. He came over here on holiday one Glasgow Fair and she fell for him in a big way.' She shook her head and then went on in a voice so low I had to lean forward to catch what she was saying, 'Yes, poor Ruby, she was a lovely girl, but so easily swayed by his glib talk.'

'And they lived on the island?'

'Yes, he got a job on the Mount Stuart estate, because of Ruby's father, I'm sure. Everything went well for a while, Millie and then the twins were born and then he started drinking again, not turning up for work and in the end he lost his job. He was well known in all the pubs in Rothesay and there were plenty of them at that time. He'd been barred from almost all of them and that took some doing in those days. He survived for a while doing odd jobs. He even worked at Rothesay Castle for a while. Some archaeologists came over from Glasgow, spent some time dredging the moat. Goodness knows why.'

I remembered the photos in the book at Mount Stuart. Perhaps this was where Ernie had worked. A swift mental calculation confirmed this was possible – the dates would match. While this background information was very helpful, I wanted to get to the bit I was really interested in – the name of the other twin.

'And the twins?'

'Oh, yes. In the end she'd had enough, but the only thing to do was to get him to leave the island, though I suspect she didn't have to do much to persuade him. By then he was in trouble with the police…petty crime, but even so, crime. It was never proved, but it was suspected he'd been stealing some items, small items, to sell. He'd had a friend who'd emigrated to America and that's where he went. She went back to using her maiden name. Perhaps when he left he intended to come home at some point, but by then Ernie had drunk himself to death.'

'And he took one of the twins with him?'

'Yes, it was terrible, but it was the only way he could be persuaded to go. Probably thought the boy could get work, support his drinking.'

'And Max went with his father?'

'Indeed, it was a terrible wrench, but what could poor Ruby do. Years later, she tried to track Max and his father down, but it was as though they didn't want to be found. It wasn't as easy as it is now with that internet thing.'

She sighed. 'And the other twin stayed here on the island, of course, with Ruby. At least for a while. So many people leave to find work. What choice do they have? Oh, Ruby understood, but she was very upset and lonely.'

My heart began to pound and my throat was so dry I could scarcely get the words out. Now at last I'd know for certain, would be able to decide what to do about Oscar. The police would have to be told. It was all over.

I swallowed. 'But the guess is Max took his mother's name and returned eventually, came looking for his twin brother. That must have been difficult for him.'

She gazed at me for a few moments, a puzzled look on her face. 'Eh? I'm not sure what you mean, dear. The other twin was a girl.'

CHAPTER FORTY-THREE

Now I knew the meaning of being stunned into silence. Unable to believe what she was saying, I asked again, 'Are you sure? There was one boy and one girl?'

'Yes, of course. You see, in those days that was what made sense to folk. That was the way the family was arranged. The girl stayed with her mother and the boy went with his father. Not that it happened often, thank goodness. And I'm sure it was the only time it happened here. Aye, a terrible tragedy for everyone concerned.'

'And do you remember the girl's name?'

Mrs Halson tutted loudly. 'Sorry, dear. That I can't remember. That's not to say I won't, but at this moment it escapes me.'

I tried to make sense of this new piece of information. If Mrs Halson was correct, Oscar was nothing to do with the Colpin family. It was merely by chance that he had also gone to America, that in his early years his mother had filled his head with stories about famous Stuart connections. He hadn't actually said he was from Bute originally and, in my rush to find an answer, I hadn't taken the trouble to ask.

I had to leave as quickly as possible, but without seeming rude, thanking her for all her help as I rose to my feet.

She didn't try to detain me. 'Think I'll have a little doze now, dear. All that talking has quite worn me out.'

And as I slipped out, she was already nodding off.

I tracked Diane down to the Residents' lounge. 'Thanks for calling me,' I said. 'That was most helpful.'

She answered in a vague kind of way, 'Glad you got what you wanted,' but it was clear she was fully occupied arbitrating in a dispute between two of the residents about which television programme they should watch.

I began to walk towards Rothesay. It would take me almost an hour, unless I waited for the bus, but an hour seemed little time to gather my thoughts about everything that had happened.

It had to be someone from the Heritage Adventurers who had killed Max. It couldn't have been a random attack. I refused to believe that – it was too far-fetched. But why come all the way to Bute to kill him? Because it wasn't until they arrived on the island that Max's twin realised who he was?

I ran through the list of possibles, but few were likely to be roughly the same age as Max, from what I could tell. But then I've never been very good on ages.

There were three of them in the right age range: Kimberley, Connie and Margie. I couldn't see Kimberley having killed Max. She'd enough on her hands trying to keep Ricky under control. Which left Connie and Margie. Could it be one of them? Connie and Oscar were too taken up with his claim to be Scottish nobility, surely? The only possibility was

Margie. The story that she was related to Max must be true. And what if she wasn't just related, but was his twin? I had intended to speak to her about her connection to Max, but somehow there hadn't been a suitable opportunity. My fault. I should have insisted on seeing her on her own.

This was hopeless, too much for me. So far I'd been completely wrong on two occasions, what made me think I could get it right now?

By now I was walking past Blethers cafe and realised I was much in need of a cup of tea.

There were a few customers, but I found a seat by the window, overlooking the bay. Gazing out on such a tranquil scene, watching as the ferry made its way steadily into the harbour, it was impossible to believe what had happened in such a short time. When I got back to the hotel, I'd have to find an opportunity to speak to Susie, tell her everything. But I'd be resolute about one thing. No more sleuthing for me. If Margie was the twin Mrs Halson had described, the police could sort it out.

That was it. I wouldn't think about it anymore, would enjoy the Pageant and the fun of the last evening on the island, then head off to join Simon for a well-deserved holiday.

When the waitress came to take my order, I added a freshly baked scone to my order of tea. It was the least I deserved.

CHAPTER FORTY-FOUR

The next morning dawned bright and clear with no more than a whisper of wind, not enough to send the high tendrils of cloud moving across the sky. Rothesay Bay sparkled in the early sunlight, a few boat owners out and about on the pontoons, preparing to sail further up the West coast. Their berths would soon be taken by others as this was coming up to the busiest time of year.

The MV Bute came sliding in to the pier, turning to dock with a grace that never failed to amaze me, given her size.

I'd been up early, before the others. I'd slept well, given my decision to let someone else sort out the problem of Max's death. Lloyd was out of hospital, but confined to his room and the police were coming and going to question him. Every time I saw one of them I broke out in a guilty sweat, wondering what he would tell them about being in the castle.

After breakfast, seeking something to distract me and determined to take advantage of my last full day on the island, I headed down to the pier, only stopping to buy a morning paper on the way. The weather was ideal for the medieval fair at the castle and hopefully it would hold for the evening Pageant and the firework display.

Susie had been very good about my lack of communication. I suspect she'd been as thankful as I was that my tendency to interfere had come to nothing. Or perhaps she was feeling guilty about involving me. I'd still no idea why Max had been murdered, though his boast about an inheritance must have had a lot to do with it. It was the business of others to find out, though I couldn't help watching Margie closely in case she gave any sign she might be guilty. She didn't. If she was responsible for the death of Max, she'd covered her tracks well.

I walked along to the benches outside the Discovery Centre and found a spot where I could watch the bustle of the day. Not that there was a lot of activity other than at the ferry terminal, but that would change as the day progressed.

After a restful hour, watching the seagulls, the ferry gliding into the bay, I stood up and stretched, ready to head back. There were gaily printed posters all around the town and a good turnout was expected for all the events at the castle. I was excited about it, though I'd a notion Susie was beginning to feel nervous about her part in the Pageant.

As I came in to the hotel dining room to join the others for lunch, I spied Ricky at a table over by the window, the scowl on his face a sign he was being scolded yet again by his mother.

'That boy,' said Susie. 'I'd like to wring his neck. If it weren't that we were heading home soon, I'd take action.'

'So what happened? Did you ask him about the baseball cap?'

'Yes, and what's more, and he seemed to think it was all a joke. He'd heard all the discussions about me being missing and when you left for the castle he guessed you knew where I'd gone, so he followed you, tried to scare you by making that noise. But he denies locking me in.'

I shook my head. 'He's been nothing but trouble. Well, he's not getting his baseball cap back. That should be some sort of punishment.'

'So what do we do now?'

'I suspect he'd something to do with Lloyd's accident, but Lloyd is saying nothing, so it's not up to me to accuse him.'

As she turned away, I grabbed her arm. 'No, wait, Susie, there is something else I have to say,' and I told her my suspicions about Margie.

'Margie is Max's twin? Are you sure.'

I nodded. 'Well, Connie told me Margie and Max were related and apparently there was bad blood between them.' I shook my head. 'But let's leave it to the police. I don't want to test another theory.'

'I don't think Connie's the most reliable person. You know she's a bit deaf and gets things wrong. It's more than likely she misheard.' She frowned. 'And Margie and Max don't look any more alike than Zachary and Max did.'

At this mention of my previous mix-up, doubts began to creep in. 'But sometimes Connie hears perfectly well.'

Susie dismissed this suggestion with a wave of her hand. 'Yes, as with all people who are hard of hearing, background noises can have an effect.'

'So you don't think she's a likely candidate?'

'No, Alison and what's more, don't go accusing her. As I've said, she doesn't look at all like Max and didn't Mrs Halson comment on how similar the twins looked? Last time you did that, it nearly caused no end of problems.'

Susie was right. I'd no proof, except what Connie had said. But it must be one of the Heritage Adventurers who was responsible. 'I've no intention of asking Margie. I told you …it's a matter for the police now.'

'I'd ask her, but we have to go soon,' said Susie.

'Of course, put this business out of your mind, think about your role tonight.' I could well understand her frustration.

'It won't be too hot, I hope,' muttered Susie as we finished our coffee. 'I'll suffocate in that costume.'

'I'm sure it'll be fine,' I comforted her. 'You know how chilly it can be in the evenings. You'll probably be glad of an extra layer or two.'

'Maybe.'

Just then, Margie came towards us. I held my breath and tried to catch Susie's attention. This wasn't the moment to be investigating the link between Max and Margie. I wished I hadn't told Susie of my suspicions.

Too late. 'Can I have a quick word?' She caught Margie's arm.

There was a look of surprise on Margie's face, but she stopped, saying. 'Sure, Susie. How can I help?'

'Don't answer this if it upsets you, but it's about you and Max,' Susie blurted out as I tried to edge away. 'You knew him, but there was some hostility between you?'

For a moment it seemed that Margie was going to ignore the question, walk away, then she sighed. 'You're right. But there was a good reason.' She didn't look at us, but gazed steadily ahead.

'Oh, well,' she said eventually. 'There was a family feud, if you must know. It was to do with his father. He came over to America thinking he could worm his way into our family. My mother was his sister. He was always borrowing money and it came to a head when he started stealing from us.'

'But Max?'

'He blamed my mother for his father's death. All nonsense. She didn't get over the bitter quarrel they had. That's why I wanted nothing to do with him. I can't pretend I'm sorry he's dead.'

Susie and I looked at each other as Margie said briskly, 'I'd better go and find the others.'

We stood and watched her leave. Thank goodness I hadn't accused her of being Max's twin. Suddenly aware we should be moving off, I said, 'Susie, we'd better go over to the castle.'

'Gosh, is that the time? I'll catch up with you. I must find Dwayne.'

Helena was standing at Reception as I came through the foyer. 'Hi, there,' I said. 'Are you joining us?'

She grinned. 'Susie's asked me to help today. The castle is bound to be very busy and I'll be there in case anyone needs assistance or information.'

'Very sensible,' I agreed, knowing Susie would be occupied for a good part of the day if Zachary had anything to do with it. I'd avoid him as much as possible, the memory of my false accusation making me cringe.

Kimberley was sitting in the far corner of the lounge with Ricky, refusing all attempts to engage her in the general discussion, but the rest of the group were clearly determined to enjoy what was left of the holiday, albeit in a quiet fashion. I spied Oscar and, coward that I am, snuck behind one of the pillars until he'd moved away. The last thing I wanted was to have to speak to him.

The plan was for the group to head over to the castle, to the various stalls and events of the medieval fair and then come back to the hotel for dinner at six, in good time for the Pageant starting at eight.

Sounds of laughter, mingled with loud ancient music drifted towards us as we made our way over, Helena leading us. Susie seemed happy to be relieved of the responsibility, even temporarily, and chatted amicably with Connie as we walked across the wooden bridge.

How this building had figured in our lives during our time on Bute and now I hoped there would be a satisfactory conclusion. I thought about the investigations Susie and I had started, all for nothing, and about how Susie had been trapped in the castle. Fortunately, she'd come to no harm and the possibility that a gust of wind had slammed the door shut had occurred to me several times. Not that I would have said to her. She was convinced someone had deliberately shut her in the turret room.

'Wait a minute.' I tapped her on the shoulder and she turned back. 'Lloyd. You're convinced Ricky took something from the dungeon when he found Max?'

'Yes, yes.'

'Could Lloyd have bought it from Ricky? That's why Ricky had money?'

There was no time to discuss this possibility as we came in to the open space in the middle of the castle. There were several gasps of surprise. What had been an empty green space was now thronged with people. The inner courtyard had been transformed. Medieval style canvas booths crowded together on the green in the centre where the living quarters and the stables had stood in the distant past. Many of the spectators were probably locals, but I heard a foreign accent or two as I began to explore. Over in the far corner a group of children were learning the intricacies of working on a large wooden spinning wheel, while at the next booth several of the older boys were enjoying instruction on how to build a coracle. 'If the weather is fine tomorrow we'll take these out on Loch Fad,' the instructor was saying, adjusting the belt of his leather jerkin.

We wandered slowly from stall to stall, pausing at the craft stall where the option was making a medieval princess headdress or a shield and sword. 'As well they're made of cardboard,' said Susie, pointing to the far corner where one or two youngsters were enjoying putting their newly made swords to good use.

A section of the green had been roped off and two men in full Viking costume, complete with fierce weapons, were staging a fight to the cheers of the crowd clustered around the rope barrier. Music started up beside the Gatehouse as a ferocious-looking group

299

of musicians, bare-chested and much-tattooed, played on a variety of drums, led by the chief drummer, his muscles rippling as he attacked his instrument with gusto.

The only jarring note was the booth dispensing modern food. 'I don't think larks' tongues or pottage would go down well,' grinned Susie.

'Yep, you can't beat a good burger, Ma'am,' said Wesley who had come up beside us. He held his generous portion up for our inspection. 'This is the real stuff, from local beef.' He wandered off, still munching.

The Heritage Adventurers had dispersed as soon as we came into the castle and from time to time we spotted one or other of them, faces obscured by cameras.

'There's Helena,' I said, pointing to where she stood, engrossed in her phone, at the bottom of the outside steps leading to the Great Hall. I had a quiet chuckle as I remembered Ricky's escapade here, annoying us by his antics on the steps. What was the truth of it all? In spite of our best attempts, I couldn't see how we were any further forward. I knew Susie was frustrated, her desire to find out what had happened over-riding her common sense, but it was too late and we'd have to trust to the police to solve this particular crime.

In spite of the distractions of the medieval fair, the death of Max still lurked in the background, the worry ever present. Lloyd had refused to speak to any of us, preferring to wait in his room, so Susie and I had no idea what explanation he'd been able to give for his being in the castle after hours.

300

'He and Max were as thick as thieves,' said Susie, unaware of the inappropriateness of her analogy. 'He must have discovered why Max had come to Bute, what he was after.'

That didn't solve the puzzle. 'Yes, but Lloyd isn't an historian so how would he realise what Max intended to do with the piece of stone?'

She shrugged. 'Perhaps he didn't, but thought it might be worth something, not understanding the value wasn't to do with money. At least, not directly.'

'So all he knew was it was something to do with the castle. He probably thought you had some information,' I said, 'and he followed you.' Susie had been luckier than she would ever realise.

'I've tried talking to him, but he just growls at me through the door,' she said. 'There's no way he's going to admit to me what he was doing. I gather he told the police he went over to have another look at the castle earlier in the afternoon and fell.' She laughed. 'As if he wouldn't have been found before closing time, if that had been true.'

The afternoon drifted on, until by five o'clock there were only a few children remaining and the stall-holders began to pack up.

'Guess we should head back. I could do with a shower before dinner,' I said at the same time as, 'You're right,' Susie said, glancing at her watch. 'We want to be in good time.'

'I'll gather everyone together,' said Helena. I had to admit she'd been a great help during the afternoon, patiently answering questions, making sure everyone was catered for and generally being a support to Susie.

'Why on earth did I agree to help with this Pageant,' Susie whispered to me as we crossed the road towards the hotel.

'Because you're well able to do it,' I reassured her, but she didn't reply, merely made a face.

Whatever happened we were almost at the end of the holiday, and now there was only the Pageant and the firework display left before we departed. How did I feel? A sense of relief.

'I can't believe I said I'd do this,' said Susie picking at her food as we sat at dinner. 'I can't eat a thing.' She pushed her plate aside. 'I have to be at the castle early to get costumed up. I'm going now.'

Jerome gazed after her. 'It's more stressful than everyone thinks, starring in a play. At least with a movie you can do several takes. I remember when I was in Desert Rats of Tobruk the weather was so hot we had to…'

I tuned out, let him ramble on. The Pageant wasn't scheduled to finish until after ten o'clock, to be followed by the firework display. Starting any earlier would spoil the effect.

Susie was anxious to make sure everyone was packed up and ready to leave before we set off for the Pageant. 'There won't be much time in the morning,' she kept cautioning us. 'An early breakfast and then straight on to the ferry, so better to have everything ready.'

'What about Lloyd?'

Susie made a face. 'He's being allowed to come back with us, though he's been warned he might have to return to Scotland at some point.'

302

The good weather had continued into the evening, in spite of a few clouds drifting across the sky late in the afternoon. They soon disappeared, though Helena advised, 'Make sure you have something warm to wear. You'll be sitting outdoors for a good part of the evening and don't be deceived by how hot it was this afternoon.'

The members of Heritage Adventurers nodded in agreement. Even this short time in Scotland had made them aware of how chilly the evenings could become.

We headed back to the castle in good time, Dwayne saying, 'Gee, I hope Susie's okay. She was pretty wound up.'

'She'll be fine,' I reassured him. 'Let's hurry to find a seat with a good view.' Although the event was ticketed, seats were to be allocated on a first come, first served, basis.

All signs of the medieval fair had been cleared away and the ground in the middle of the castle had once again been transformed. In front of the staircase outside the Great Hall several tiers of seats had been arranged to maximise the viewing area. This promised to be an excellent end to the tour, I thought, as the musicians struck up, a group less boisterous than those who'd been playing earlier in the day.

Thankfully for Susie's sake, if nothing else, the play went off without a hitch, if you ignored the occasional horseplay of the Vikings at the back of the stage when they thought no one was looking.

As was his custom, Zachary fretted back and forth, but there was no need. The rapturous applause at the end as the Brandanes defeated the last of the Vikings was testament to the audience's enjoyment, and I guessed no one was likely to complain about the historical accuracy of the story.

And now, with the drama over, it was time for the firework display. A full moon had risen above the castle and the darkened sky appeared to be sprinkled with stars as we waited, chatting quietly, for the event to begin.

Susie came over to join us, still in costume. 'I didn't want to miss any of this.'

'Where's Helena?' I scanned the audience, but there was no sign of her. 'She won't want to miss the firework display. I hope she's all right?'

Susie looked concerned. 'Where did she go?'

'I'm not sure. She said she'd something to do and wouldn't be long. But that was some time ago.' I stood up as the announcer said, 'Take your places, everyone. The firework display will begin in ten minutes.'

'I'd better see if I can find her.' I didn't want to admit that the prospect of another 'accident' at the castle was my main concern.

CHAPTER FORTY-FIVE

I went to the Gatehouse where I'd last seen Helena and checked the toilets, but there was no sign of her. What made me decide to go into the Great Hall, I'll never know, but at a loss where else to look, I headed up there.

Helena was standing in the Great Hall, the lights from the Pageant shining through the window on the grand fireplace. She was gazing earnestly at the painting on the wall, the depiction of a royal banquet at the castle we'd seen on our earlier visit.

'The firework display is about to start. If we don't hurry, we'll miss it.'

She kept her back to me and I walked over to stand behind her. 'We have to hurry.'

'See this painting? What do you think of it? It's a pretty scene, isn't it? There's the King, dressed in his beautiful robes, his happy nobles clustered around him, the skilful musician playing a cheerful tune and the pet dogs running around, part of the household. It's all a lie, of course. The room would be stinking, an odour no number of sweet-smelling herbs could disguise, the nobles would only bathe once a year, the dogs would be alive with fleas. So you see, Alison, nothing is ever as it seems.'

While this discourse on the painting might be interesting, I'd no idea why she was standing here chattering on about it, rather than enjoying the firework display with the Heritage Adventurers.

'Yes, but we'll miss the fireworks if we don't go now.'

As though I hadn't spoken, she went on, 'I can't keep up the pretence. I thought it would be easy, but it isn't. He came back, thinking all he had to do was claim his inheritance. Why did he have to go boasting about it? How was I to know? He came here, a rich American, saying how he would be even richer.'

'I don't understand. You mean Max?' What possible connection could Helena have with Max? 'You've some kind of inheritance? You thought Max was after it? But why?'

As she turned towards me for a moment, pushing back her hair, I caught sight of her profile and felt my heart give a lurch. That aquiline nose and high forehead could only mean one thing. 'You're Max's twin,' I breathed.

'Yes, strange isn't it. He didn't it realise, of course, but when he came here, talking about an inheritance, I thought he'd somehow discovered what I'd inherited from my mother. Would you believe it was to do with a painting? I found it when I came back to clear out her stuff. It was in the attic - she'd always hated it, but know what? It turned out to be a painting by one of the group known as The Glasgow Girls, Annie French. I'd only the vaguest recollection of seeing it as a child, but I did remember my mother didn't like it.' She laughed.

'That's why it ended up in the attic. Of course now I knew what it would be worth. Selling it would end all my financial problems. Well, it was my right and I wasn't going to share it with him.'

'You thought Max had come back because of a painting?'

A look of cunning came over her face. 'I thought he'd seen the article in The Buteman a few months ago.'

'That's not very likely, is it? The Heritage Adventurers have only been on Bute for a couple of weeks.'

She frowned. 'How was I to know that? You can get newspapers online now.'

'I see. He came over with the tour and spoke to you about it.'

'No,' a sigh, 'it wasn't like that. I recognised him because he's so like my father was at his age, but he didn't know me.'

'But Max wasn't interested in the painting: he was interested in another kind of inheritance. It was the artefact he was left by his father, the one stolen from the castle. If Max could prove the castle was built earlier than believed, his reputation would be made – a book, a lecture tour, even a television series.'

'Yes,' yelled Helena, advancing towards me, 'but I didn't know that, did I? I spent years with that awful husband of mine, scratching every penny, only to find when my mother died that there was money in the family after all. I wasn't going to risk Max wanting his share.'

She stopped and put her hands over her eyes. 'It was all for nothing. He was a greedy fool. Desperate for recognition in the academic community. I told him I'd some information that might be useful, set him up to go down into the dungeon.'

'But he didn't fall – the police said it wasn't an accident.'

She laughed loudly. 'I had it all planned. I went down behind him and stood on the step just above him. I hit him hard and watched as he fell.'

My mouth was so dry, I couldn't get the words out, but eventually croaked, 'And you arranged it so one of the Heritage Adventurers would find the body.'

'Yes, good idea, wasn't it! It had to be that silly boy, Ricky. Stupid enough to steal the artefact from Max's body.'

She turned back to the painting. 'Nothing is as it seems,' she whispered. 'I thought I could cope with it, but you see, he was my twin, my own flesh and blood. How could I have killed him like that over some money. How could I?'

She moved in front of me. 'You do understand, don't you, Alison?'

I tried to think of a way out of the hall, but Helena was standing between me and the door. Then I remembered there was a door leading out on to the parapet. If I could divert her attention, I could get out there and down to join the others.

But she wasn't finished yet. 'He sold it to Lloyd, you know and Lloyd came to me, trying to find out if it was of value. What did it matter then?'

I moved towards the door, slowly, very slowly, trying not to make a sound on the wooden floorboards, managing to open it, but she was too quick for me.

'Where are you going?' she demanded.

There was no way I could struggle with her. She was so much bigger than I was, I'd come off worse in any fight. Perhaps heading for the parapet wasn't such a good idea after all, though surely she wouldn't push me off in full view of such a large audience.

There was a great din outside, a whoosh and loud bangs and streams of colourful light illuminated the room. The firework display had started. If Helena managed to push me over now, the sound of the fireworks would cover up any other noises, including my screams as I toppled over the wall.

Could I appeal to her better nature, suggest killing me would only make matters worse for her?

'It's all over, Helena. Trying to get rid of me won't help.' The words came out in a high pitched tone, almost like a song, and I wondered if she'd actually heard me.

She came closer and closer. I couldn't move, was rooted to the spot as though my shoes were glued to the floor.

Without any warning, she crumpled and slid down against the wall, covering her eyes again and wailing, 'I didn't mean for it to happen like that, I didn't mean it. If only he'd said what he meant by his inheritance. How was I to know it was all about a stupid piece of stone.'

My hands were shaking so much, it took me a minute to find my mobile phone in the pocket of my jacket and speed dial Susie's number. 'Pick up, pick up,' I muttered.

And, luckily for me, she did.

EPILOGUE

Simon was waiting on the platform for me as the train pulled into Central Station.

He hugged me tightly, though he couldn't resist a barbed comment. 'Glad to see you made it back safely – again.'

I didn't reply, but said, 'Did you manage to get in touch with Deborah? Is she in Glasgow?'

'Yes. I've booked us into the Stuart Hotel in Buchanan Street for two nights. I thought it best to be in the centre of town. Deborah's meeting us for dinner there.'

I didn't reply. The last thing I wanted was to be reminded of my trip, but I'd no intention of giving him the details. A broad outline would be enough.

We left the station by the main entrance, weaving our way through the rush hour crowds.

'So, is there a story to tell?' He took my hand.

'It wasn't really anything to do with me,' I lied, thinking about the way I'd become entangled in the lives of the Heritage Adventurers. I'd said goodbye to Susie and Dwayne earlier that morning as they left the island. I'd waited on for a while, taking a last opportunity for a walk out to Port Bannatyne, mindful that it might be some time before I was again on Bute.

Simon didn't look at me, but I could imagine him lifting his eyebrows as he said, 'Oh, really? But you did get involved, didn't you?'

'Mmm. I felt sorry for Helena in the end. She'd had a terrible marriage and selling the painting was a way out of her troubles. Even if she'd had to share the proceeds with Max, she'd still have been well off.'

'And this Lloyd chap? How would he benefit?'

I laughed. 'He wouldn't. He thought what Ricky had sold him was of value, but it was only of interest to an historian like Max who could use the information to make a 'great discovery' that would prove Rothesay castle was built much earlier than currently believed.'

'And was it?'

'That wasn't the point. It was the debate that would have brought him fame. The books, the lecture tours – those were what he was after. I daresay there will be lots of discussion now the stone artefact is back in safe hands.'

Simon shook his head and before he could speak I added, 'Anyway, it's all over now. Once we're back in London I'll finish off the rest of this commission.' I stopped. 'We are going back to London, aren't we?'

There was a moment's hesitation. 'Yes, we are, at least for a while. I'll update you later. In the meantime, let's enjoy our time here.'

He chattered on, suggesting far too many possible options for the short time we had in Glasgow.

No matter. He was right. Tomorrow's problems were for tomorrow.

Acknowledgements

Thanks to Joan Fleming and to Bill Daly for reading the
manuscript and making many helpful comments and to
Joan Weeple and to Judith Vallely for proof-reading
and comments.

Special thanks in matters geographical and historical
and for technical support to

Brandanii Archaeology and Heritage

www.discoverbutearchaeology.co.uk

Historical Note for Bad Blood at Rothesay Castle

ROTHESAY CASTLE

Rothesay Castle, on the Isle of Bute, is one of the earliest castles in Scotland which still survives. Much of its history relates to the Stuarts who were originally the Stewards to the Scots Kings and the title was hereditary.

There are various theories as to the exact date at which the castle was built. In its present form most experts believe it was started in the early 13th Century, though it is likely there was a timber castle on the site much earlier.

As with most castles, Rothesay Castle has seen its fair share of combat, including several Viking incursions facilitated by the present moat being linked to the sea, which was much nearer the castle than it is today.

Rothesay Castle is one of over 300 properties maintained by Historic Scotland and is open to the public. If you wish to visit this castle, with its unusual circular shape, check details at
www.historic-scotland.gov.uk

MOUNT STUART HOUSE

Mount Stuart House is a spectacular Victorian Gothic building, once the home to the Marquesses of Bute.

The fantastic interiors were the creation of the 3rd Marquess and reflect his many interests including heraldry, astrology and mythology. The Stuart family has been on the Isle of Bute for over 700 years.

The house also has a fine art collection, many by Old Masters. There is an excellent Visitor Centre and Restaurant, as well as a Tearoom for lighter refreshments.

The House is set in extensive grounds including a Kitchen Garden and a Victorian Pinetum.

Recent innovations include eco-friendly holiday cottages to rent.

The House is open to the public from March to October. Full details are available at
www.mountstuart.com

Lightning Source UK Ltd.
Milton Keynes UK
UKOW02f0312061116
286934UK00002B/3/P